Sandra Gurvis

Loconeal Publishing
Amherst, OH

Country Club Wives

This book is a work of fiction. The names, characters, places, and events in this novel are either fictitious or are used fictitiously. Any resemblance to actual events or persons is entirely coincidental.

Copyright © 2011 by Sandra Gurvis
Cover Design by Craig Rusnak
Edited by Jennifer Midkiff
All rights reserved. No part of this publication may be copied, reproduced, stored, archived or transmitted in any form or by any means without prior written permission from the publisher.

Loconeal books may be ordered through booksellers or by contacting:
www.loconeal.com
216-772-8380

Loconeal Publishing can bring authors to your live event.
Contact Loconeal Publishing at 216-772-8380.

Published by Loconeal Publishing, LLC
Printed in the United States of America

First Loconeal Publishing edition: February, 2012

Visit our website: www.loconeal.com

ISBN 978-0-9825653-6-0 (Trade Paperback)

Table of Contents

PROLOGUE AS EPILOGUE
From Blue Blood to Blue Light Special   1

PART ONE: QUEEN FOR A DAY
Chapter 1 - New Wellington: The Final Frontier   6
Chapter 2 - The Three Rules   17
Chapter 3 - To the Manor Born   29

PART TWO: QUEEN OF DENIAL
Chapter 4 - The Truth about Birds and Dogs   40
Chapter 5 - Grand Illusions   52
Chapter 6 - Meltdown   62

PART THREE: QUEEN OF PAIN
Chapter 7 - The Death Card   81
Chapter 8 - Joker's Wild   96
Chapter 9 - With a Little Help   111
Chapter 10 - Cashing Out   128

PART FOUR: QUEEN OF HEARTS
Chapter 11 - Hairball to the Throne   142
Chapter 12 - Paper Cuts from Pushing the Envelope   154
Chapter 13 - Off with His Head!   169
Chapter 14 - Catfish Wedding Fantasy   182
Chapter 15 - Gimme Shelter   194
Chapter 16 - Who Let the Dogs Out?   201

EPILOGUE AS PROLOGUE
Lassie, Come Home   217

Dedication

To my friends. You know who you are.

To my parents. They loved the good life and lived it wisely.

To my sister, Judy Roth, for helping show me the path. And to her husband, Sam, who's always there to lend a hand.

And last but not least, to my daughter Amy, for her grace, humor, and wisdom beyond her years and her wonderful, insightful comments. And my son Alex, whose growing-up years provided some really good fodder.

Acknowledgements

No person is an island, and nowhere is this more evident than an undertaking as challenging and time-consuming as writing a novel. I would like to thank the following for their invaluable assistance during the eight years it took me to complete COUNTRY CLUB WIVES:

- Sherry Paprocki and Nancy Richison, fellow writers, good friends, and a constant source of encouragement
- Barbara Buscarello and the staff at Good Mews, the first stop in what proved to be a long journey
- The Eli Lilly Book Club, Indianapolis for their initial encouragement
- The Class of April '03 at the Vermont Studio Center and the writers and artists there; especially Alan, who suggested "Thomas Edison"
- Rikki Ducornet, for her on-target and insightful comments during the early stages of the manuscript
- The Mary Anderson Center for the Arts in Mt. St. Francis, Indiana, who generously provided a brief fellowship
- Wendy Avner and Janine Vince-Killiea at Hope's Boutique
- Angela Palazzolo, Karen Harper and the Columbus Writers' Conference for keeping the fire lit
- The Reading Room at the New Albany Public Library, a great place to focus which allows snacks (as long as you eat and drink quietly and pick up after yourself)
- Viviane and Andrew, who rented me the Bienvenue cottage in San Diego, allowing a few more lovely, quiet, and productive days
- Lee Lofland, for his crime-busting expertise (and realistic suggestions)
- Kim Cristofoli for introducing me to Lee and for her encouragement and support
- The Capital Area Humane Society animal shelter, for providing ideas for Paws That Refresh
- Wade Beane and the Humane Society of Delaware County for having an actual "Fur Ball" at an genuine country club and whose shelter also served as an excellent model
- Marcia McLane, Kelley Nichols Krutko, Amy Gurvis, and Rian Gurvis for their editorial eyes and suggestions.
- Stephanie Springfeldt Mounts for her invaluable help with the promotional video
- Craig Rusnak for his brilliant cover design
- To my agent Nancy Ellis for her belief in this book and openness to new ideas.

Women are like tea bags. They don't know how strong they are until they get into hot water.
Eleanor Roosevelt

There is risk, but life itself is risk. For a higher life, there will be higher risks. You move on a dangerous path. But remember, there is only one error in life, and that is not moving at all; that is, just afraid, sitting; just afraid that if you move something may go wrong... This is the only error.
Osho, *The Path of Yoga*

If someone is not treating you with love and respect, it is a gift if they walk away from you... Walking away may hurt for a while, but your heart will eventually heal. Then you can choose what you really want. You will find that you don't need to trust others as much as you need to trust yourself to make the right choices.
Don Miguel Ruiz, *The Four Agreements*

PROLOGUE AS EPILOGUE

From Blue Blood to Blue Light Special

Not many women can say they've been left for season tickets to seats on the 50-yard-line at Ohio State football games. Susan's late husband Gary, a cum laude graduate of OSU medical school and one of the city's leading OB/GYNs, had finagled these prizes, worth thousands of dollars in college football-crazy Columbus, and Susan, riding on the crest of sympathy, had managed to keep them after he died. And now my ex-husband Brian no longer has to worry about scrounging for tickets to his favorite sporting event.

If someone had told me two years ago that I would be standing here on a Friday night in the customer service section at Reich's Discount Department store a few blocks from my apartment, thrilled to be getting $40 back for a outfit, I would have said, "No way." That I'd be divorced and almost penniless, I would have said, "Bite your tongue. That's a terrible thought! Brian and I were together for over two decades, we've been through everything. He's my best friend!" But I'd overlooked the fact that the grass was greener on the other side—especially when it was seeded with dead Presidents.

When I was a kid, I would flip to the back of the book when I got to about the middle. It gave me a sense of security to know how things would come out. Besides, it was the process of the story's drama that fascinated me, not the conclusion. How do the characters overcome their obstacles and extract themselves from various situations? Some of them create awful messes for themselves yet things are always resolved. I take comfort in that, because it's so untrue in real life. If only our lives were as safe as books and we could open and shut them at will, rereading them for reassurance of a definite outcome.

My story and that of my friends is fraught with peril and hypocrisy. Terrible things have happened to all of us, even the one who betrayed me the most. Over the past ten years, the four of us have seen two divorces, a death of a spouse, and breast cancer that has possibly spread. Not to mention financial problems, infidelity, kids running amok with drugs and the law, the usual mid-life bullshit. And to think we started out jokingly calling ourselves the Drama Queens, tennis buddies at the New Wellington Country Club who made a big to-do—in jest, of course—over breaking a nail on the court.

But now my turn in line has come at the department store and I hand over the blouse and pants, pointing out to the saleslady that, although I'd charged it, I'd immediately paid off the purchase, so I get cash back. Thus the system is manipulated to its ultimate advantage: you accumulate points for additional discounts by charging X amount, make payment on the spot and voila, no bill at the end of the month. That's the new order: cash for everything. When you don't earn much you have to remember there are all kinds of sharks out there who will gladly give you credit. They will then equally happily nail you with 18-25 percent interest until such time as you die owing the exact amount you initially paid for the rest of your life, coughing up money like a terminal patient with emphysema hacks up phlegm and sinking even deeper into debt.

I'm ready to leave with the $42.18 when I remember my friend Emily, a woman I work with at the Banford Veterinary Clinic, had given me a $25 gift certificate for my birthday from this, my now-favorite store due to its combination of reasonably-priced yet trendy clothes. Granted, they do not have the selection of, say, a Nordstrom's or a Saks, but what they lack in range they make up for in such-a-deals. So I might be able to buy something. But nothing appeals, and I really do have enough for this season. There will be plenty of opportunities later on.

Inordinately proud of my new sensibility, I head towards the exit. I am just about to walk out the door when I see them…my ex-husband Brian and Susan, one of the other drama queens.

Brian and I had been divorced almost a year when they began dating. Susan was the one friend I'd spent weekends with as everyone else was married or otherwise involved. Shortly after my divorce, Susan and I went to Florida to the condo she'd bought with her dead husband's proceeds. We spent several (for me) boring hours by the pool, while she read the latest romance novel and I worried about getting skin cancer and how I would make the rent once the house sold. I probably would not have gone at all if it hadn't been for that free ticket left over from an aborted trip to Boca Raton, canceled because Brian's mother had yet another "episode" resulting in her pending demise from a smorgasbord of ailments ranging from kidney failure to an ingrown toenail. My mother-in-law expired several months before the ticket, much to my amazement. With so many dress rehearsals, it was almost impossible to believe that the real event had occurred. I knew our son Evan grieved for his grandmother, but did I really miss the old girl's velvet-covered iron-fisted ways?

Susan had never said a word to me about seeing Brian, instead sneaking around behind my back until my ex did the wet work of revealing every detail of their budding romance, concluding with "We haven't had sex yet. We've just started going out."

Oh, please. Tell me more! Are plump women better in bed than thin ones? And I *know* she has more cellulite than I do.

It's been almost three months since I found out about Brian and Susan. I am making good progress in focusing on not wreaking havoc a la Betty Broderick, another country club ex-wife due for parole sometime in the next few years. Instead I've been directing my energies towards pursuing my seemingly impossible dream of opening a shelter for homeless animals. As well as trying to avoid thoughts about my former almost-partner in the venture, Nick Fairchild, DVM, who is even more unattainable, thanks to that ring on his fourth left finger which he actually seems to honor.

But seeing my ex's balding blonde head (more grey than blonde, actually) bent close to her streaky dark curls in real time—or "meat space" as my son Evan would call it—immediately wipes out my superego. For starters, her 'do came courtesy of my hairdresser, the one I recommended to her just after Gary died when she was feeling so down. Now I can no longer afford that beautician's services and have to color my own fucking hair, even though it's mostly stayed blonde, unlike some son-of-a-bitch's.

The rage seizing me is so sudden and intense that it knocks the air out of me. I cannot breathe, yet I need to get away from them NOW. I know I must run, run to the nearest safe place—and in a flash I know that would be the women's dressing room towards the middle of the store. A quick gasp, "Oh my, God!" and an almost direct collision with a rack of clothes labeled "Sag Harbor"—that's just what that twat needs, a sanctuary for her drooping ass—and within moments I am huddled in the cubicle there, the smallest, safest one I can find. But I still cannot breathe and now along with being angrier than I've ever been, I'm also scared.

I hate them, oh God how I hate them. I've never hated anyone so much in my life. I did not think it was possible to feel so much rage. I did not know who I was more furious with, Brian for unceremoniously dumping me, in spite of his no-divorce-in-the-family-ever pedigree. Or Susan (Susan!), The Club's answer to Martha Stewart (pre-incarceration), for doing the one thing she'd, unsolicited, told me she'd never do: date a friend's ex-husband. I was raised to nurture and love, first the dogs we had when we were kids, the cats I later adopted and then my own family. Now I was seriously considering assassination.

"Get a salesperson, please," I gasp at a shocked customer. I needed to speak, I needed the kindness of strangers. If I can talk to someone about this, I might be able to breathe again. It seems like ages, but is probably only a couple of minutes, before a young girl with a Reich's department store badge comes into the room. A few women have gathered around, their faces mostly sympathetic as I begin an epithet-laden explanation of my near-encounter with Brian and Susan. They still live in New Wellington, which is partially why I am so shocked to run into them several miles away, near my neighborhood. Located squarely in a middle-class section in the city of Columbus, no self-respecting country clubber would deign to claim a ZIP code around here, even if they did send their kid to private schools. But then, Susan always loved a bargain—she felt it justified her often-extravagant purchases, which of course she could afford, and me, being the ever-loyal guppy, had told her about Reich's.

It is humiliating yet liberating to lay bare my sordid tale to a group of total strangers. The part of my brain still capable of analyzing realizes that, as an emotional train wreck, I'm providing reality-TV style entertainment but without the cable fees. Hopefully I'll never come across these people again, but what if I do…My anxiety ratchets up even more, causing my breath to come in quick puffs and my hands to shake. Someone asks me if I can get up, and I find that I can't. Right now this is the only safe haven, the ladies' dressing room at Reich's discount department store.

Finally the store manager—the same solid-looking woman who gave me my refund—comes over and tells me the emergency squad is on the way. So here I sit huddled, on the floor, wheezing and trembling, waiting to be whisked away by an ambulance. I am only a few hundred dollars away from the streets and I'd once inherited a nearly quarter of a million. I had grown up in a nice house, in an upper-class neighborhood near Boston, in the country club life. And until recently, I'd continued with that lifestyle, never imagining that it could come to an end or that people could be so ugly and deceitful.

I ask for water, hoping it might help. Like love, water is soothing and free and has absolutely no calories. But these days, they sell water in bottles and charge you a minimum of a dollar.

PART ONE: QUEEN FOR A DAY

Chapter 1 – New Wellington: The Final Frontier

About Ten Years Earlier
    "It is pretty," I grudgingly admitted as we pulled into the entryway of the New Wellington Country Club. I could think of a dozen reasons why I shouldn't join, but here we were. For starters, my sister-in-law Cecilia, or CeCe as everyone calls her, had roped me into taking a complimentary tennis lesson.
    CeCe's mission—and she'd chosen to accept it—was to try to persuade my husband Brian and me to become members. It had just opened that spring and I'd recently inherited a large chunk of cash when my father died. Aside from investing four years' tuition into the state college trust authority for our ten-year-old son Evan, we hadn't quite decided what to do with the rest. A new house? Maybe. A new car? Probably. A trip to Europe? Perhaps.
    My older sister Lisa and her husband Nate had suggested that I talk to a financial adviser but I had no idea what those people did or how to find them. If I put the funds into a stranger's hands, would he or she abscond with them? The whole idea made me nervous, and besides Brian took care of the finances. A few more thousand had already gone to his parents for repayment of a loan for a down payment on our smallish split-level in Upper Arlington, a few blocks away from their elaborate 1950s ranch. How CeCe had convinced Brian's older brother Brett to remain in her home suburb of Bexley probably had a lot to do with sex, I reflected, not for the first time, and not without envy. He was forever fawning over her, saying how he couldn't wait to go home and get her alone. When had Brian stopped treating me that way?
    The elder McLeans were also high on the New Wellington Country Club or "The Club" as members generally called it, in the tradition of country clubs everywhere as if their particular enclave

was unique in the universe. And the rest of us generally followed their lead. After all, McLean's Fine Furniture ("The Largest in Ohio!") had been started by Brian's great-grandfather and had served as the primary source of the family income for nearly 100 years. Although Brett made twice as much as my husband, he and CeCe were in deep debt, having recently purchased a 5200 square-foot, falling-apart habitat on a prestigious street in Bexley and rehabbing it as well as paying for their two daughters' private school, giving new meaning to the expression "living large." Older than Brian by a whopping fifteen months, he was president, while my husband was rather ambiguously titled Chief Operating Officer. Unless one resided in Upper Arlington, Mable McLean frowned upon public education so she and my father-in-law, mild mannered Jack, supplemented the tuition. Unlike Brian, Brett seemed to have no pressing desire to expedite reimbursement.

CeCe was always enthusiastic about anything that involved spending other people's money, be it Brett's, the in-laws, or in this case, mine.

Plus The Club was really something, according to my in-laws. They applied every cliché with enthusiasm: The state-of-the-art, world-class facility had three—count 'em, three!—Jack Nicklaus-designed golf courses; two Olympic-sized swimming pools (one indoor and another outside); four dining options (casual, formal, sports bar and snack); a workout facility with all the latest equipment and exercise programs du jour, including an on-call personal trainer; and two locker rooms, one for tennis and social members and another for golf members.

And women were actually welcome—they even had their own tee times. You didn't have to be "Mrs." anything to get accepted. This was quite different from the country club of my childhood, when divorcees and widows lost their membership along with their spouses and the ladies always ceded tennis courts and greens to the gents. (Single men were always embraced with enthusiasm, unless they were overtly gay.) Females were listed according to their husbands' name and occupation. In TV-land, for instance, Donna Stone (aka

"Donna Reed") would be "Mrs. Alex Stone" with (pediatrician) behind it and then their spawn Mary and Jeff. June Cleaver would be Mrs. Ward Cleaver (businessman), then "Wally" and "The Beav."

New Wellington seemed unlike any other club I'd ever heard about, and Brian -- who was still quite the golfer, even though he'd given up his dream of being a pro decades ago—and I had been guests at several around the area, including my in-law's latest venture, the Northside Country Club. That ended badly last year when CeCe's youngest daughter Whitney invited two nonmembers from her third-grade class to the pool on a hot afternoon, and Brett got a letter of reprimand for bringing guests who resided in the area, rather than being from out-of-town as was permitted by Club rules. Mable was furious and resigned in a huff, practically forcing CeCe and Brett to follow suit. It had been the topic of family conversation for months.

Set among rolling hills, the facing three-story Georgian Palladian structures were bisected by a tree-filled road divider and had touches of Britain, Scotland and the Eastern and Southern U.S. in their architecture and landscaping. They were actually visible from the street, not hidden from the teeming masses of migrant workers and illegal aliens who customarily only pass through the doors of such bastions of exclusivity as employees. Of course, the suburbs of Columbus weren't exactly bubbling over with ethnic diversity.

The red brick, white pillars, and slate roofs harked back to my and Brian's alma mater, University of Virginia in Charlottesville, where we'd met. That fact alone began to reel me in. If we could return to our romantic roots, we might be able to recapture the magic of our early years.

It also brought back unpleasant memories of times when Mom and Dad left me and my four sisters at the pool while they golfed. As the dead middle, third in a group of five girls ranging from 10 months to 7 years apart, when I wasn't being ignored, I was the butt of gang-ups. Still my siblings were more palatable than the other country club kids, who had no compunction about dunking your head or tickling you until you thought you'd die or at least pee in your pants. Then they'd turn around and ask to borrow your snack coupons, upper-middle-class food stamps purchased by parents so kiddies didn't have to handle filthy lucre or sign for charges that may have been just a little bit padded. I had hated that club, and in fact the whole lifestyle. For a while I'd even fantasized about moving to Boston and living the romantic life of the inner city, joining in freedom marches and being on the front lines of the War on Poverty, dodging drug dealers and gang slayings as I carried out my good works. Which is why I could relate to my ten-year-old's budding fascination with gangsta life.

Perhaps most intimidating of all was the fact that I hadn't played tennis since high school. Most of my free time was taken up with Evan, with juggling volunteer duties for the Humane Society and Cat Welfare, and with taking the occasional course in business administration, upon whose completion of an associate's degree would guarantee me, in the words of mother-in-law Mable, who never worked a day in her life, a "real" job. I was busy. When did I have time for tennis? And according to Brian's increasingly grim dispatches, business had not been great lately so the funds would also have to come from my inheritance.

"I really don't want to do this. Do I have to do this?" I struggled to leach the whining tone from my voice. "Evan's going to be back from camp at 3 and I need to be there…"

"Jesus, Tish, he's almost 11! He knows how to use a key." CeCe's older girl Britney, now 12, had already completed a babysitting class, although her schedule of soccer, piano, and tap dancing prevented her from taking on any actual customers. She often left Britney alone with her younger sister Whitney, 10, and they seemed fine. But then those Barbie-doll toting angels never had a propensity for putting firecrackers in old gym shoes and blowing them up or hanging their action figures from light fixtures and railings, causing a melee of string and yarn that took hours to untangle.

"You'd think you were getting a root canal!" CeCe swung her red Mercedes convertible into the parking lot. It contrasted perfectly with her bright blonde hair.

"What about Duke? He needs to be walked." Duke was our ancient but still hyperactive cocker spaniel who urinated with exponential frequency on items according to their newness. I had just gotten a dining room set and was understandably nervous.

"Oh, hell, he'll pee anyway," CeCe pulled confidently into a space next to the tennis courts, as if she'd been a member forever. "And if he messes up a chair or whatever, you can always replace it." One of the advantages of the furniture business was getting things at cost, or in some cases, free. "Why don't you put that mutt to sleep?"

"Well we've had him since we were married…" My voice faded out. "You don't abandon him just because he's old and sick."

"It's an animal, for Christ's sake!" CeCe grabbed a racquet, and tossed me her other one. She had several, since she played three times a week. "I can tell you Brian would be happy if you got rid of him. And the cats, too." Teddy and Freddy were two little boys slated to be put down at the Humane Society a couple of years ago. I'd gotten Brian in a weak moment and he'd consented to allow me to adopt them. Unlike Duke, who was constantly underfoot, they mostly played with Evan and me and pretty much stayed out of the way. They were the first felines I'd ever owned and I adored them.

"I don't know who else will be here because they've just started the program. You have your whites, don't you?" One was forbidden to step onto The Club's courts unless clad in the traditional non-color, a nod to the pristine pants and long skirts that dominated the sport when it first became popular in the late 19th century. "At least pretend like you're having a good time!"

"Whatever…" I sighed and reached for my duffle bag. I would have to go inside and change before coming onto the courts. At least the tennis clothes were fun. I'd spent an enjoyable afternoon at a specialty shop with supposedly the best selection in the city. I'd be good for a couple of lessons and get to wear everything once, thus justifying my purchase of few hundred dollars' worth of outfits, shoes, and something to carry them in.

*****

Although the promotional brochures state that the gentrified, white-picket-fence laden suburb of New Wellington was established in 1841, real money didn't pour into the area until the late 1980s. That was when resident billionaire Eli Katz, who made his fortune manufacturing inexpensive but quality home accessories, took it upon himself to create his own little fiefdom.

Labeled the male Martha Stewart by Wall Street wags, the attendant gossip about his sexuality was only quieted by his recent marriage late in life and the quick and efficient production of four little "Kittens" at intervals of approximately 1.5 years. At first local jokels nicknamed New Wellington "Eli's second coming" or "Katzberg," an underhanded if rather anti-Semitic, barb. But dollars have a way of silencing even the most vocal critics, some of whom became New Wellington's most upstanding boosters.

1841 indeed….Although some might look older, most homes were built in the 1990s. And the farmers and blue and lower-level white-collar workers, looking to escape from what they considered the encroachment of the big city, turned their cow pastures into cuds of cash and relocated to Florida or larger homes elsewhere in the area.

Having grown up near Boston which refers to itself as the hub (as in "of the universe"), I had a different view of urban sprawl, and, even after over a dozen years, still regarded Columbus and environs as more rural than anything ("Oh, look at the cute little skyline!"). Few of the original New Wellington inhabitants remained, but of those who did, many had poor dental hygiene, drove beaters as opposed to urban assault Hummers, and went from a blank stare to "fuck you" in three seconds, making for an interesting demographic mix. And I found it highly amusing when recently relocated yuppies acted like country squires whose families go back generations— undoubtedly they did, but to some Eastern European country where it was get out or get kebabed. My mother's ancestors came over a few decades after the Mayflower and it was never a big deal with us.

The Club's tennis/exercise facility was less old money and more upscale gym than anticipated. My childhood country club in Milton had been heavy into taxidermy and matching overstuffed chairs, and this place was all windows, light-colored furniture and indoor/outdoor plaid carpet. I later learned that its user-friendly design—large workout room, mirrored studio for aerobics, tennis shop directly facing the courts—was a model for subsequent facilities. The heads of dead boars and stags worked in neither this temple to improve your body nor the building across the street, another type of shrine altogether.

Despite my reservations, I felt at ease in the plush but surprisingly homey locker room where all of my favorite bath and hair accessories and perfume—manufactured by a subsidiary of Katz Enterprises, of course—were strewn on sparkling vanities. Women in various states of undress chatted freely and the atmosphere was friendly, a cross between a health club and a college dorm. When I mentioned that I was a tennis virgin—well, almost—everyone had lots of advice, which mostly concerned the fact that I would have to hit about a million balls before becoming competent and not to get easily discouraged.

This was where I first encountered Shelia. With short, wildly curly bright red hair, big green eyes, and a well- proportioned petite body, she was a beginner and also in my group. "Are you a member yet?" she asked as we laced up our Reeboks. Hers had a daring blue stripe.

"I will be if my sister-in-law has her way. I'm not athletic and it seems silly to take up a sport at this point in my life." I was 37.

"I disagree. The more active you are, the younger you stay. You might even grow to love it. You say you came with your sister-in-law?" She seemed incredulous, as if I'd arrived with Attila the Hun.

"You know her?" CeCe's flamboyant dress and mannerisms never failed to draw attention, not always positive among some females.

"No. It's just that I find it amazing that you hang out with your sister-in-law," Shelia said as we headed towards the courts. "My sister-in-laws would never play with me. I'm just learning and it might screw up their game."

"Well, that seems stupid...How many do you have, anyway?" As someone who came from a large family, I was always curious about the size of others.'

Shelia rolled her expressive eyes. "Three. They're all trying to outrank each other. And not just in tennis, either."

"Well, there's really no rivaling CeCe. She's got a hard exterior but underneath her pretensions, she's all right." I remembered CeCe's admonition to act like I was having a good time. "I have to admit it, though, sometimes she gets on my nerves."

What was with this family that made appearances so goddamn important? I pasted on a smile as Shelia and I clomped towards CeCe and a gaggle of women. Aside from Shelia who seemed amazingly down-to-earth, I was rarely comfortable among strangers, unless they were attached to a four-legged friend. What if they laughed at my clumsiness?

Of course, I already knew CeCe who, like me, was tall and blonde, but unlike me, had internalized the confident walk and talk that seemed genetically implanted with the looks. A boyfriend once described me as beautiful but with the soul of a nerd, and the second part is pretty close, although the first was undoubtedly an exaggeration as he was attempting to deprive me of my virginity. But he almost succeeded because of his charming combination of flattery and honesty.

CeCe had had a boob job, liposuction and was trying to talk me into some new facelift thing call Botox. I preferred to let nature take its course unless it was in the form of creams, lotions, and noninvasive surgery. Soft lighting and loose-fitting clothes worked well and who was I trying to impress anyway? I lived in the eighth fattest city in the nation and was a size eight and not complaining. Nor was Brian, who only got upset anyway when I spent too much money on clothes for myself or for Evan.

I'd grown up in a country club, too, and my parents never fussed if we wanted to discuss something or were displeased. Of course they had perfected the fine art of talking about someone who'd entered the room without turning around, their mouths barely moving. That's the thing about country clubs. Unlike high school, you could be an object of discussion and never know it.

As it turned out, except for CeCe who was an experienced player, most of us were klutzes. Another woman, Susan, was also new to the sport and she, Shelia, and I bonded immediately, laughing as our returns sailed wildly over the fence and, in one case, almost knocked off a golfer's hat. Shelia's ball got stuck in the net and we wondered if they gave extra points for that. Of course I hadn't yet pegged Susan as the social chameleon who would slither away with my ex-husband. On that clear and crisp May day, she seemed like a sweet person with almost-frizzy hair, lots of curves, and a ready laugh.

"You ladies need work but you have potential. Same time next week?" This came from Scott. A swarthy hunk, he looked more like the son of a New Jersey wiseguy than a tennis pro. His glance included me.

"Well, I'm not a member yet…" It had been a blast and wonderful to run around in the fresh air and sunshine. But I was reluctant to make such a large commitment. Besides, Brian and I had only briefly talked about joining.

"Oh come on, Tish, admit that you loved it," said CeCe. "I can't remember the last time I saw you having such a good time."

"Yes, but…" I flashed her a warning glance, mentally telegraphing her not to put words in my mouth. "I need to discuss this with my husband…"

"She'll be here," CeCe told Scott. "I'll be back too, to provide immoral support. I'll also see you at our regular time next Wednesday." She flipped her long hair at Scott and slid her eyes towards him as if acknowledging a connection. If I hadn't known her better I would have thought she was trying to seduce him, although he was at least 15 years younger.

We started back towards CeCe's Mercedes. "You really shouldn't talk for me," I told her, more angry with her than I'd been in a while. "Brian needs to agree to this, too."

CeCe cast me an incredulous glance. "How could he not? He loves golf and now he can join Brett and the others in their Sunday game. Besides, it's your money," she added, referring to my inheritance.

"Not according to Brian. It's our money. And I haven't worked in ages." Between raising Evan, volunteering, and the occasional course I'd hardly added to our net worth. Hopefully once I got my associate degree in business that would change. Although how I would apply it to employment I might enjoy I had no clue. No way was I ever returning to nursing, although that's what I'd gotten my degree in.

"Now you won't have to. A quarter of a million dollars is a lot."

That's what I loved about this clan, I thought bitterly, but clamped my mouth shut, not wanting to acknowledge the accuracy of the dollar amount. Nothing was secret. I'd asked Brian not to reveal the exact sum I'd received from my father's estate. I wished, just once, that my husband would keep something between the two of us and not feel compelled to share it with his family.

It was then that I spotted a gold Lexus sitting in front of the clubhouse. What an improvement even a lesser version would be over my five-year-old Chevy wagon that broke down on cue once its 36-month warranty had expired. It was especially fond of dying when I had to be someplace important.

CeCe followed my gaze. "Hell, you could afford that,"

"Those things cost, what? Thirty-nine grand? And look at that license plate—SHE WON," I observed. "What did she win? The Olympics? The lottery?" The Club already counted a couple of major local sports figures among its burgeoning ranks. "A free turkey dinner? I've got it…The battle of the bulge. It's the local president of Weight Watchers!" Now I was stretching, but I'd always found country club pretentiousness amusing.

"Tell me you're joking, Tish. You *can't* be that naive." CeCe flipped on her dark sunglasses, obscuring her face and making her look even more a part of the scene. "That car belongs to Laura Klein, the ex-wife of Marty Klein of Laser Vision Centers USA." She slipped into the country club vernacular which automatically inferred that the business cited was owned by the person named. "You should see the Corniche that Marty got his second wife," she continued.

"That license plate reads 'EYE 1, TOO.'"

"It's about divorce," CeCe went on. "She won the *divorce.*"

Chapter 2 - The Three Rules

After we joined The Club, it seemed natural to move to New Wellington. It was something Brian and I both wanted. Not only could we get a nicer and newer home, but Evan just didn't fit into Upper Arlington schools. That child must have been a throwback to his great-grandfather who fled Boston at age 14 and joined the Navy to see the world. Evan was a great kid, but wild, a misfit in a primarily white-bread suburb where anal retentiveness had been honed to a fine art over generations.

An apprenticeship to snobbery seemed a problem in old, established neighborhoods. CeCe had similar issues with her daughters in Bexley. Which was why she agreed to send them to Columbus Academy, a private boys' school turned co-ed, instead of what Mable had originally planned, the oh-so-proper Columbus School for Girls. One thing about my sister-in-law; she took shit from no one.

Now it was my turn to defy the elder McLeans; specifically, Mable. Jack was generally no problem; he usually went along with everything, although once in a while he'd show a flash of determination that would even give Mable pause. The good news was that Brian was on my side on this issue. He wanted what was best for Evan and that meant going to a smaller, more liberal school district where "different" (read: attention-deficient or hyperactive) children were dealt with on an individual basis, rather than being given a blanket prescription for Ritalin.

As the daughter of a doctor and trained as a nurse, I knew enough about the side effects, including kidney failure and stunted growth, to keep my son away from that panacea for pampered miscreants. Besides, he'd been tested and although ADD was a possibility, the psychologist had pointed out that his IQ of 140 was at least partially responsible for his boredom with school and subsequent acting out.

The underbelly of the McLean opinion was that it was also my fault because I failed to discipline and control my son. Mable said she had no such problem with hers, although Brett's pictures from his early 20s when he had long hair and a joint hanging out one end while he bared the other told an entirely different story. Still she'd had dinner on the table every night—thanks to her three-times-a-week maid who made fried chicken, tuna casserole, and hamburgers—and her boys always went to church cleaned-up and respectable (said maid also did the laundry and ironing). I didn't even want to think about our Sunday-morning battles with Evan when Mable insisted we go en masse to Long Ridge Methodist.

Brian decided that the best way to approach a move to New Wellington would be to do the fait accompli thing. That is, pick out a lot, put a down payment on it, and start building. I, or rather, we—it was always "our" money and only "his" when his family gave out bonuses during years when business was reasonably good—now had the means. There were several neighborhoods to choose from, so I decided to consult Shelia. Somewhat of a pioneer, she had been part of the initial infestation of yuppies four years ago.

I invited her to lunch after our weekly tennis lesson, which CeCe, Shelia, Susan, and I had arranged on Saturday mornings in addition to our regular Tuesday clinic. We'd joined The Club, and would get half our deposit back when we moved to New Wellington. The King, as I privately called Eli Katz, was a genius when it came to providing incentives to buy into his realm. Finding the coins was your problem, however.

CeCe and I had become friends with Shelia and Susan, despite the fact that CeCe was the far superior tennis player and Shelia's pedigree was a tad ostentatious, even for Mable. Along with having her own family money, Shelia had married into one of the wealthiest and most high-profile dynasties in Columbus. Shelia was Jewish to boot, locating her outside my mother-in-law's point of reference, which included the cliché that people only need to have their names in the paper three times—at birth, for marriage, and upon death. Shelia's large and extended family was forever donating to various causes, so the Weintraub moniker was emblazoned on research facilities and entertainment venues throughout Columbus. Nevertheless Mable seemed pleased that I had met some "nice" people. My tendency towards being alone and general lack of interest in all things social was an ongoing concern.

CeCe and her damn fake nails started the whole drama queen thing. She slammed into the ball using the full force of her racquet and both hands and voila! A good portion of her French manicure lay on the court, a pile of pink and white slivers.

She crumpled over, holding her right arm in a gesture of pain. "That hurt like hell!" she cried, loud enough to garner the attention of two couples on the next court who immediately stopped playing.

"Are you all right?" The man asked with concern. Scott the pro, Shelia, Susan, and I stood around CeCe in what Brian calls a clusterfuck, usually personified by a bunch of people, most often guys, gathered around and staring at something most of them know absolutely nothing about fixing, such as a sewage drain or an airplane engine.

"I guess I am..." CeCe glared at her fingers in disgust. They had turned an unbecoming red and the real nails stood revealed in all their jagged non-glory. "I don't believe it! I just got a new set!"

"A prosthesis?" The man looked incredulous.

The woman next to him laughed and said, "No, she's talking about fake nails, Herb." To CeCe she said, "Do you have wraps or acrylics? If they're silk, they'll rip off for sure."

"The girl who does them told me the wraps looked more real." CeCe's Botoxed brow failed to wrinkle from distress, giving her face an almost bipolar appearance. "The other kind you have to fill and the tips can get thick, which makes it hard to pick things up."

"But wraps are very fragile," the woman explained. "And if you get the right nail tech who knows what she's doing, acrylics are great...I go to a Vietnamese place down the street. My new set only cost $25, plus tip." She held out her perfectly buffed hands.

CeCe scowled, although her brow remained unruffled. "I paid twice as much for mine at DelCarlos," a day spa which everyone knows overcharges its customers for the privilege of getting their hair cut among marble pilasters, bronze sconces, New Age music and all the decaf herbal tea their bladders could handle. "I'm going back there and insist that they do it over again."

"Can we get back to playing tennis, Marcy?" Herb, obviously the woman's husband, remarked in annoyance. "Nobody here wants to stand around the court all day talking about your damn fake nails." The other man was trying not to smirk, and even his female companion turned her head, as if to hide a smile.

Susan said, "For God's sakes CeCe, it's only a manicure. You'd think you'd sprained something." Of all of us, Susan had started out with the least. She'd grown up on a farm near Cincinnati and, although her husband was a successful doctor, she did homey things like needlepoint and canning, skills about as familiar as astronaut training to the rest of us.

"They could have torn off at the quick, and I could have lost the nail underneath" CeCe huffed. "Even now, one might get infected."

"That's true," I swung into full worst case scenario mode. "You could get a blackened nail bed, which is almost impossible to disguise and takes forever to grow out. Or if someone stepped on one of those suckers barefoot, it could have caused serious damage to their heel. And then you'd have a lawsuit to deal with…"

"Very funny Tish. So call me melodramatic."

"More like a drama queen if you ask me," the woman's companion observed, rather insolently I thought.

"Shut up, Herb," Marcy snapped. "I'd like to see you put your hands in cold water for an hour during a soak-off . You complain when you have to have your blood pressure taken because the cuff gets too tight." She turned to CeCe. "Don't mind my husband, dear. Men can be the biggest drama queens around."

"It's all a matter of perspective," said Scott, defusing what was shaping up to be a major marital blowout. "You're having the time of your life playing tennis, a peak experience."

"And then you break a nail. What a disaster!" Shelia pretended to faint. "Let that be the worst thing that happens to any of us."

"Well, it's back to the lesson for you drama queens," Scott lifted up his racquet, tossed a ball high into the air, and whipped out a perfect serve. "Let's practice our serves. Don't be afraid to hit hard, even it goes out." He was referring to the box inside the court where serves were supposed to be placed, not into the adjoining courts, where thankfully, fewer of our efforts had been landing.

"I can see it now," I observed as I attempted my own clumsy interpretation of Scott's topspin. "Instead of saying 'break a leg' during matches, it'll be…"

"Break a nail!" Shelia and CeCe chorused and everyone laughed.

*****

Susan went home to cook her kids' lunch – they were about the same age as CeCe's and had been cooped up with colds – and CeCe had another appointment. With children the same ages, Susan and CeCe knew each other through various activities at Columbus Academy. Susan expressed interest in learning tennis, and CeCe hooked her up with our clinic.

CeCe had changed her mind about returning to DelCarlos. Instead, she'd gotten the number of the Vietnamese nail salon from Marcy and had called them on the phone from the pro shop but couldn't get in until 4:00. Like most of our friends, she had a phone in her car, which was only convenient when you were driving. She declined to join us for lunch, claiming she needed to make several calls, the numbers of which had been left in her Mercedes, and had yet another meeting related to the renovation. She was still chatting with Scott when we left.

"Marcy's not very smart, talking that way to her husband in public," Shelia observed as we strolled through the tree-lined path towards the clubhouse for a quick salad at the sports bar. Less kid-intensive than the grill adjoining the tennis facility, it allowed for conversation uninterrupted by marauding toddlers and zealous mommies who felt compelled to stop by to share their little darling's latest accomplishment. The latter sort of socializing seemed directly proportional to the total gross income of the other mommy's spouse. The presence of Eli Katz's wife, Janice, for example, elicited the kind of response usually found at the Vatican during the appearance of the

Pope.

"Why do you say that?" Not that I ever had the nerve to talk that way to Brian in public. Or privately, for that matter. "It's the '90s, Shelia. Can you say equal rights for women?"

"Ah, but she violated the three rules." A look of half amusement and half seriousness crossed Shelia's pixyish features.

"What are you talking about?" This was going to be good, I thought. Shelia's sense of the absurd equaled my own. Unlike me, however, her timing was impeccable.

"You don't know? The three rules of The Club?" Shelia pretended to be shocked. She held up three fingers and ticked them off. "Number one: Money is no object. Number two: My marriage is perfect. Number three: My children are faultless."

I failed to see the humor. Especially since I'd nearly always felt out of place: First as a tall, gangly child whom boys teased. Although I was bigger, I was uncoordinated and could never outrun them or excel in sports. Now as the wife of a man who seemed more interested in accommodating his parents and covering up for his brother than caring for me or upon occasion even his own son. A man who at times made me feel as if we were one step from financial failure even though we had almost $250,000 in the bank. Shelia's comment held more truth than I wanted to acknowledge. "Well, where the hell does that put me?" I blurted. "Would we be better off staying in Upper Arlington and not spending the money to move?"

"Oh come on, Tish. You hate it there. And what about Evan? New Wellington schools are great. The middle school even has a class for high IQ ADD kids that helps them plan their homework so they won't get behind."

"I know that. I checked it out." Evan was starting seventh grade, and he'd been making noises about leaving behind the few friends he'd made. But a tour of the just-built New Wellington campus with its deluxe Georgian buildings, indoor swimming pool and tennis courts, and state-of-the-art computer and graphics lab turned him into an enthusiastic convert.

"Besides, the three rules don't apply to everyone. Some people just pretend that they do."

*****

Sensing my hesitation, Shelia spent our lunch convincing me that a move to New Wellington was the best thing we could do for ourselves and our son. Like me, her husband was in a family-owned business—selling and recycling spare auto parts—and she was especially sensitive to the politics and rivalries therein. Unlike us, there seemed to be plenty of money for everyone. "The neat thing is that most people in New Wellington are from somewhere else, so you don't have the whole damn family history thing to deal with." When they first married, her husband Todd drove her through Bexley and pointed who lived in what residence and what they did for a living, providing a running commentary on their personal and economic provenance. The price and size of their homes as well as how much was spent on the necessary remodeling was also common knowledge. Even though Shelia was from Shaker Heights, another wealthy predominately Jewish suburb in Cleveland, she had been appalled by the incestuousness of it all.

So as soon as Todd's father retired and divided up the business between Todd and his three brothers, Shelia took their newfound prosperity—Todd refused to use her family money for anything other than investments—and built a home in Upper Crescent. Its picket fences had two boards instead of the usual three so you could appreciate the beauty of the nearby golf course without that extra white line marring your field of vision. A pond surrounded by walking paths with benches and cunning little boxes with baggies and gloves for dog poop was another perk. However, I suspected that the bottom of that pond was lined in plastic, and I don't mean credit cards.

Still, no matter what the price, all homes in New Wellington had to meet certain criteria: Georgian architecture, slate roofs, even windows and ceilings a certain width and height. In selected subdivisions, the grass had to be cut a particular way. It was like going to a foreign country where everyone looks alike at first. But as you get to know the culture, you become acutely aware of the differences among the natives. Some shutters are blue or green or even brown; other homes have more white-painted wood trim; still others have "widow's walks" on the roof which I thought was really bizarre, considering that the nearest ocean was several thousand miles away and the only fishing some husbands did was for newer models once their financial ship came in. Of course, the largest disparities were in the size of the homes and lots and layouts of the neighborhoods. People seemed acutely conscious of this, although nothing derogatory was ever mentioned about any particular area, at least among the general groups that congregated at The Club.

But no one in my acquaintance was more aware of these gradations than Shelia. Even CeCe had limited grasp of the machinations that went on among some women in New Wellington: the ones who "cared," the ones who strove to be inside the circle dominated by Eli and Janice Katz and the rest of their multimillionaire crowd. They got invited to the best parties at the biggest houses and then compared their progress or lack thereof.

Everything this inner group said and did was subject to analysis. During our regular tennis clinic, Chloe, a friend of Shelia's who was building a home in Balfour Farms, the most exclusive area of all, was agonizing over what kind of built-in soap dispenser to install in their downstairs bathroom. Not the guest bath, but the everyday one to be used by the kids, the nanny, and other household help. Should she go all out with the Optima Plus, a battery-powered automatic job made with solid cast brass construction and heavy chrome plating? Or the workmanlike and sensible (read: considerably less expensive) OneShot Automatic Hand Soap system which came in a satin or brass finish (the chrome option being immediately dismissed as too tacky-looking).

Befuddled by choices, Chloe had phoned her husband, one of Katz Enterprises' multitudinous vice-presidents. As chance would have it, he was in a meeting with Alan Donnelly, Eli's right-hand associate, almost as well-known as the King himself, at least within the boundaries of New Wellington. After apologizing for the interruption and explaining her predicament, she was told by her husband, "Whatever you want to do is fine with me, dear. I trust your judgment."

Five minutes later, hubby called back in a panic, hoping she hadn't ordered anything. It turned out the Donnelly family bath products remained in Katz Enterprises' tastefully designed containers, effectively washing any other soap dispenser idea down the drain. The real clincher: Chloe's reference to Alan was immediately understood by all listeners as *the* Alan. As if no other Alan existed.

One's social outlook was even brighter if the kids were invited to a bash of a company executive or other wealthy burgher. Shortly after we moved to New Wellington, I overheard two women behind me in line at the grocery discussing what sounded like an extravaganza, with decorations, entertainers, and so on. I found myself wishing I'd been invited; it would give me a chance to wear a great-looking formal dress I'd purchased for a cousin's wedding a few months ago. As I paid the bill, their conversation turned towards the fact that Barney was being used as a theme way too much and I realized they were talking about a preschooler's party, not an adult's.

And it wasn't enough to pass every single school levy, no matter how excessive or seemingly extraneous—did they really need scuba classes at the indoor pool?—or micromanage all your kids' activities, including doing their homework every night. While such helicoptering was also common in Bexley, Upper Arlington, Dublin and Worthington, New Wellington parents took it one step further. On Evan's first day of school, I walked with him to the bus stop, despite his half-hearted protests that he was perfectly capable of facing an unknown group of children on his own. I watched incredulously as the line of Volvos, Lexii, and Beamers grew along the street, clogging traffic. Moms and even dads were videotaping and clapping as their offspring clambered aboard the bus, despite the fact that they were middle-school kids, not kindergarteners.

No doubt it was also an expression of joy from parents overstressed by a full summer of schlepping (a term learned from Shelia) to swim meets and tennis and karate lessons at The Club. Would it be like this every day? I wondered. Had I accidentally moved into the set of "The Stepford Wives"? Or perhaps New Wellington was a test market for Pod People.

Thank God, no. After that, kids trudged to the stop unaccompanied for the rest of the year. And they still misbehaved in public, although unlike other suburbs where their parents blithely ignored their screams and tears, mothers went to great extremes to hush or placate them. Almost as if they were afraid that Janice—area helmswoman for such noble causes as shaken baby syndrome and prevention of domestic violence, two things she'd undoubtedly never experienced—would step out from behind the frozen peas and give them a gently disapproving look.

Although Shelia acted as if all the jockeying were beneath her, she gently steered me towards the Crescent. Had I been left on my own I would have built a home in Pickett Village, a lower-priced subdivision, almost—gasp!—tract housing, the standard 4br, 2 ½ bath layout. That would be plenty of room for the three of us and the animals, although I was no longer sure about Duke. The aging cocker was declining rapidly and along with a continuing lack of bowel control, was sleeping more and more. Brian had been after me to do something about it, although I resisted because Duke seemed happy and peaceful and continued to eat, although he often dropped his food everywhere, adding to his mess.

Along with sidewalks, which the larger homes in the Crescent lacked (because such concrete strips were aesthetically jarring, I supposed), Pickett Village seemed genuinely friendly, with street parties and summertime picnics for the neighborhood families. And it was affordable, with prices in the $200,000 range. Anything costing more than $250,000 made me as nervous as a ewe on a submarine.

The much larger Crescent was divided into three levels, sort of like Frodo's universe in *Lord of the Rings*. Homes cost $500,000-$750,000 in Upper Crescent, where she lived. Middle Crescent had a price range of about $350,000, while Crescent Mews, whose close-together dwellings resembled an English village with bricked walkways and a center square, nonetheless ran between $400,000-800,000.

Shelia's argument was that the value of the real estate would only skyrocket and wouldn't it be nice if Brian had a downstairs office in addition to a fully furnished basement. Evan loved playing pool and pinball and Shelia knew where I could get discounts on equipment for both. Besides, we could work with our own architect/builder and get exactly what we wanted for only about $50,000 more then the costliest model in Pickett Village. "Would you rather have a smaller home on a more expensive street or live in a neighborhood where the houses are identical?"

But *all* the homes were similar, I wanted to retort. I knew that two out of three of her sister-in-laws were planning construction of their own mini-mansions in the even more prestigious 'hood of Lambdon Park, whose widely spaced abodes boasted mature trees and green spaces with playground equipment every couple of blocks. This was a point of contention between her and Todd. As the oldest brother and the president of the company, shouldn't he have the biggest house? So I kept silent, figuring that Shelia wanted a friend nearby. Susan had been talking about building as well—she lived in the nearby suburb of Gahanna. And although her children went to Columbus Academy, her husband Gary was a golf aficionado. They could easily afford a golf course lot at Lambdon Park, which was also within walking distance of The Club. So they'd probably end up there as well.

Shelia told me she regretted being so conservative in her choice of a home. Her daughters were rapidly approaching their teens and would need private bathrooms, dressing areas, and a separate room for entertaining guests and having parties: all under parental guidance, of course. Arranging and managing were vastly different concepts, however, as Evan's middle and high school years would reveal.

I had to admit her argument made sense. But it was an investment and—my God!—I had a almost a quarter of a million dollars, less the few thousand I'd already spent on joining The Club and odds and ends, such as new towels and sheets, a big-screen TV, car phones for me and Brian, and computer equipment and games for

Evan. So we could put a major down payment on the house and still have an affordable mortgage. And I could still get the luxury sedan I'd been contemplating. I'd lease a BMW instead of buy one, saving on a hefty monthly payment.

I promised Shelia I'd talk it over with Brian. She invited us to dinner with Susan and Gary at The Club the following night and I accepted. I was thrilled. Other than his parents and occasionally Brett and CeCe, Brian and I rarely socialized with other couples. Maybe we'd found our niche after all.

Chapter 3 - To the Manor Born

My wonder years were pretty average, although at the time I thought I was oppressed. We lived in the affluent suburb of Milton, which was largely Protestant and Catholic, with a sprinkling of Jews. The latter two had their own country clubs, just as we had ours, which included nearly every species of WASP, short of Baptists and what people back then called "holy rollers." For years I thought they were referring to perforated plastic curlers I used to straighten my already linear hair. Whenever friends slept over, I took pains to hide the bristly instruments of torture. No reason to add to the ammunition brought on by my height and clumsiness.

The cultural mix made kids from my neighborhood a little less acceptable to the lace-curtain snobs who ruled Boston social circles, where Mom had grown up and where we girls were often shuttled to Cotillion events to mix with other Daughters of the American Revolution spawn.

The only African-Americans I ever came into contact with were maids—no one had heard of the PC term "house cleaner"—and waitresses and gardeners at the country club. Our maid Nancy received a Master's in English from Morehouse College in Atlanta. But when her Navy husband got transferred to Boston in the 1950s, the only work she could find was as a domestic. Ironic, considering that better jobs for Negroes—as they were called back then—were supposed to be up North.

Every day at 4:00 the maids would congregate at the bus stop at the end of the street. I often wondered what they talked about—surely it was more interesting than what went on in my closely transcribed life. I wished I could go home with them and play with their pigtailed, afroed children. During the hot summer months, I'd seen newscasts of black kids fooling around with makeshift bats and balls and jumping in water streaming from fire hydrants. It looked more fun—and certainly more exciting—than lounging around the pool and fighting with my sisters and the other country club brats.

Nancy turned out to be my best friend, even before Mom got sick. It's easy to get overlooked when you're a middle child and Nancy, who also came from a large family, understood this. She took the time to seek out my thoughts on various matters, both personal and political, sharing her views as well. Every so often she'd let slip that the families of the other domestics mistreated their help, had marital problems, or shipped their wayward offspring to military school for some misdeed or another. Afterwards, Nancy swore me to secrecy, and I kept my word. So when my next-door neighbor Mrs. Kehoe came back from a two-week "vacation" wearing sunglasses, I knew that she'd really been away at a private hospital having a facelift. How cool was that for a twelve-year-old to know?

My father, Vincent Spinoza, MD, was a family practitioner before the era of specialization. He worked long hours and even made house calls when we were little. And my sisters—two older and two younger – were forever excluding me. Each had found a playmate in the sibling closest to her own age, and whenever there was a falling-out I was bypassed. They skipped over the middle stair-step—me—for the older or younger sibling who could more easily relate to the flare-ups that occur between sisters who are at the same time best friends and worst enemies. Plus, I was so tall and fair-haired that, given Daddy's Italian heritage—he'd grown up Catholic and converted to the Episcopalian church to please Mom's family—I was a standout physically in a family of petite, brunette munchkins. Even Mom's pale, patrician blondeness paled next to my Viking features. Hats with horns and fake braids still cause me to cringe—I've received more than I care to admit as gag gifts for various birthdays.

But the worst time came during my freshman year in high school, when Mom was diagnosed with ovarian cancer. Just a few months before I'd decided to become a veterinarian. Our house was a way station for stray dogs, cats, parakeets, hamsters, and anything else my fickle sisters decided to adopt and equally as quickly lost interest in.

Mom had always been busy with golf and charities and I ended up taking care of the pets, under the tutelage of Nancy, who had grown up on a farm in Alabama. Large and small animals shared the same basic physiology and she'd nursed her share of sick cows and sheep, passing along the knowledge to me.

It seemed as if one day Mom was racing about, instructing us with warmth and care about schoolwork and boys in her intelligent, distracted way and the next, she was gone forever. She'd spent most of her last months in the hospital trying various treatments, rather than with us. Daddy had been desperate to save her and spared no cost or effort. If it hadn't been for Nancy, we would have probably ended up on drugs or in Juvenile Court. As it was my two youngest sisters, Cassie and Robin, got in trouble for smoking and sneaking out with boys. The older ones, Lisa and Caroline, were a freshman in college and a senior in high school, respectively, and already halfway out of the nest. Once again, I was the odd girl out, except for Nancy, who was always there to listen. She stayed over during Mom's last few days and just after the funeral. Daddy plunged right back into work, pretending there was no huge gaping hole in our lives.

Our once-nuclear family reached critical mass, and it was about this time I became conscious of the fact that we were semi-wealthy. I kept hearing discussions about trust funds and wills and learned that Mom had died with nearly $2 million to her name. And that was after taxes.

Suddenly we had carte blanche to purchase whatever we wanted. Caroline decided to go for a red Ford Mustang loaded with extras; she got it. Cassie and Robin developed a taste for the most expensive toys, and later clothes, that money could buy. It was the mid-1970s and materialism was becoming cool again. Only Lisa seemed not to want to spend excessively; she was and always has been practical. And I was too distraught to even think about buying things, feeling somehow responsible for my mother's death. As the one most on her own, shouldn't I have immediately noticed her quickness to fatigue and paler than usual complexion?

It was Nancy who convinced me that our decimated family unit was no one's fault. "We can't see what the future holds, honey," she said in her thick Southern accent. Daddy kept reassuring me that I'd always be "taken care of"—whatever that meant—asking me if I needed clothes or money. I didn't, I just wanted him to spend time with me.

So if I overspent my allowance or monthly allotment in college, I was given more. I never worried about finances and whenever people talked about stocks, bonds, savings, and interest rates, a switch in my brain shut off. As a girl who was guaranteed an education and would marry a man at least as well off as she was, I didn't need to know about that boring stuff. Besides, such topics were in the male genetic code, like golf or football. Women's lib only extended so far.

Except for Lisa, whose husband Nate actually taught her about finances, my sisters felt that way too. After investing her inheritance in a commune, Caroline no longer cared about material things and believed she would be taken care of for the rest of her life. Cassie and Robin, both beautiful girls, married into old, established East Coast families and are part of the East Coast social scene. They make the New Wellington crowd look like the Beverly Hillbillies.

So when Brian and I arrived at that fateful dinner with Susan, Gary, Shelia, and Todd, I was susceptible to that uniquely American syndrome, Jonesus Keepupwithus. With over $225,000 tax-free dollars burning a hole in our savings account, I thought we were financial equals to our new friends. What they don't tell you about money is that it's the opposite of losing weight – easy to get rid of and twice as hard to replenish. With both, you must work like hell to maintain, watching every cent and calorie.

All during the drive to The Club, Brian and I discussed the new house. Not surprisingly, Mable had ferreted out our plans, although amazingly, she offered little resistance. Looking back, it made sense, considering it was my inheritance and had nothing to do with McLean's Fine Furniture. Despite the conversation with Shelia, I had reverted to my original position and Brian agreed that we would be better off buying in the more modest Pickett Village. There were several layouts to choose from and we both liked the one with three bedrooms upstairs, a great room and a first-floor study. Any remaining money would be used to finish the basement, a lair for

Evan and his friends.

"If there's anything left over," Brian observed grimly as we pulled in The Club's circular driveway. "We'll have to spend thousands of extra dollars to conform to New Wellington codes" such as putting sod on the lawn and not seed, constructing ceilings to a certain height, and making sure window and roof materials met certain specifications. "I wish there was some way around it."

He peeled off a five for the valet, handing him the keys to his still new-smelling Grand Cherokee, purchased just weeks before my father's death. "So far I've managed to avoid any scratches, so please make sure you park it away from everyone else." As the valet walked around to open the door for me, Brian turned to me and smirked. "If it had been your p.o.s, I would have only given him a dollar."

"That's going to change," I retorted, annoyed at his habit of making jokes about things that he meant seriously. His inevitable response was that he was only kidding. If I had it to do all over again, I would have made him sign a truth-in-jest prenup, avoiding comments with hurtful, hidden meanings. "Evan and I are going to the BMW dealership tomorrow."

"Don't make any decisions until this house thing is settled and we've sold ours," Brian warned as we stepped into the subtle opulence of the main entryway.

I opened my mouth to frame a rebuttal—something on the order of any moment expecting to being asked to park my scratched and dented station wagon, labeled the "Purse on Wheels" by Evan, in the employee's lot—when Susan and Gary and Shelia and Todd came over to greet us. Brian, who'd not met either couple, tensed. "We'll discuss this later," he told me quietly in a terse voice. I hated when he said that.

I hadn't met the husbands either, but right away I could tell who belonged to whom. Shelia's shortness and intensity were matched by the bespectacled, balding Todd, who although he was a businessman, had the scattered look of a college professor. Gary was the exact opposite. An imposing six-footer with a shock of thick, dark hair, he radiated ebullience and confidence, seeming to dwarf the other three by the sheer force of his personality.

He was the first to reach us and pumped both our hands. "It's so good to finally meet you! Susan says great things about you, Tish."

I smiled at Susan. "Surely not about my tennis game." We'd discussed the possibility of joining a fall league at an indoor court then decided against it, opting for a play-and-learn which catered to peons such as us. Even the lower-level players at The Club took the game with a seriousness which still intimidated.

"What would you like to drink?" Gary asked, looking at me. "I'll get you something from the bar." I noticed the others held wine glasses.

"I'll go with you," Brian said. It was a McLean trait to never allow anyone to pay for anything. Otherwise, you might owe them something.

"No, I'll get you guys something to drink. It's on me. I'm just glad to finally meet you!"

No one could argue with such force of will, not even Brian. "Well, thank you. But I'll come with you, anyway. I'm not much of a wine drinker and I know what Tish likes. Chardonnay, right? "

"Not tonight dear," I said as the others laughed. "A Riesling. Blue Nun if they have it." Usually I went for the more traditional stuff, but I was feeling adventuresome.

"Have it or habit?" Gary smiled while Susan rolled her eyes.

"I'll warn you—My husband is king of the corny jokes," she said.

"As is Tish...." Brian smiled and gave me an indulgent wave to let me know he meant it in the kindest of ways.

Mentally I breathed a sign of relief. Brian seemed at ease, at least with Gary. With Evan finally getting older, we'd been wanting to expand our circle of friends, a luxury denied us since moving to Columbus. First it was his father's illness, then Evan's birth and trying toddler years, then my Dad's death.

I turned to the others. "I invited CeCe, but she and Brett had other plans." Lately CeCe had been dodging family functions, claiming issues with the rehab project and her sudden, totally uncharacteristic desire to obtain full-time employment to help pay for it. The latter sent Mable into orbit, although business was slow and even Brett's annual request for a raise was denied. Never mind that Brian hadn't had one in five years—four years longer than Brett—and Mable frequently inquired about progress on my associate's degree. Brian never asked for a salary increase and put the pressure on me to work when money got tight. I could never figure out why it was acceptable for me to go out and find a job I despised, while CeCe could gallivant as she pleased.

"I haven't seen much of her lately," Susan observed. "I hope everything's all right."

Of course it was. Nothing bad ever happened to a mistress of the universe.

*****

Dinner was as much fun as we'd had since college. It was the rarest of chemistries, when women who genuinely like each other get together and their husbands form a similar rapport. Each couple ordered a bottle of wine, which disappeared quickly as the six of us shared in consuming it. Even Brian, who never drank wine, joined in and ordered a couple of martinis.

And miracle of miracles, he was giving me amorous looks and squeezing my leg under the table. Could tonight be a night? The last time we'd made love was when we took Evan on a Disney cruise three months ago. Lately Brian seemed to have lost interest, claiming exhaustion or stress every time I proposed we "go upstairs," his euphemism for sex, which I initially found amusing when we moved into our ranch house a few years back. Maybe the Mickey Mouse and Donald Duck tableau painted on the door of our cabin fueled his ardor. Or perhaps it was the fact that we could hear our neighbors banging away the other side of the wall, a mental picture I tried to block out because collectively the couple weighed about 450 pounds.

Shortly after the main course, discussion turned to houses. Susan and Gary had just met with an architect who specialized in Lambdon Park and were in the process of fixing up their current home for sale. Already realtors were fighting over the listing. The Raders seemed to live a charmed life, with homemaker Mom, happy-doctor Dad, a boy and girl who were both honor students and a not-so-bright but ironically named labradoodle, Thomas Edison. Their large circle of friends encompassed Gary's medical colleagues and contacts from his part-time teaching gig at OSU and Susan's buddies from Columbus Academy and the Gahanna public schools, where she generously donated her efforts, although her kids only attended the former.

Gary and Brett were the same age and when they both turned 40 last year, CeCe compared the turnout of her husband's party to that of Gary's. "They had so many people that the street was parked up on both sides. People were coming in and out the whole night and the house was so mobbed you could barely move."

On the other hand, CeCe held Brett's at a restaurant to downplay the fact that only ten couples (including Mable and Jack and me and Brian) attended. "I must have invited fifty people and half of them didn't bother to respond. And do you think they'd reciprocate and invite *us* to their fucking parties? Hell no!" I'd never seen her so angry.

There was a pause in the conversation and Shelia turned to me and Brian. "Have you two made any decision about where you're going to move?"

Brian looked almost embarrassed. "Well, we were thinking about Pickett Village, but after hearing you guys talk...." He let the sentence trail off, as if implicating me as being the instigator of so tacky an alternative.

"I'm going to tell you the same thing I told Tish," Shelia jumped in, her eagerness reminding me of my cat Teddy. Whenever I opened a package of baloney, he'd come running, no matter where he was in the house, even if he'd been sleeping. "This is an investment which can only accrue. There's really not much difference cost-wise between Pickett and the Crescent."

"Well, you've got these damn building requirements," Brian grumbled. "And they can add up to tens of thousands of dollars. So a house that's a quarter of a million someplace else is $300,000 in New Wellington." When it came to money, Brian knew the cost of things down to the penny.

"That's true," Shelia conceded. "But what if you buy a house that's already built? All the homes in Pickett Village are new builds but that's not true of the Crescent. I know of a gal on Gunnison Hall who just listed theirs. Eli fired her husband and they're going back to New Jersey. And I bet they'd negotiate to your price range, especially since they're desperate to sell."

Her expression was so similar to Teddy's as I tore off a small piece of lunch meat that I almost laughed, although the situation was hardly amusing. Upper-echelon employees of Katz Enterprises regularly felt the heel of Eli's boot for reasons that were only hinted at. Only the handful who'd known Eli since he began his business two decades ago seemed to have job security.

"For goodness sakes, Shelia. How do you know what they can afford?" Todd reprimanded in his quiet, gentle way. "Let Tish and Brian make their own decisions."

"All the houses in New Wellington are nice," Gary added. "And other than size, there's not much difference between them."

I raised my wine glass in silent agreement and took a sip. Gary smiled. "The only reason we're moving is so I can be on top of the golf course." Between his busy practice and lecture schedule, his free time was at a premium.

"Actually Shelia has a point," Brian looked thoughtful. "If we can get a home that's already built, it would save a lot of money and aggravation."

I'd been looking forward to adding my own personal touch to the design, after so many years of living in someone else's prefab space and taste. We hadn't done much to the Upper Arlington residence, mostly because it was so old and borderline shabby and the upkeep sucked away any extra funds that might have been used for decorating. "It depends upon what the house is like," I hedged. "There are certain things I want."

"Of course you have a say-so Tish," Brian said in a reasonable tone, most recently utilized when Evan begged for a $700 mountain bike for his 11th birthday. Although Evan was disappointed he understood that he'd have to wait a few years for such a prize. But he was also beginning to realize it might never come at all.

In all fairness, though, kids' demands were sometimes downright thorny and the only way to placate them was with "some day" or "maybe." And I could be just as guilty about not keeping promises, especially if it had anything to do with my animals, such as containing them in certain rooms so they wouldn't shed on our good furniture or sending loyal Duke to his final reward. Even though, thanks to the family business, we got quality furnishings at cost and could replace them easily.

The ride home was mostly silent, which I took to be a positive sign. I had drunk more than normal and was still hoping for an amorous end to the evening. Brian seemed to have had a good time; otherwise I would have heard about it the moment we entered the car. Finally he spoke. "Wherever we move, Tish, you're going to have do something about that dog. We can't have him ruining the carpets and furniture in a new house."

"I know." Best not to start a discussion of Pickett Village vs. the Crescent.

But Brian seemed to read my thoughts. "It does make more sense financially to buy something that's already built. You can't argue with that."

When I stayed silent, he continued. "If not that place, then another one you like better. I'm just looking out for our best interests. We're just asking for headaches and hidden costs if we build. And we can buy in a better neighborhood for about the same amount."

It was alcohol vs. sexual desire and alcohol won. "But why is it important to live in a neighborhood because someone says it's more prestigious?" I blurted. "There's a real sense of community in Pickett Village," something I had never experienced in Upper Arlington. "And besides, I'm tired of being practical. For once, I'd like to pick out our colors and layout." I know -- I should have waited for a more opportune time to present my side of things.

"Jesus, Tish, why are you so stubborn?" Brian raised his fist towards the steering wheel as if to pound it in frustration. "We just had a great evening. I really like your friends, especially Susan and Gary." Always pleasant, Susan had kept the conversation sparkling when the rare dead silence emerged. "Why can't you see things my way? It's a real turnoff." No one could read me better than Brian. And I don't know if I'll ever give anyone else that chance again.

Nothing I say or do is good enough, I thought. I wanted to retort, "I'll agree with everything you say whenever I lose my free will. Too bad they stopped doing lobotomies." But I kept quiet. The punishment for my insubordination had been meted out. No sex tonight for me. But that probably would have been the outcome anyway.

PART TWO: QUEEN OF DENIAL

Chapter 4 - The Truth about Birds and Dogs

"Do dogs worry about retirement?" The veterinarian standing before me was a complete stranger, albeit a very good-looking one. His sparkling eyes brimmed with humor.

"Excuse me?" I stood in the examining room of the Upper Arlington Animal Hospital in my tennis whites, my blonde hair stuck unceremoniously beneath my New Wellington Country Club cap. It matched my pleated skirt and sleeveless top, also both with NWCC monograms. The only splotch of color in the whole ensemble was my cocker spaniel, Duke, who lay in my arms, trembling. Evan was in the waiting room. He had called me off the court in the middle of the game, saying that Duke was having some sort of seizure.

"Where is Dr. Exeter?" I demanded, struggling against tears. "I'd asked for him." Dr. Exeter had been with Duke since we'd first moved to Columbus, since he—Duke, that is—had been a puppy. It seemed fitting that he should do the final procedure.

The young doctor's expression changed abruptly, his expression going from merry to aloof and professional. "When you called, you asked if you could get in right away. I was the first one available. What is going on with Duke? I'm Dr. Fairchild, by the way." He did not bother to extend his hand. Both of mine were busy, trying to maintain my rapidly failing pet's physical equilibrium.

I could see where this was headed. He thought I was another kind of bitch, a two-legged, country club purebred insisting on special treatment. "Duke is dying," I said coldly. "He was lying on the floor shaking when I came home. His pulse and respiration are thready and his breathing is shallow. I was trained as a nurse, although not in veterinary medicine," I added, making sure he knew that I was more than just some rich man's wife.

Dr. Fairchild looked at me closely. "I certainly understand why you wanted Dr. Exeter. I would get him, but he's left for the day. Do you know any of the other doctors? Perhaps one of them..." He reached over, as if to take Duke from me.

Then I did burst into tears. "I don't want anyone!" I sobbed. "I want my dog to be better! I want him to be healthy again! I don't want him to die..." It was embarrassing crying in front of this handsome veterinarian—now closer to my age than I initially thought, although his shaggy hair bespoke a familiarity with a collegiate lifestyle in which locks went untrimmed, jeans were worn until their holes became larger than the body part they were covering, among other questionable acts. But I couldn't help myself. I was losing a best friend.

"I have to examine Duke," Dr. Fairchild said gently. "We won't decide anything until I've had a chance to look at him first. OK, Patricia? Can I call you that, or do you prefer Mrs. McLean?" His voice was like caramel, rich but not oversweet.

"It's Tish." At his questioning look at my unusual choice of a nickname, I explained, "Pat is so neuter and Tricia's, well, too Republican." I had grown up during the Nixon era and in no way wanted to be associated with the daughter of a man who resembled a failed used car salesman and went around proclaiming "I am not a crook!"

I handed him the dog, who proceeded to pee all over both of us. "Oh no," I moaned, trying to wipe up the mess with my short skirt.

"Don't do that," Dr. Fairchild looked away. "You, uh, don't want that to stain. Let's get you a towel so you can clean yourself off." He seemed oblivious to his own ruined lab coat. " Poor old fellow." Gently he patted the cocker spaniel, who could barely lift his head in acknowledgement. Just yesterday, Duke was a squirmy golden puppy, a perpetual motion machine whose level of activity was only surpassed by Evan's growth from zany toddlerhood to full-fledged wild child. How was my son faring in the waiting room, anyway? He was unusually quiet—normally he would have wandered back here long ago.

Dr. Fairchild left, only to return almost immediately with a nurse and several wet towels. The nurse and I wiped up the mess, while he examined Duke. "I was afraid of this," he said after a few minutes. "It looks like a progression of the heart failure Dr. Exeter diagnosed several months ago. Duke's really having trouble breathing. We could put him on oxygen and leave him here for a few days but given his age and general physical condition…"

"I know," I sighed. "My son wanted to be there if we put him to sleep. He's only eleven. What do you think?" Here I was asking this man I barely knew for advice. Once every ten years or so I meet a man I find attractive and of course it would be under the worst possible conditions. Not that I was looking, of course.

"There's a young boy who just went outside," said the nurse. "Do you want me to get him, Dr. Fairchild?"

"Yes, please do," the doctor replied, as the nurse left. He turned to me. "I've not had much experience with children. My kids are still very young," he said, and it was then that I noticed his wedding ring. It was similar to the slim gold band I'd purchased for Brian when we'd first married. He'd worn it for maybe six months and then it disappeared into a drawer. Brian maintained that jewelry made his skin break out, although he had no trouble with the matching jumbo gold and diamond-studded pinky rings his parents had bought him and Brett.

"I hope you don't think I was being flip when I made that remark about dogs and retirement plans," he continued. "My wife is a stockbroker and last Sunday she and her golf group were discussing 401ks in great detail. When I saw your tennis outfit, it reminded me of that and occurred to me that animals are very much in the moment, which isn't always such a bad thing."

"Do you belong to New Wellington?" I'd hardly pegged Dr. Fairchild as clubbable. Like many of the women, most of the men there were tanned, barbered, and groomed to excess, with an aura of smugness I invariably found annoying. Although it had supposedly been said in jest, Shelia's comment about the three rules—money is no object, my marriage is perfect and children equally faultless—seemed to apply to them as well.

Dr. Fairchild seemed uncomfortable, as if he'd regretted turning the conversation in this direction in the first place. "No, we joined Lakeview," he said, referring to another club that had sprouted in the suburb of Powell a few months ago. "It's mostly for my wife's business. Taking clients out to dinner, playing golf…" He trailed off.

"We just bought a house in New Wellington, and I'm learning how to play tennis." I jumped in to fill the gap, trying to distract myself from the real purpose of my visit. "My husband is a great golfer and he's thrilled about having a course close to our house."

"I could take golf or leave it," Dr. Fairchild admitted. "There's something about people in mismatched clothing riding around in funny little carts that doesn't quite resonate. But my wife likes it, and Jason and Jessica will probably enjoy it when they get older. But at ages one and three, they're hardly concerned with getting in with the right crowd."

Interesting how, when a man and woman connect—even if it's a flurry of a flirtation—they rarely reveal the name of their respective spouses. It's as if by personalizing their significant other they are taking them out of the role of wife or husband and making them more real. I didn't realize this until much later, of course.

I was about to tell him I had to deal with country club phoniness as a child and never particularly enjoyed it either when the nurse came in with Evan. The defiant look on my son's face revealed volumes about how upset he was about losing his lifelong companion. "I can watch, Mom," he announced. "I'm not a baby. Dad said I could."

"Evan," I began. "I don't even know if I can stand it…" Duke whimpered and put his head between his paws. My son pretended to be a tough guy, but inside he felt the loss as keenly as I.

"How about this?" Dr. Fairchild said. "Why don't you come back with me while I get the stuff ready for Duke, and then we can decide. Your Mom can have a moment alone with him to say goodbye and then you tell me whether you want to help your Mom here or be with Duke." He cast me a significant glance.

"Thank you, Dr. Fairchild," I said. I had to admit that Dr. Exeter, who was nearing retirement age, would hardly have had the finesse or patience to make Evan feel like he had a choice in the matter. In fact, it was Dr. Exeter who kept telling me that I would "know" when it would be the right time to put Duke to sleep. Had I listened to Brian, it would have been two years ago, when the dog started becoming incontinent. If I had listened to myself, it would have been never.

"Call me Nick," he said. "Mostly everyone does, except the staff, who insists on preceding everything with 'Dr.' Come along, Evan." Then Duke and I were alone.

"You've been such a good companion," I whispered into the dog's soft yellow fur, which was wet with my tears. "I'm really going to miss you." He sighed, as if in acceptance. Retirement funds, indeed. I managed a half-smile.

*****

Meeting Dr. Fairchild or Nick or whatever he called himself had gotten me thinking. What *had* attracted me to Brian all those years ago?

Of course I still loved him but even if I didn't, I'd been raised to stay married—no one in our immediate family had ever had a divorce, except for my paternal grandmother, whose ex-husband, an alcoholic, beat her regularly. She always joked that she might have been in it for the long maul, except she met my grandfather, the lawyer she'd gone to see about getting the divorce.

Brian was a nice-looking man, a good provider, and reasonably intelligent. I told myself that I should have had no complaints but whenever I saw couples who truly seemed to be in love, I was consumed with envy. But walking away because I felt unfulfilled seemed foolish and self-indulgent.

Susan and Gary were a classic example. Unlike CeCe, Susan never discussed her sex life or acted flirty. You just knew they were happy, by the relaxed way they acted around each other and the constant interchange of affectionate glances. People say no one knows what goes on behind closed doors and this is true, but some couples seem to have a special magic.

We'd had it, too, when we first met and during our early years in

Columbus. My sophomore year at the University of Virginia, I was getting over a relationship with a rock-star wannabe, a 4-F man whose "find 'em, 'feel 'em, etc, fuck 'em, and 'forget 'em" attitude may have worked with naive girls such as myself but was not effective in his own attempt to matriculate and resulted in even more "Fs". My friends kept telling me what a loser he was, hardly a brilliant insight since he'd been in and out of college for six years. But he was cute and had a great butt. And he knew how to make a woman sing, even if she'd been sexually tone-deaf before meeting him.

So when this earnest and considerate jock type from my English class started hanging around, I refused to take him seriously, at least at first. But Brian has a way of charming people by being steady, consistent, and considerate, and perhaps most important of all, good in a crisis.

When my father called me in a panic because my 13-year-old sister Robin had gone to a Kiss concert and not come back that night, Brian drove me all the way from Charlottesville to Boston. Although it was a 10-hour trip, we made it in eight. By that time Robin had been located, her brief career as a groupie cut short when a roadie expected an "audition." Having so recently experienced my own rock 'n roll trauma, Daddy thought I'd make a good counselor. But it was Brian who gently explained to Robin that Gene Simmons probably had wrinkles and hair growing out of his ears and nose under all that makeup.

More than anything, Brian's thoughtful mending of my littlest sister's broken heart won me over. Here was this guy who was really sweet, in addition to being attractive in his own way. And we could talk about anything. He confided that although his mother initially expected him to follow the family tradition of the furniture business, he'd been a crack golfer in high school and dreamed of going pro. His father encouraged him, but being practical, suggested that Brian get a college degree.

Brian was the first in the family to attend an out-of-state college; he'd gotten an athletic scholarship to University of Virginia and spent summers winning regional competitions. His mother Mable was thrilled by the fact that their youngest son might possibly follow in the footsteps of Upper Arlington's own Golden Bear, Jack Nicklaus. It would be up to the older brother, Brett, a former high school football star, to ensure the continuation of McLean's Fine Furniture.

Years afterward, when Mable nostalgically recounted Brian's "glory years"—and it was often, especially when the business started becoming less profitable—she lamented that if he'd only been able to fulfill his potential, he would be raking in millions or at least hundreds of thousands. The implication was that Evan and especially I held him back. Naturally, the truth is far more complex. But for a while there, between Brett's gridiron talents which earned him temporary status as a legend, and Brian's all-star duffing, the McLeans were quite the notable Upper Arlington family, particularly among country club cognoscenti.

Brian and I got engaged our junior year, shortly after Brett announced plans to wed his high school girlfriend, CeCe Stephens. It wasn't until after the divorce when I was sorting through photos that I noticed the shocking resemblance between me and CeCe. A bridesmaid in her wedding, I could have been a sister, or at least a first cousin. The years have diminished our likeness: CeCe tended towards flashy and sexy designer clothes and highlighted her hair while I went with a basic blonde rinse and shopped at the department store. She also had several plastic surgery interventions and worked out regularly, making sure every square inch of that fabulous body was firm and fit. It's a demanding job for which I had neither interest nor income but is one of the more common vocations among country club wives.

I had little time to mourn Duke because we were in the process of moving. And both Mable and Brian castigated me whenever I mentioned my sorrow over the loss of our beloved pet. "It's only an animal," Mable, who never so much as allowed a goldfish into her perpetually redecorated, spotless haven, chided. "I don't know what the big fuss is about. And you still have the cats." At which Brian rolled his eyes. He'd tried to persuade me to give up Teddy and

Freddy, citing they'd ruin the new house with hairballs and back claws, but I refused to even consider it. He especially hated it when one of the cats slipped in the room when we made love, staring at us with a "what the hell is this" expression in its wide yellow eyes. It was Felinus interruptus until the perpetrator, usually Teddy, was ejected.

And besides, there was Evan to consider, my tough and tender-hearted son who cared for animals as much as I. So Evan and I kept our feelings to ourselves, sharing stories about Duke's silly antics while I reminisced about his puppyhood.

Finally I had a chance to start unpacking boxes at 5205 Chiswick Court in Middle Crescent. Although Brian had won the location war, I had gotten my wish for a new build because we had nabbed the last demo in the lowest economic stratum of the *Lord of the Rings* subdivision, a model now surrounded by larger versions whose residents no longer wished to deal with the looky-loos who made regular forays into New Wellington. The area had become so popular that most home sales were through speculative custom models built by developers, rather than a range of tract homes found in many suburbs. So, aside from things like kitchen cabinets and the color of wood (a bit dark for my taste but Brian loved it), I got to pick out appliances, carpet, even the tile for the entryway. And it had a new smell that almost equaled the heady fragrance of my recently leased BMW 325i.

So when I heard a "thump" against the front door glass I nearly panicked. It sounded as if something had collided with the window and such repairs could be expensive. We'd spent a considerable amount of my inheritance on The Club, the house, and my car and needed the rest for decorating and the dozens of unexpected expenses that come with hauling your worldly possessions from point A to point B, even if it was only halfway across town. I peered outside—the cats were already there, tails and ears on high alert, whiskers trembling—but saw nothing. I opened the door. A robin lay face up, still as death itself.

My heart sank. What to do? I couldn't bear the thought of

picking up and throwing into the trash a poor, unknowing creature whose intellect could not process the concept of glass vs. air. Humans have done stupider things. So I called the Upper Arlington Animal Hospital. Upon explaining the situation, I was immediately put through to Dr. Fairchild. Didn't the man have any other patients? I wondered. He certainly seemed competent enough.

"The nurse grabbed me just I was coming back from lunch break," the rich voice informed me, as if reading my mind. "I understand you have an unconscious bird on your doorstep?" I sensed his amusement and could practically hear the rest of the unsaid sentence, "Do you want me to call an ambulance?"

"Well, it just happened," I dithered, feeling like a birdbrain myself. "There was this awful sound as the bird hit but he looks intact. It's a robin. He's lying in the middle of my front porch. Should I bring him inside?" Was it my imagination or did I see the tiniest bit of movement? "He might be alive...."

"Whatever you do, don't touch him," Nick instructed. "The fellow might be stunned. He might surprise you and just fly away when he gets some sense back into him."

Then I saw something that shocked me even more. Brian and Jack had pulled up into our driveway, and it was the middle of the day. Why weren't they at McLean's Fine Furniture? Mable followed behind them in her Caddy, her expression even grimmer than her stiffly sprayed, gunmetal grey helmet of hair. My heart thudded; had someone died? My first thought was of Evan and I felt sick. "Something's happened...I have to get off. My husband and his family are here. I'll let you know about the bird later." Without waiting for a reply, I hung up.

It was only my presence that prevented Rigor Robin from getting squashed as they marched towards me. Even Mable failed to notice the moribund-looking avian lying on the front porch of her son's new house.

"Let's go inside," Brian ordered.

"Evan...is he all right?" I gasped.

Brian looked at me in surprise. "He's in school unless he talked you into another sick day." Evan's ruses ranged from pressing a thermometer against a light bulb (it read 107 degrees which fooled no one) to throwing oatmeal into to the toilet to mimic vomit. I had to give the kid points for creativity, although he hadn't tried anything since we'd moved to New Wellington. Still, it was only October.

As soon as we got inside, Mable started to cry. Although I'd seen her weep several times, she seemed truly upset. I put my arm around her. "What's going on?"

Brian looked at me, almost accusingly. "Have you talked to CeCe?"

"Not since we all had dinner a couple of weeks ago." What the hell was he getting at? Between the move and some serious thought about switching my associate degree training from business administration to veterinary technician, I'd hardly had any time for my friends. And CeCe had dropped out of our tennis group months ago, claiming that the demands of her own renovations greatly limited her schedule. Though she was still at the gym quite a bit, according to Shelia who took such defections personally.

Jack spoke out. "CeCe is divorcing Brett and suing him for half ownership of McLean's." Unlike the rest of the family, the man rarely minced words, so when he talked it was usually worth listening.

"What?" I was as astounded as the bird lying dead (or unconscious) on our doorstep. "Why is she doing that? And what about the kids?" I'd thought they were happy, at least Brett was with CeCe. And in the still mostly male-dominated country club world, that counted for a lot. "And what's this thing about McLean's? She's never even worked there." It was an unwritten rule that although I, and now even lately, CeCe could get outside jobs, we would never so much as answer a phone at the furniture store. Even Mable was forbidden to do anything, and her grandfather started the damn thing.

Jack, Mable, and Brian exchanged glances. During the early years of our marriage, Brian had told me stories about Brett's improprieties, gambling, bribes, and foolish investments. But I thought that was behind him once he'd settled down. Perhaps not.

"Well, she has some things on him and it's put us in a bad

position," Mable admitted.

"That doesn't concern Tish, Mother," Brian reprimanded. "What we wanted to know is if she's seen CeCe lately or was privy to what she's been planning." His murky eyes gleamed with suspicion.

Now it was my turn to get heated. "You think I'd hold out on you, Brian? I have no idea what the fuck you're talking about." Although I did it plenty in private, I had never dropped the "F" bomb in front of his parents, so they looked at me, shocked.

"I didn't mean it like that, Tish," Brian quickly backpedaled, his face arranging itself back into its usual bland expression. "I just wanted to know if CeCe sought you out or was complaining about anything…"

"Well, hell, Brian, we all complain," I retorted. "You complain about me constantly and if I ran to CeCe every time that happened, I'd be at their house 24-7." Then I caught myself and saw the devastated look on my in-law's faces. "Sorry. I just don't like being accused of things. I knew nothing about this until just this second."

"I realize that, dear," Mable placated. "We're all upset. CeCe's been sneaking around for months. Apparently she's been having an affair with the Vice-President of Soaps 'n Scents"—yet another subsidiary of Katz Enterprises—"but wanted to make sure his divorce was final before springing her bombshell on Brett. He hadn't a clue about this, either."

I sat down at the kitchen table, maneuvering around more boxes. "Well, I'm sorry about that, I truly am." When I first joined The Club, the thought had flickered through my mind that CeCe might be sneaking around but with Scott, the Italianate tennis pro. Rumor had it that he resembled Michelangelo's "David" in more ways than one. But Scott had recently confided that he wanted to marry a girl from Seattle and was moving there as soon as he saved enough money. Shelia had mentioned something about CeCe's regular workouts with a wealthy single fellow at the gym but she'd also said she'd heard the guy was gay. Besides, lately I'd been too preoccupied to concern myself with country club intrigues. "Maybe I'm not as plugged in as I should be so I'm not going to be much help."

"Look, Mom, Dad, why don't you go home for now," Brian said. "Since I'm not going back to work today, I'll help Tish unpack. Maybe we can come over tonight with Evan."

After letting his parents though the garage, Brian came over and gave me a hug and a kiss. "Look, honey, I'm really sorry. I know how bad that must have sounded and it just didn't come out right."

"I can't believe you'd even think I'd hide something like that from you. And although we're friendly, CeCe's hardly a close confidante. When would I have time for her anyway?" Yet my heart thudded at the remembrance of my brief encounters with Nick.

"You're right," Brian released me. "Evan's going to be home from school in a couple of hours so let's get as much done as we can. Then we can all relax and go out to dinner before stopping at Mom and Dad's."

It was a small concession, but enough for me. I didn't think to question why CeCe had left Brett nor the reasons behind her threat to take over McLean's. And I failed to remember the bird until just before we left for the restaurant. When I finally checked, the front stoop was empty.

Apparently Rigor Robin had survived and flown away. It would be years before I recognized the parallel to my own life.

Chapter 5 - Grand Illusions

One of my high school buddies, Patsy Kennedy Shapiro, often asks me why I stayed so long with Brian, tolerating the chaos generated by him and his family. To borrow her vernacular, long before he requested a divorce, I should have performed a CeCe section. "Spinoza," Patsy said, falling into our old habit of calling each other by our maiden names, "take him for every penny, even if you make a couple of lawyers richer."

Patsy, a plastic surgeon who married an urologist ("If I don't get 'em on one end, Bob does at the other"), only sees that I dreamed of being a veterinarian, and ended up a nurse, a job I hated. The inequities of the family business made her furious: how could Brian let his parents and brother use him like that? They lived high, while we struggled.

The fact that Brian was generally uninterested in me as a woman also aroused her suspicions. During the last years of our marriage, I'd gotten him to admit that he cheated with a 24-year-old warehouse worker. When I confided this to Patsy, she sighed. "I hate to say that I told you so."

"Oh, but it won't happen again, he promised me. And it was only that one time, PK." Unlike the rest of our small but deadly serious group of girlfriends from Milton High, she was referred to by her initials, rather than her maiden name, a homage to JFK and RFK. Anyone with the last name of "Kennedy"—whether or not related to the famous political family as Patsy certainly wasn't—were treated with just a little more respect. Not much, given that we were kids, but a skosh. "Everyone's entitled to a mistake." By then I had made mine with Nick, so I was more empathetic than I might have otherwise been. After that, I talked to Patsy less until after the divorce when we took up our friendship again.

But Monday morning quarterbacking is just that—a bunch of spectators sitting around and discussing what they would have done had they been in the professional athlete's Nikes. When you're in the middle of something—whether it's the death of a relationship or a 275 pound linebacker headed your way—it's almost impossible to be cool and analytical. You just feint towards the sidelines and hope not to get too badly mauled.

Brian and I wed the summer between our junior and senior years in college. We rationalized that since we were the same age, and my plans were to go to veterinary school which would be at least four more years, why wait?. Brian would find a job as a coach—he'd majored in Phys. Ed., minored in business—or, preferably, as a golf pro, wherever I got accepted into vet school. Always generous, my father was willing to send me wherever I wanted so I worked hard for excellent grades. Anything was possible, unless you were a female in a primarily male-dominated and highly competitive profession in the late 1970s.

I didn't know Brian's family well, but to me, a girl who had lost her mother at a vulnerable age and whose own family had been diffused and shattered as a result of that tragedy, they seemed to have stepped directly out of a Norman Rockwell painting. His parents lived in a lovely home in one of the most prestigious areas of Columbus. Mable was animated and vivacious, and eager to share her vast knowledge of social graces. She took me to lunch and shopping and suggested clothes that were classic and more flattering than my shapeless college uniform of jeans and peasant tops.

Whenever we went to their country club—at that time, they were members of the city's oldest and most prestigious Marble Cliff Golf Links and Social Club—people made a fuss over Brian and Brett. They were as different as two brothers could be: Although athletic, Brian was of medium build and height with straight, sand-colored hair. The more striking-looking Brett was bigger overall, with a thatch of wavy dark curls with coarse features, a sort of Anglo O.J. Simpson with touches of Tom Selleck. Brett had been a star football player in high school and his freshman year at Ohio State until something had happened and he'd had to drop out. He'd also followed the family tradition of pledging Sigma Chi, Mable informed me, and had been nominated for Homecoming Court, a rare honor for a first-year student. Married to CeCe only a few months, he was now working in the family business and taking occasional courses at Franklin University, a small secular college in town, although he still exuded that oily prom king/senior class president zealousness. Constant smiles and promises of great things always make me uneasy and at the time I wondered how they could have sprung from the same parents.

It didn't come out until later, but Brett and CeCe "had" to get married, thus the reason for their hasty nuptials. Britney, their eldest daughter arrived just short of seven months after their wedding day. CeCe always claimed that Britney was premature, but the kid weighed in at eight pounds, six and a half ounces.

With weddings less than a year apart (and not having to pay for them) Mable was in a frenzied glory. She helped quite a bit with mine; this was before the era of self-propelled Bridezillas who micromanage every detail of the Big Day That Will Change Everyone's Life Forever. Back then mothers did most of the planning, while the daughters just showed up for an engagement party or shower. Since I was dealing with finals and vet school applications, I was grateful, because I had no idea how to even begin to handle invitations and seating arrangements, although I did insist that the affair be at my church in Milton, rather than in Upper Arlington. I had a family too, and my father's relatives were Catholics of the "be fruitful and multiply" persuasion, despite the fact that Vincenzo, as they still called him, had converted to the Episcopalian faith. (My aunt Tessie told me that having five children kept him Catholic in spirit.) They loved weddings and even third cousins would be highly insulted for decades if the festivities were in an unaffordable outpost in flyover country rather than in their (and the bride's!) hometown. Fortunately, Dad's expansive guest list was counterbalanced by my late mother's socially aloof Blue Blood kin, who'd had little time for us when she was alive and even less after she passed on.

"Please understand that Mom can be over-enthusiastic," Brian apologized after yet another seemingly endless discussion about how much more convenient the ceremonies would be if they were held in

Columbus. "She's always trying to run people's lives unless you stand up to her." That summer, Brian and Mable had argued over his decision to be a golf pro, rather than using his teaching degree when he graduated. She felt it was beneath his social standing to be an employee of a country club and he just as firmly stated it was the only viable and affordable path to the pro tournament circuit.

"I had the same crap when I first got to U. of VA," Brian told me as we drove back to Boston, shortly before the wedding. "Mom wanted me to pledge Sigma Chi, which has been the family tradition. Well, I didn't like the guys; they were a bunch of dumb jocks and hopheads and disrespected girls, talking about who they 'got it on' with, high school stuff. So although I was invited to join, I turned them down."

"I wish I had your courage of conviction," I replied. "I've hardly stood up to anyone in my life…" Nervously I nibbled at a fingernail. "I don't know what I'm going to do if I don't get into a vet school."

"Don't worry about that," Brian reached over and squeezed my knee. "I know you will. I have faith in you, Tish."

*****

Brian was right, but he was also very wrong. About six months after we married, Jack suffered a major heart attack, leaving McLean's Fine Furniture under the dubious guidance of Brett. By now, I'd been let in on some of the family skeletons: Brett had been expelled from OSU for taking a bribe from a bookie to meet a certain point spread. It had all been very hush-hush and only Mable's father's friendship with the newspaper owner had kept it from the media. (Lucky for Brett, this was just before Watergate.)

However, it eventually resulted in their resignation from the Marble Cliff Country Club, of which Mable's family had been a member of for three generations. Subtle pressure had been brought to bear and since the president and board had decided it was time to admit a token black before the NAACP and ACLU made an example, the McLean's' troubles provided a perfect excuse to carve space in a membership already bloated with trustafarians and legacies.

It took several months for the family to finally get the hint;

things came to a head during a Fourth of July party when the club sergeant-at-arms, who also happened to own a rival home furnishings store, made loud, drunken insinuations about Brett's "little problem with the ponies" in front of all their friends. Humiliated, Mable and Jack left, never to return. They immediately joined the less exclusive but equally expensive Upper Arlington Country Club, the first of many unsatisfactory ventures until they finally landed at The Club—the one in New Wellington. For years, however, Marble Cliff was the gold standard against which all others fell short.

About a year before Jack fell ill, Mable's father, George K. Smith, also had a heart attack, a fatal one. It was he who had renamed the company McLean's in the 1940s when Mable married Jack, because, according to Brian, it sounded so much "thriftier" than Smith's and they'd hoped to expand their customer base to what George had called "ethnics and coloreds."

Brian was worried, not only about his Dad, but also about the business. "I don't know if Brett can handle it. He's a great outside man for sales, but when comes to the office, he doesn't know anything about dealing with employees or suppliers." Brian had worked at McLean's summers and weekends from the time he was twelve.

"Why don't you fly back to Columbus and finish your courses by correspondence?" I suggested. Finals were only a few weeks away and professors were flexible, especially when it came to family matters. I would miss this beautiful campus with its lush Georgian architecture, quirky traditions, and Jeffersonian graciousness. Charlottesville offered the best of the Old South without the underside of racism – at least not overtly, in view of Yankee eyes. I would also miss sharing with Brian the bittersweet nostalgia of parting with our carefree college years. But I also understood what needed to be done. "That way you could be with Jack and watch over the business. By the fall, everything should be back to normal and we can move to Sacramento like we planned."

Much to my delight I had gotten accepted into two veterinary schools, one at University of Missouri and another at UC-Davis. We opted for California, on the basis that it had more golf courses and a great climate. And I'd never been there, although Brian had always teased me about looking like a California girl. "Now you'll fulfill your destiny." Of the six colleges I'd applied to, only two—Ohio State and Cornell—turned me down. I'd been wait-listed for the rest.

The rejection from OSU had really frosted Brian. "Jesus Christ, what do they expect?" he fumed. "You have a 3.8 in pre-med, your GRE scores are out the roof, and you've got great recommendations from your professors."

I shrugged. "What difference does it make? Sometimes they're looking for experience with animals, and frankly, they don't take many women, although I've heard that is changing." Secretly I'd been hoping for UC-Davis and when I got the acceptance, none of the others mattered. "It's not like we were planning on living in Columbus, anyway." I paused. "Were we?"

"No, no," Brian replied, avoiding my eyes. "I just wanted to know that the option was there." A few weeks before Jack's heart attack, Mable had called with the news that a plum coaching job was available at Worthington High School, a suburb close to Upper Arlington.

Be that as it may, we're going to California no matter what, I told myself as I helped Brian pack. I would close out the apartment and if necessary, find us a place in Sacramento and stay there alone until Jack was better and Brian could fly out and look for a job. No way was I going to end up in Columbus, Ohio, surrounded by Mable, whom I had begun to recognize as manipulative, and ex-beauty queen CeCe, who acted as if she was a sex goddess, despite the fact that she had just had a baby. No way.

But that's exactly what happened. Jack ended up with complications, a minor stroke and a scary staph infection which left him hospitalized for nearly eight months. He came close to death twice, and Brian never left his side, unless it was to deal with some problem at McLean's. We found a small ranch home near theirs and rented it with an option to buy. And since I could do little with a pre-med degree and needed to work, I went back to school and got an RN.

A couple of years later, we had Evan.

Brian and I did both walk for graduation, however, although only my family could attend. Shortly before we were to return to Columbus, leaving Charlottesville for the last time, he went out for a brief while then came back with a shy smile. In his arms was a squirming golden puppy, the purebred cocker spaniel I'd talked so much about wanting since I'd been a child. "It's just a way of saying 'Thank you,' Tish," he told me, his normally mild expression full of genuine regret. "And that I really appreciate all you're giving up for me. I love you."

I burst into tears. "I love you, too." And the three of us stood there for a long while, a canine and human group grope, caught in circumstances beyond our control, lacking the maturity and confidence to fight back.

******

"I'd like to speak to Dr. Fairchild," I grasped the phone so hard I was afraid it would come apart in my hand. It was several weeks later and we'd finally settled into our new home. Evan seemed to be enjoying eighth grade and Brian and I were spending lots of time with Shelia and Todd and Susan and Gary, going out to dinner and to the country club. We'd half-jokingly given CeCe a dishonorable discharge from the drama queens and rarely saw Brett. Although he'd moved in with Mable and Jack, he'd already developed his own friends, mostly singles with whom he went skiing and bar-hopping.

The initial splurge on the golf membership had been in the low five figures, but Brian was good about making sure monthly fees were paid from McLean funds as a corporate expense, rather than from our family coffers. He also seemed to appreciate the time and effort I put into the house. One of the perks of the business was that we were able to furnish every room, including a pool table and bar for the basement.

Brett and my in-laws had engaged a lawyer, and it had become an all-out war on CeCe that looked to be headed to the courts. Along with half of the business, CeCe was determined to gain full custody of Britney and Whitney, in addition to occupation of their now fully renovated home in Bexley. She claimed to have proof of Brett's misconduct, which ranged from false tax claims to using corporate funds to invest in race horses and stock cars, questionable activities in even a privately held company. If CeCe was to be believed, Brett had been stealing from McLean's for years.

"Is this true?" I asked Brian one night when we were in bed.

He looked everywhere but my eyes, a sure-fire indication that he was being evasive, if not lying outright. At least I'd figured that much out about this man whom I lived with for so many years and thought I knew. "To some degree… Of course Dad and I didn't realize it then, but now we do." Wearily he put his book in front of his face. "I don't know what's going to happen but let's not discuss it now. I need some sleep."

During the increasingly rare times we went to The Club with Mable and Jack, Mable constantly speculated that people were staring and talking about us. I suggested she might be overreacting, but Brian chided me, saying, "Tish, you always were oblivious about social things and what others are thinking."

Look who's talking, I wanted to reply. Your own damn brother was robbing you and you claimed to never notice. But I shrugged instead. "Our friends don't gossip or ask questions and that's all that matters to me. And the other members come from all over the city and even the country, so how could they know anything?" Or even care, I thought but did not add.

To which Jack observed, "Who gives a shit what these schmucks say, anyway? Let's just enjoy our meal, Mable." Lately he'd become more assertive and less tolerant of his wife's obsession over appearances.

My purpose for calling Nick was, on the surface, innocent. I'd pretty much made up my mind to switch from business, much to the dismay of the McLeans. Except for Evan, who thought that it was "phat" that I was going to be spending my working life with animals. As part of my introductory course to veterinary technician work, I was to "shadow" a busy office for a day or two.

Since I was familiar with the Upper Arlington clinic, it seemed a logical choice. Viewing the setup firsthand would help me finalize this big decision. The two-year training program in anatomy, physiology, applied mathematics, biochemistry, animal husbandry and more would be at least as intensive as any college curriculum. And I would be expected to work summers at a clinic or animal shelter, getting minimum wage if I was lucky.

"Who shall I say is calling?"

My mouth tasted like cotton and I swallowed. "Tish McLean."

A pause and the receptionist came back over the phone. "He's with a patient right now. What's your number? He'll call you back as soon as he gets a moment."

Yeah, right, I thought as I gave her the exchange. Just like all those guys that I had a crush on in high school that never did. But then, he probably would, if he believed it was a veterinary matter.

Fifteen minutes later, the phone rang and I snatched it up like Evan waiting for a call from his latest girlfriend. "Hello?" I tried to borrow some of my son's seeming cool and braggadocio.

"Mrs. McLean? It's Antonio Fairchild." His warm voice held undertones of formality.

So that was his full name. "Nick" had to be the Americanization of the Italian nickname "Nico." In Boston, where I grew up, a person's moniker was vital in making a first impression, providing a provenance to not only his country of origin but an opening to further inquiries such as, "Are you related to the Fairchilds of Beacon Hill?" In Ohio, it seemed not to matter as much but I couldn't help noting with pleasure that Nick probably had both Italian and Anglo-Saxon roots like me. We exchanged pleasantries and then Nick asked, "How is the bird?"

The bird? I wondered wildly, worried that I'd accidentally flipped him off on the freeway. At times I was less than patient with overcautious Columbus drivers, the direct opposite of the cowboys in my home state, called Massholes by locals.

"The robin…the one on your front porch?" he prodded.

"Oh, yes! Well, you know I think it was fine because when I went back to check later, he was gone. I had a family emergency so I had to get off the phone. I thought something had happened to my son but there was a problem with my brother-in-law." When flustered, I tend to give out what Evan calls TMI—too much information. "Anyway, that's not why I called. I'm thinking about becoming a veterinary technician and would like to spend some time observing your office. Would that be all right?"

"That would be great," Nick's response was immediate and enthusiastic. "I sensed that you had a real feel for animals. You can come in during the morning or at lunchtime, and we can talk about some of the job opportunities. It's not much money but it's very rewarding in other ways." He went on to describe the various aspects of the work, from taking histories to providing nursing care to helping with routine procedures and surgeries.

I felt as if I'd come home, as if I'd struck the mother lode of what I was supposed to be doing. "That sounds wonderful. How about next Thursday?"

We set on 8 AM. I had a sense of taking the first step on an important journey, a feeling I'd not experienced since being accepted into UC-Davis over 15 years before.

Chapter 6 - Meltdown

Mable might have been disappointed to learn that the big news, rather than centering on the divorce of her eldest son and the subsequent perils his soon-to-be ex-wife had brought to the family business, was what people at The Club called "the nanny problem" and the mansion in Balfour Farms that Shelia and Todd were building adjacent to Eli and Janice Katz's. Shelia had finally convinced her doting husband that, as the president of a booming recycling business, he needed to have a home to match his image as a lion of industry, which he was, despite his lamblike exterior. Her three catty sister-in-laws were furious and had basically stopped speaking to her on all but social occasions, when they went out of their way to ooh and ahh over each updated window treatment and kitchen fixture in each other's homes, ignoring the fact that Shelia was going to have everything entirely new, at least for a couple of years. Which suited her fine, since she couldn't stand them anyway. "They're nothing but a bunch of social climbing bitches who hate it when someone else betters themselves," she pronounced.

It was an unwritten New Wellington rule was that you were not to construct anything more elaborate than Briarcliff Cottage, the "King's" deceptively named palace. Appraised at $50 million, not even she and Todd could begin to match it. So what they lacked in capital they hoped to make up for in distinction. Outside touches included Art Deco sconces and lintels, a shocking deviation in terms of both lighting and window and door decorations and (gasp!) selecting bricks different from those approved by the New Wellington Planning Board. Upon submitting the blueprints, they were cited for building violations from both the Board and The New Wellington Group, who had sold them the lot.

Eventually they'd caved and gone the mini-me route, which was the original intention anyway. Imitation paid homage to the King's excellent taste in creating what had been "simply a vision," according to a brochure I'd picked up when we first started looking for a house in New Wellington. "An ideal of what life would be like if all portions of a community came together as part of a single master plan." And it had worked, which made the concept even scarier. "Apple pie's a little more flavorful in New Wellington" raved another tag line next to a photo of three smiling cherubs at what was obviously a Fourth of July celebration. "Our Club is so extraordinary, residents spend vacations there," the inadvertent subtext being that they're so financially strapped they couldn't afford to travel elsewhere anyway.

Anyway, Jonesing (as in "Jonesus Keepupwithus") Eli would be physically impossible. His acreage was about 15 times the size of the biggest parcel at Balfour Farms, which, incidentally, had been purchased by Shelia and Todd. Much of the interior of the so-called cottage, at least the 25,000 square feet that had been seen by outsiders (the Katzes had another 20,000 square feet to themselves) had been brought over from England, Scotland, and France and included a huge gallery for Eli's museum-quality art collection.

Another highlight was a marble and teak dinner table that emerged from the lower level. This enabled the servants to lay the Spode china and Buccellati silver atop the hand-embroidered Italian tablecloth and napkins without disturbing the guests. And then the table slowly lifted, like a crypt from the dead.

My questions, which I posed to our group over dinner one Saturday night a little over a year after we'd moved, were: what did the guests do while the table was completing its journey? Did they peer down anxiously or scoot their chairs away from the edge? Had anyone ever had too much to drink and fallen *into* the opening? While the others were laughing, Susan shook her dark curls. "Tish, you can be so silly. The table is elevated before the guests even reach the front parlor. It's already there by the time they sit down to eat."

"And you know this because…" Up went Shelia's ever-present social radar.

"I was invited to a luncheon there last month," Susan lowered her head as if humbled by the admission. "Janice wanted to thank the girls who helped her organize a workshop on shaken baby syndrome." One of Janice's biggest causes was domestic violence, an odd choice for a woman who'd grown up in a sheltered Orthodox Jewish community just outside of Philadelphia. It reminded me of Miss America hopefuls spouting about how they wanted to establish world peace. As if conflicts in Bosnia and Afghanistan could be patched up with butt tape, hair extensions, and spray tans.

"You *are* holding out on us," Shelia's voice was shrill. As the house had gone up so had her level of obsession with all things New Wellington and Katz. "What was it like? Tell me everything. "

"Here we go again," said Todd and even Gary rolled his eyes. "It's not like you've never been there yourself, Shelia."

"The last time was years ago, when it was just built... Todd, remember the United Jewish Appeals fundraiser? What we got was a tour of basically empty rooms. Since then, we've been relegated to the Shed"—the huge party barn so far removed from the residence that large groups had to be transported by bus—"But that was it. From what I hear, Janice has added a fully equipped gym and spa with a full-time masseuse and personal trainer. And didn't Troy McHugh build a dog house to match the Cottage?"

Troy McHugh was *the* interior designer for New Wellington. I'd met him on a couple of occasions and found him surprisingly down-to-earth although we could hardly afford his services. But Gary and Susan (who moved about the same time we did) could and did, and now Shelia had hired him.

"For someone who hasn't seen it in a while, you certainly know a lot," Gary drained his glass of wine (his fourth? fifth?) and without waiting for the server, poured himself another.

"I don't," Shelia looked frustrated. "And Troy refuses to discuss his other clients. He won't even hint at what their ideas are."

"Which is probably why he remains successful," said Gary. "Why don't you just do what pleases you and Todd?"

"Amen to that," added Susan. "Besides, I signed a nondisclosure statement." Thanks to a scathing article in *Esquire* about Eli's over-the-top lifestyle and manipulation of governmental bodies to build roads, museums and office space (not to mention an entire fiefdom, er, suburb), he refused most interviews and according to Club gossip, had become almost fanatical about his privacy. As one local columnist had observed, the house had a media room but it wasn't a reception hall for reporters.

I had to admit I was curious, too. "You're among friends, Susan. You can tell *us*."

"I didn't pay much attention anyway," Susan replied primly. "I was too busy talking."

Oh, please, I thought. While agreeable most of the time, occasionally Susan could be annoyingly self-righteous.

"You guys are no help at all," Shelia glanced at Todd. "I guess you're tired of hearing about this. What's the weather going to be like for your golf game tomorrow?" Todd smiled and took her hand.

"Well, I've got something juicy," Susan leaned forward, her large chest drooping over the table. "Did you hear about Mary Filson's nanny?"

Susan's breasts were another topic of speculation, mostly because of their size and lack of buoyancy. When we first joined The Club and many months before she left Brett, CeCe and I went to the grocery one day after a round of tennis to pick up menu items for a surprise 60th dinner party for Jack. She'd just finished remodeling her dining room and wanted to show it off. We passed by a bin full with several types of squash and she burst out laughing.

"What's so funny?"

"Have you ever seen Susan naked?"

"Nooo." I usually bathed at home, foregoing the nude confab that was a part of The Club's female locker room culture. Though the few times I'd overcome my modesty and changed there, I'd found it deliciously self-indulgent, thanks to the large, multi-jet showers, luxurious towels and cornucopia of soap, deodorant, and hair accoutrements.

CeCe held up a long but thick banana squash. "Susan's breasts without a bra," she chortled, barely able to speak. She topped it with another gourd with a large, turban shaped cap. "Susan's nipple. It's been on vine waay too long." She collapsed with glee, placing two smaller acorn varieties with short, upturned vines against her own chest. "At least mine are pointed in the right direction!"

I smiled at the memory. Despite everything, I missed CeCe's observations, which although sometimes brutal, often had the accuracy of a heat-seeking missile.

Unlike boobs and other body parts that may or may not have been surgically enhanced, the Nanny Problem was discussed between both sexes. When you mix attractive women, usually in their 20s, who have access to the same amenities as the wives, who are a decade or two older, it causes problems, especially when said girls are unaccompanied by their young charges and can flirt with the husbands. Nannies were constantly being told not to dine in the main clubhouse or use the workout facilities. They could play tennis and eat at the snack bar as long as they were with the children. There was even talk of making a separate lounge for nannies when The Club was remodeled and expanded in a few years.

"Apparently, Elise"—the nanny—"had a thing for Scott,"—the tennis pro—"and someone caught them in the supply shack doing, as they say, the wild thing." Susan wagged her fingers at the last three words. The visible portion of her massive cleavage in its tastefully cut, scoop-necked top jiggled, as if in sympathy with the act being discussed.

I found that story hard to believe. "I know for a fact that Scott's quitting and moving to Seattle to marry his girlfriend."

"I heard this from a very reliable source," Susan retorted, a touch arrogantly. "Scott and Elise have been eyeing and rubbing up against each other for weeks. And this person, who shall remain unnamed, went back to get an extra hopper of balls because there were no pros around and walked in on them..." She let the sentence trail off, leaving the rest to our imaginations.

"Yeah, but the girlfriend's in Seattle and he's here," countered Brian. "Why not get some strange before clamping on the old ball and chain?" And this from the man who refused to join one of the most prestigious fraternities at U.Va because he'd found them too crude.

Todd and Gary snickered but I flushed in anger. How could

Brian say such a thing? Didn't he realize that such statements made both of us look bad, and our marriage look even worse?

"Well, needless to say, Elise got fired and Mary's now desperate for another nanny," Susan concluded in the same tone she probably used when telling her kids their favorite bedtime story.

Suddenly I was disgusted with them, my allegedly loving husband and these people who were supposed to be my friends. Compared to the veterinary world that had become a part of my daily life, the things they considered important seemed petty and irrelevant. Although Brian was unhappy with the salary I'd be making as a vet tech, which would be much lower than what I'd earn in a corporation or even as a nurse, I prevailed. Thanks to a suggestion by Nick, I'd applied for and received a federal grant which paid for my classes. In addition to getting straight A's and loving the work, it cost us nothing and even looked as if I'd be graduating early, because I'd placed out of some of the pre-med courses I'd already completed in college.

"Yeah, poor Mary," sarcasm dripped from my voice. "What's she gonna do? She'll have to take care of those two brats by herself. No more daily massages and manicures for her! And Elise? She's out of a job with no references but that's what you get for being young and beautiful. Scott? Well, he's a man," I drawled, with deep emphasis on the last word. "He can't help himself. Excuse me." I fled, knowing that an explosion of tears was just a few more words away. Some people had a short fuse; while mine was longer, it was of the "thar she blows" variety.

Before I had a chance to reach the ladies' room and compose myself, Shelia hurried up behind me and grabbed my arm. "C'mon, Tish, don't be upset. It's no big deal."

I jerked it away. "You don't get it, do you? These are real people with real problems. You've got more money than God, so you can't possibly understand what it's like to lose a job or have someone make up lies about you. You have money and they don't, so what you say is true, right?"

"No, it's not like that at all. The Club is a wonderful place. It's like living in a fantasy world which caters to your every need. But sometimes people overstep their bounds and measures need to be taken."

"You're right about the fantasy part. I'll tell you what I think," I took a deep breath to douse my flaming emotions. "I've noticed Mary's husband flirting with the nannies and some of the more attractive staff members. I think Mary caught on and made up that story about Elise to get her out of the way." Come to think of it, I'd seen Susan and Mary deep in conversation at the snack bar a few days ago.

"Then speak up. We're not heartless people. There are two sides to everything."

"Why? And contribute to the endless round of gossip and speculation that goes around on here? I don't know for sure, I'm just telling you what I observed. You need to get out and see what the real world is like…" At Shelia's injured expression, I stopped and remembered what my anatomy professor had said about compartmentalizing. When an animal is dying or an emergency occurring, emotions need to be put away in a box and the situation dealt with objectively. The same was true here. "Look, I'm sorry I went off like that. I've been studying a lot, under a lot of pressure." And here came Brian around the corner, an upset look on his face, probably mad at me for making a scene.

"That's OK. I understand." Shelia reached over and gave me a quick hug, turning to go back to the table.

I faced Brian. "Don't you say a word. That crack about the ball and chain was just uncalled for."

"I know. I just want you to join us. I realize what set you off." That was as close to an apology as I was going to get.

"If you don't like being married, just tell me. And don't say I'm being too sensitive."

Brian sighed deeply. "It was a joke, Tish. A joke. Can't you tell?" Then why was neither one of us was laughing?

*****

The dust-up at what was to become one of our last dinners at The Club gave me an idea. If people in New Wellington were so keen on helping the disadvantaged, why not get them involved in something that directly affected their community? If charity begins at home, then surely the dispossessed animals that were inevitable in any area would benefit from a no-kill shelter. Although there were a couple in Columbus, scandals about mistreatment and misuse of funds had either closed their doors or reduced their operations to mostly ineffectual.

The problem was worsened by college students whose transient lifestyles resulted in the desertion of dozen s of dogs and cats at the end of each term. Lacking money and a sense of responsibility, the students let the poor creatures, who were neither spayed or neutered, roam the streets, further increasing the itinerant population. Along with being a moral transgression, abandoning a pet was a crime under Ohio law.

I decided to bring up the subject at the meeting of the Columbus Veterinary Society. Consisting of doctors, techs, and other animal care professionals as well as concerned citizens, we gathered on the third Thursday of every month in the basement of the First Lutheran Church on Broad Street. Nick had told me about this group when I first visited his office before embarking on my training. He occasionally came to meetings, his attendance often curtailed by his erratic schedule. When I did see him there, we talked for a long time afterwards, lingering until after the last pot of coffee had been washed out and the church janitor started closing up.

This particular evening he showed up late, slipping into in the back row. It was almost as if I had a sixth sense about him; if we were in the same room I knew where he was at all times. Our eyes met frequently, usually accompanied by a smile at both ends. But today I didn't turn around to acknowledge him. I was preoccupied, worried as to how I, a relative newcomer, could present this idea to experienced professionals who'd seen so many shelters come and go. A few months away from taking my certification exam as a vet tech, I wanted to make a good impression on these people, some of whom could be potential employers.

When it came time for new business, I tentatively raised my

hand. "Tish?" I was surprised that James Gladstone, DVM, knew my name. Along with being president of the Society, he was head of the Banford Veterinary Clinic, one of mid-Ohio's largest and most successful practices.

I stood up awkwardly. Public speaking has never been my strength but if this thing was going to succeed I would have to start learning how to talk in front of people. My father had always advised us that it would be easier if we sought out a friendly face. So I focused on Nick and he nodded encouragingly. "I know we've discussed no-kill shelters before," I said. "But they're usually in less desirable areas or near campus. What about a shelter in a well-to-do suburb?"

"You mean like New Wellington? That's where you live, isn't it?" This came from Arnie Freeman, who'd opened a shelter on the West Side, only to have it shut down by the Board of Health. He'd been written up in the paper several times, claiming that he'd been discriminated against; by exactly who, though, he'd never made clear.

"Yes to both questions, although I don't know what the second has to do with the first," I retorted, trying to keep my voice even. Several people chuckled, including Nick and Dr. Gladstone. Thank God.

I took a deep breath. Few liked Arnie and most of the others' expressions seemed sympathetic or interested, so perhaps I had stumbled across a valid issue. "It's like bringing the mountain to Mohammed. If we make the indigent animals easily available to those most likely to give them the best homes then we'll probably have a higher rate of successful adoption." It was one thing to place an animal, and quite another to make sure the dog or cat would be well taken care of for the rest of its days. People who moved frequently or had otherwise unstable lifestyles in their jobs or relationships were generally poor risks. The minute something went wrong—the pet got sick or misbehaved—it ended up back at the shelter or worse, on the streets. And too often, the previous owner lied about the animal's health, another cause of recidivism. As with foster children, frequent changes of domicile caused trauma, mistrust and disobedience.

"I think it's a great idea," Nick spoke up. "We've never tried to open a shelter in a suburb before. And I think New Wellington, or even Powell, where I live, might be ideal."

"Getting the money for a project might not be as difficult as, say, in Columbus, because we're focusing on a specific neighborhood or community," added a woman named Leann who ran a pet hotel and grooming center in Gahanna. "Plus you won't encounter as much red tape or grandstanding by the vultures on City Council." This got a laugh; it was well known that during election years local Humane Societies came under intense scrutiny as they were easy targets for politicians. It took very little effort to get a news crew to the animal shelter and highlight the problems there, while the politician promised reform if he or she was elected. Nothing ever came of it, and thousands of dogs, cats, and even rabbits continued to be euthanized and crammed in cages under too-crowded conditions, receiving limited care because of lack of public involvement and government support.

The group tossed around the idea for several minutes, coming to the consensus that it needed further research, which was to be done by Nick and me. Afterwards, we spoke briefly, agreeing to meet over the next few weeks and outline a plan for fund-raising, along with deciding on a location. I was thrilled; not only had they liked it, really liked it, but it I would be seeing more of Nick.

*****

Although Evan started his New Wellington career with great promise, by the end of his eighth grade year, he had become sullen and confrontational. He and Brian argued constantly, and even if I wasn't present when the quarrel began I was always caught in the middle by the time it reached fruition. My sweet son, who loved to jump out from behind corners and shout "Boo!" and picked flowers from the neighbor's yard to give as gifts (and even asked me to marry him when he was four) had turned into a monosyllabic thug, whose main passions ranged from misogynistic rap music to gangs to guns. The last time I'd seen him exhibit genuine enthusiasm was when he came home with a charred gym shoe in his hand, one that, to his credit, he'd already outgrown. "Me and Clay blew this up with M-80s," he exclaimed with a big grin. "It was so cool!" M-80s being a popular type of firecracker, rather than actual ordnance.

The one kid I really disliked was a new acquaintance, Trey Unger, whose divorced mother rented a run-down ranch home at the edge of New Wellington. Oddly enough, she still belonged to The Club. Rumor was that her ex had given her the choice of keeping her membership there or staying in a huge new house with all expenses paid. Apparently she'd opted for the first; the property was littered with a rusted-out car, lawn mower and other broken-down household appliances and attracted equally malfunctioning kids. Trey himself had already had several minor run-ins with the law.

It was also said that the mother, who had no visible means of employment, entertained various gentlemen (or maybe not) callers on the premises at all hours. Although I had no problem with Evan's other friends who came from single-parent or blended families, there was something sleazy about this one. But there was little I could do. Especially with teenagers, forbidding companionship with a particular person only breeds sneaking around to see said individual behind your back -- if nothing more, having four sisters had shown me that. You have to give the kid a damn good reason not to associate with the undesirable. I only prayed that my son would be spared harm while I waited for the right excuse.

I'd offered to host Evan and his crew (his vernacular) at our house, but Brian was always in a bad mood, making it uncomfortable for everyone. He seemed especially intent upon curtailing our activities at The Club, claiming there was no money. So we saw less and less of Susan, Shelia, and their respective families. Brett's divorce, now close to being final, had run into the hundreds of thousands, thanks to a hefty lump-sum settlement to CeCe and his payoff on their Bexley residence. Brett's inattention to the business and Brian and Jack's preoccupation with damage control had taken a toll: where there were once a dozen stores all over the state, there were now only three in and around Columbus. Apparently CeCe had had no designs on McLean's but had been advised to ask for the most she could possibly get by her high-powered attorney and negotiate downward. She hadn't missed by much.

I found myself resenting her more and more as Brian continually hounded me about finances. "You need to start bringing in some money, Tish," he said, and I tried to explain that although I'd done well on my certification tests, it took time to find a decent job. I could work for minimum wage, but that would barely pay for gas and my meals and after taxes very little would be left. Besides, if the animal shelter got off the ground I could be my own boss… But I kept quiet about that, instinctively knowing Brian would chide me for chasing a dream when things were so tough. And I was reluctant to explain my friendship and possible partnership with Nick.

There was no denying my growing attraction to Nick. I told myself that we were just friends, that he was married and had young children. But in the middle of the night or when I had an occasional quiet moment, I found myself fantasizing about him, wondering what it would be like if we made love. Then other times, I'd burst into tears, feeling absurdly guilty. For what? He hadn't so much as touched me, other than to shake my hand when we saw each other, which wasn't often since most of our conversations took place over the phone.

As if our mounting debt and troubled teenager weren't enough, Brian decided to take out a second mortgage. It was to pay off the credit cards I'd run up, he said, but even I could do the math; you didn't need a $50,000 line of credit for a total of $10,000 worth of charges.

And then a 24-year-old warehouse worker fell and broke her leg while unloading several rolls of fabric. Brian and Jack were worried about a lawsuit, so Brian spent a good deal of time making sure she received the proper care, as she lived alone and her family was in West Virginia. He took groceries over at least twice a week, stopping by for a few hours on Saturday or Sunday to check if she was all right.

When I questioned him about this—his depth of participation seemed out of synch with the situation—all I got was that she came from "poor white trash" who, if they became involved, would see an opportunity to sue an old, established company. So apparently it was in McLean's best interest to keep her happy.

Meanwhile piles of Brian's mail remained unopened on the dining room table and bills went unpaid, until one day the electricity was turned off—somehow several warning notices were discarded before I saw them—and I decided to take over the checkbook. Uncharacteristically, he didn't even argue with me, a total 180 from early in our marriage when he wanted every penny accounted for. Brian also developed an affinity for country music, which he'd openly mocked before. His mood swings ranged from jovial to "things have to change around here", the particulars of which I had no idea.

Yes, the signs were telegraphed for all to see. But when you're with someone day after day, it is hard to recognize dramatic change, especially when it's gradual. And it's even harder to let go of the illusion of normalcy when it's propped up with lies, especially if you deny your own gut feelings. And whenever I asked Brian if anything was wrong, he claimed fatigue and overwork.

So I accepted his responses at face value. If he'd been cheating, he would never have been so open about seeing this woman, I told myself. And I had plenty of my own issues to deal with.

By the time Evan was in the middle of his freshman year, Nick and I were almost ready to present our plan to the Veterinary Society. We decided to call the shelter Paws That Refresh, a title suggested by my clever but underachieving son. The first one would be in New Wellington. I would manage the shelter, while Nick and other volunteers provided medical care.

The problem, as always, was raising money. Having funded his own education through scholarships and loans, Nick was adept at navigating the circuitous and confusing procedures involved with obtaining grants. But we also needed a way to acquire matching funds. My first thought was to go to Shelia for guidance; as one who'd sat on many boards and charities, she'd know the right people to contact and avenues to pursue. But Shelia was in the throes of finishing her house and kept putting me off, saying she'd call me back and we'd get together when she had time. But that moment never came and I was beginning to wonder if word about our troubled financial situation had gotten out and she and Todd were avoiding us.

So I went ahead and did my own research. There were a myriad of details: obtaining community, government, and political support, along with financing and finding an appropriate site that would allow for the safe intake and segregation of animals. This was far more complex than it initially seemed; for cats alone, to prevent the spread of disease and pests, you needed a separate space for the intake of new animals that hadn't been yet checked by the vet. There should be another room for kittens, many of who required extra attention; another area for ill and unsociable felines; and still another spot for the general population that was ready for adoption. The same was basically true for dogs, complicated even further by their need to go outside both to the bathroom and for regular exercise, and for lots of human interaction. Potential adopters also had to be more carefully screened to make sure they could deal with the additional time and care necessitated by dog ownership. No one is quite sure what Scooby will do until they have him around for several days.

Euthanasia was yet another challenge; some animals were quite elderly, chronically ill or troublesome and therefore nearly impossible to place. How could you deal with them? By not accepting them at all and allowing them to become homeless? But if you gave them space and care, where would you put the dogs and cats that might be adoptable?

It was these and a myriad of other questions—for example, choosing and organizing the all-important board of directors to provide counsel and enhance our public image—that I began to pose to Nick during our biweekly conference call. Finally he cut me off with, "Look, Tish, why don't we talk about this over dinner?"

At first I thought he was trying to placate me. "I know you have your own things to deal with on this project. I don't mean to throw all this stuff at you."

"No, no. It's not that. I just think you're getting ahead of yourself here. We've worked hard and it would do us both good to celebrate our progress so far." At this, his rich voice dropped a few octaves, as if something more was at stake than just the business at hand.

"Oh." I paused, taken aback. "Well, OK. Where?" I almost suggested The Club, then remembered Brian's last fit over the bill. And that was because Evan had gone to the snack bar twice. I hadn't had a tennis lesson in months. That would change, once I got a decent job and had more money. If I could find one – good positions for certified vet techs were hard to find and although I didn't mind cleaning cages and doing some of the so-called scut work, I wanted to be able to use my other skills. And no way was I working at the shelter where euthanasia occurred on a regular basis. I couldn't stomach that.

"How about Three's Company?" he suggested, referring to a popular eatery Downtown. It was in the artsy Short North area, a place rarely frequented by either myself or my friends. Unless it was Gallery Hop weekend, when we went in a herd to gawk at the trendies and purchase overpriced gewgaws.

"Do you know how to get there?" I asked. As he gave me directions I could tell that he wasn't particularly familiar with that part of town himself. We agreed to meet on Thursday.

Fortunately, that night Brian had a late meeting with his lawyers and Evan had plans at his friend Clay's. So I had no one to fend for and the whole afternoon to get ready and agonize over choosing the right outfit. Finally I selected the sartorial equivalent of a mullet haircut, a tailored jacket with a scoop-necked, flowered shift with a short skirt, a combination of party and business that I didn't care to examine too closely myself.

I arrived a couple of minutes before seven and much to my delight Nick was already there, waiting for me. He'd dressed for the occasion as well, with a sport coat, crisply ironed shirt and chino pants. His usually disheveled hair was freshly washed, hanging over his ears in soft waves. How I wanted to run my fingers through it, and blushed at the thought as he took my hand in its usual warm, welcoming clasp.

He'd already made reservations and touched the small of my back as the host guided us to our table. The restaurant served what Brian disdainfully called designer food, eclectic combinations of various flavors that usually involved smaller portions and higher prices. Although Mable loved going to trendy eateries and seeing all her friends, taking Brett and CeCe with us before their divorce, we'd accompanied them less and less in recent years. Brian preferred chains or places that accepted coupons, although he usually complained that the food was overdone or too cold.

But tonight was not about Brian, I told myself as Nick asked me about my choice of wine. Since the restaurant was known for its seafood we decided on a nice white. As it turned out, Nick was a recently converted wine aficionado like me. Wine had become popular and it was fun to learn about the different varieties. However, I'd always take a glass of wine over hard liquor any time.

"My wife only likes reds," he said, after the waiter had poured a small amount into his goblet for approval. "So it's a real treat to share a bottle of this." I wanted to ask more about his wife—whose name I still didn't know—but decided not to. He didn't often mention her, and her presence at the table might spoil the mood.

We discussed the shelter, and Nick reassured me that it would fall together on its own schedule. His calmness and laid-back demeanor were an almost shocking counterpoint to Brian's unswerving intensity and demands for immediate answers. "There are a lot of factors to consider, but we'll take it one step at a time," he said. "The important thing is to have a business plan, potential funding, and a possible location. Then we can go ahead and tackle the details like the board of directors, fund-raising, publicity, layout, and the rest. Would you like some more?" He swept his hand towards my nearly empty glass in an unusually expansive gesture.

I rarely had a second, or was it a third? I'd been too busy listening to Nick—achingly conscious of his knees close to mine under our stylishly small table—to worry about my blood alcohol level or concern myself with food, although what I'd tasted of the tilapia was delicious. In fact, I hadn't eaten much all day. But the wine made me feel wonderful, better than I had—since when? I couldn't remember. I felt…like a woman. I felt…alive. "Sure. Why not?" I moved my legs a little closer to his, instinctively seeking the comfort of his hearty, male warmth.

A cell phone trilled, a ring sounding suspiciously like mine. I ignored it, telling myself I'd switched mine to vibrate before coming into the restaurant. It had to be someone else's.

Nick had moved onto the topic of his childhood. He'd grown up in Mentor, a small town near Cleveland and gone to OSU. He was impressed when I told him about being accepted into UC Davis. "That's one of the best programs in the country. Why didn't you go?"

"Well, my husband's father became ill…" And there it was again. That damned phone.

"Ma'am I think your purse is ringing," said the college-aged waiter, reaching for my half-eaten meal. "Are you finished or still working?"

I've been working since you were in diapers, I wanted to retort but said, "I'm done, thanks." With a sigh, I picked up my bag. It had to be Evan. He and Clay were probably at the mall and needed a ride home. Why couldn't he call Brian for once or Clay's parents? "Hello?" I said, struggling to disguise my annoyance.

"Tish, it's Brian," My husband's voice sounded ragged, cutting through my mood like a machete. "I know you must be out somewhere so don't say a word. I'm down at the police station. Evan's been arrested for shoplifting."

I immediately sobered up. "Oh my God. What happened!"

"I told you not to say anything; we don't want people to know. Mom and Dad are on the way. You don't need to come down here. It was a good thing I was Downtown though…"

"Of course I'll be there," I practically shouted, momentarily forgetting Nick and my elegant surroundings. "Isn't the courthouse on Front Street, near Spring?"

"You never listen, do you?" Brian was yelling now. "Where are you, anyway? Out spending more money? By now the whole store knows that your son's going to jail."

"He's our son, Brian, *our* son," I was dangerously near tears. "And don't you talk to me that way. Whatever happened, it's not my fault."

"It never is. Where the hell are you, anyway? Evan said he tried to call you a bunch of times and so did I…"

"I'm having dinner with a friend."

"Of course. You won't cook unless you have to. Tell her that your son got ill and for God's sake, don't make a scene in the restaurant. Stay there and finish your dinner. We have it under control." Before I had a chance to reply he hung up.

I felt sick to my stomach, then remembered where I was. I looked at Nick's shocked face. "What's going on? Is everything all right?" *Her*, I thought, *her*. Brian would never, for one moment, think that I'd be with another man. Well, he was wrong, I fumed, fucking wrong.

"Well, that certainly was a buzz kill," I tried to sound flippant, downing the rest of my glass of wine. "But Brian says it's all under control. So I'll just stay here and finish the bottle." I reached for the Pinot Grigio wondering if poor Evan would have to spend the night in a cell. The McLean influence could only go so far. And I just knew that that low-rent white trash gangbanger wannabe Trey Unger had something to do with it.

"You're upset, so maybe that's not such a good idea," Nick gently took the bottle away from me, his fingers brushing mine. "Why don't you talk about it?"

"I can't," I had the sense of the room closing in on me, of every sight, sound, and color being intensified. I could hear the silverware clattering on the table next to us and the whispers of the couple in the corner booth. "Nick, please take care of the bill. I'll send you a check for my half," I rose to leave, knowing that if I didn't get out of there soon, I would lose my rapidly deteriorating decorum. "I'll call you later."

"Don't be ridiculous. This is my treat—I was going to pay anyway and you're in no condition to drive," Nick's voice became stern, reminding me, absurdly, of the time I went to observe at his office, before I'd started my vet tech training. A tiny Asian woman had brought in a huge Doberman that exhibited flu-like symptoms. After several failed attempts at inserting the rectal thermometer into the increasingly freaked-out canine, Nick asked the flustered woman if she wouldn't mind going into the waiting room. After she left, he told me he wanted me to try.

It was my turn to panic. "I've never done anything like that. That dog will bite my hand off!"

"No, he won't. Under normal circumstances, Zeus is as gentle a lamb," Nick reached for a muzzle, putting it over the dog's mouth with a deft motion. "That's a good boy… If you stay focused and let him know you're in charge he'll quiet down. I'll hold onto his middle and it will just take a second." After selecting the a correct-sized thermometer ("It all depends upon the weight and structure of the animal, something they'll teach you in school"), he instructed me as to the appropriate procedure and amazingly I got it in on the first try, while Zeus looked at me with big sad eyes and whimpered. "It's easier if the owner's not around because the animal picks up on his or her anxiety. The trick is to be gentle and calm and move slowly."

Seeing my frantic expression now, Nick took on the demeanor that I'd seen so often when he was dealing with frightened animals or distraught owners. "It's not safe to get behind the wheel of a car when you're like this. Plus, you've had alcohol. We'll get some coffee down the street and then you can go."

As we headed for the Cup O' Joe, Nick took my arm. How I loved the feel of his fingers, I thought, how I want them all over my body, even though my son, whom I love more than life itself, is in terrible peril. "If you don't want to discuss it, that's fine. But you need to calm down."

"I've changed my mind, Nick. I do want to talk about it," I opened the door and hurried towards the furthest, most secluded table. "Even though we can't do anything about it at this particular moment, I want to go to bed with you. First, though, I have to get my son out of jail."

PART THREE: QUEEN OF PAIN (WITH APOLOGIES TO THE ROCK GROUP POLICE)

Chapter 7 - The Death Card

It took several weeks, but things finally settled down. I kept telling myself that now that Brian and I had really talked, things would go back to the way they'd been when we'd first married. The trick was keeping Brett away from McLean's so Brian and Jack could make it profitable again.

Once that was accomplished, I was convinced, life would be good again. Through her callous disregard of her marriage, CeCe had destroyed so many lives, causing us all hardship. Brett, too, was at fault but not much could be done about him, other than making sure he stayed away from company coffers. If CeCe had kept her mouth shut and greedy hands from McLean's, things would have never gotten this bad in the first place.

But now not only was she living in the huge house in Bexley, but she'd wed her Soaps 'n Scents magnate. From what I heard, she had a new red Mercedes—this time a SL500 roadster, ticket price about $85 grand—and made regular trips to Beverly Hills for shopping and no doubt, more plastic surgery. According to Susan—occasionally we still went to dinner with her and Gary—CeCe and several of the "girls" who were married to high-level Katz execs and local docs had jetted to Italy for two weeks, spending several days at a villa in Tuscany.

I was furious. Although I'd finally found a job at the Banford Veterinary Clinic, it was entry-level and thirty-five hours a week of hard physical work. Between that and making sure Evan stayed within the requirements of his probation and went to counseling sessions, I was lucky to have ten minutes to read a magazine.

"They invited me to go, but of course I could never leave Gary and the kids," Susan said, flitting her bovine-shaped eyes from Gary to Brian. "And I could never do that to you guys." She included me in her gaze. "It would be disloyal."

"It's awfully nice of you, Susan," Brian took her hand and squeezed it. "We appreciate your friendship."

Funny how I'd never noticed how physical Brian was with other women until the night of the living meltdown, as I called it in my mind. When I finally made it to the police station the night of Evan's arrest, Clay's parents and Trey's mother Crystal were waiting with Brian for the boys to be released. I'd been right, Trey had been present, as had William Millman, a 19-year-old dropout with a criminal record and a reputation for hanging around high school kids. I'd not yet had the pleasure of meeting that particular degenerate but had heard about his dyed green hair, tattoos, and piercings hanging from his eyebrows, mouth, and God knew where else. In fact, I would have never thought he'd be spending time with such amateur gangbangers as my son and his friends. But apparently he and Trey went back a few years and was a regular at the junkyard, as I referred to Trey's house.

Crystal and Brian were deep in discussion when I entered the holding area. It had been a struggle but I'd managed to pull myself together after the conversation with Nick. But I would not allow myself to think about that now. I had to deal with my son.

Brian glanced up and saw me. "It's OK, Tish. We've got it under control. We've posted bail and Mom and Dad didn't even have to come down. The boys should be out shortly." He seemed calm and almost cheerful, a 180 from the way he'd been over the phone. But then Brian was always at his best in the middle of a calamity–especially when other people were around.

"As it turns out, they were with a kid who was over 18 so it looks like the charges will be reduced," Jenny, Clay's mother told me. The Millman boy had been arrested before and was being detained as an adult in a different part of the jail. Jenny and her husband Earl were good-natured if perhaps too lenient, and their son seemed a lot like them. So I doubted if Clay was the instigator.

Trey, however was a different story. "Are you sure that it was the older kid's idea?" I narrowed my eyes at Crystal. With her rough grammar, bad dye job and tight clothes, she personified everything I disliked. That and the fact that she always seemed like a victim—things constantly happened to her, yet were never her fault.

"Now's not the time to figure who did what," Brian said diplomatically. He seemed to be hitting it off with Crystal and I again wondered about the warehouse girl, the one whose lawsuit was taking up most of his time. Maybe I was doing what the psychologists called projecting—putting my own misdemeanors onto another person rather than facing them directly.

*****

Nothing happened between me and Nick. We merely sat in the coffee shop and talked. And nothing was going to happen. Although he found me attractive—or so he claimed, obviously trying to soften the blow of rejection—he and Elena were happy, he said, mentioning his wife's name for the first time ever. He avoided my eyes during the last statement.

By then I was completely sober. "I really have to go, Nick," I begged, not wanting him to witness the explosion of tears that bubbled beneath the surface. "My son is at the Franklin County Courthouse and I need to be with him."

I could tell that for some reason, Nick did not want me to leave, although he said he understood. If I'd stayed any longer, I would have spilled my guts—about my almost sexless marriage, about the miserable situation with my in-laws and my husband's work, about how money just seemed to disappear, now matter how hard I tried to manage funds. And good God, what was I going to do about my son? But I managed to escape before all that came out. Then I bit my lip and sucked it up and went to find Evan.

After we got home, with Evan safely ensconced in his room, Brian and I sat at the kitchen table so Evan couldn't overhear our conversation. Although I suspected he probably sensed if not knew what was going on, hence at least part of the reason for his acting out.

Because of the way Brian had treated me on the phone and his recent preoccupation with other women—or maybe my relationship with Nick had just opened my eyes, I didn't know—I could no longer avoid facing the truth. I said that if he didn't want me as his wife or find me desirable, he needed to tell me. "If you're unhappy, we shouldn't be married. I realize you have this problem at work, but you've got to stop. I know all about it." Meaning, I could relate to how a situation outside your family could color your dealings with your loved ones, not to mention other aspects of your life. My marriage and especially Evan's well-being were much more important and valuable than any difficulty, even if McLean's Fine Furniture went under.

My next words would have been to tell him about Nick, about how in order for our marriage to succeed we needed to completely honest with each other, when he blurted, "How did you find out about Amber?"

"Who?" Seeing my confused expression, Brian realized his blunder and tried to backtrack.

"We were just good friends, that's all. She needed someone to depend on and misinterpreted my actions as more that just trying to help." Then I remembered: Amber was the girl who'd initiated the lawsuit against McLean's. It hadn't made sense before. Because she'd broken her leg on the job, the company had paid for her medical bills and her time off work during her recuperation so she had no grounds for a complaint. But if she'd had an affair with Brian; well, that was entirely different. And although I'd voiced my suspicions, I'd believed Brian when he denied it.

"What did she do, threaten to expose you?" I spat out. "No wonder she wanted so much money. She had you by the short hairs, Brian." His inability to keep his dick in his pants would ruin not only our marriage but likely push his already unstable business over the edge. Momentarily forgetting that, only a few short hours ago, I'd been ready to commit the same act myself.

By now Brian was practically begging. "I swear it will never happen again, Tish. It was just for a few weeks. And it's over, I already told her that, which is why we've been having trouble with the lawsuit. I met with Amber's lawyer several days ago and we just now settled it out of court."

Before I had a chance to reply or even react, he took it one step farther. "Tish, if you leave me, I don't know what I'll do. You know I love you more than life itself. I couldn't go on."

He sounded so insincere, so much like a bad Lifetime movie, that I almost burst out laughing. The thought of Brian considering suicide over anything—especially me—was the most ridiculous thing I'd heard in a long time. And I'd been privy to a lot of crazy stuff lately. So in order to cover up my inappropriate response, I attempted a joke: "OK, but only if we stay members of New Wellington."

One of our major recurring arguments was over dropping out of The Club. Along with seeing far less of the Drama Queens and their husbands, Brian had switched his athletic interests from playing golf to the local baseball league, which among most of our former peers was the equivalent of hanging out in a bowling alley. These days, in fact, the people we mostly socialized with were the team members and their wives, the working class of New Wellington, the few diehards who still lived on the outskirts. Lacking good grammar and often overweight and sloppy-looking, they were the exact group we'd made fun of not so long ago.

Brian practically salivated at the prospect of getting back the second half of our initial $10,000 deposit—$5000 had been refunded when we moved into New Wellington—not to mention the savings from dues, now a minimum of $250 a month. In the four or so years since we'd joined The Club, they'd been raised semiannually, from about $100 before any other expenses. Although management offered a consolation prize of a $50 food credit, that barely covered the cost of dinner for two, even if you ordered the cheapest items on the menu.

It had seemed unfair that we should sacrifice the one place where Evan had friends who spoke more than white-boy gangsta and I could play tennis and relax, especially since I'd purchased the membership with my inheritance and paid for it with my salary. I didn't see Mable and Jack offering to give up The Club. They wouldn't even change their annual cruise dates to get the off-season discount because they traveled with the moneyed geezer set who only went during the most expensive time of the year. Meanwhile CeCe benefited, Amber the adulteress walked away with money, and even Brett purchased whatever he liked, buying expensive clothes and a condo in Palm Beach, Florida.

But both Brian and I had both made serious mistakes and perhaps we needed to regroup. Quitting The Club might be one way to simplify our lives and get back to where we'd been before.

And although it had more to offer than most, New Wellington was only a country club. When you're out, part of you thinks you're missing something—one of its allures, I suppose—but when you're there you sometimes wonder why the hell you joined in the first place. Sort of like the Groucho Marx line, "I wouldn't want to belong to any club that would accept me as a member."

Because he'd been Jewish, Groucho had been rejected from a Protestant country club in Los Angeles, or so the story went. Of course country clubs were a uniquely American phenomenon, started because the suddenly affluent, post Civil-War WASPs needed a place to get away from the riff-raff and pretend they were landed, old-money gentry like the Brits they'd kicked off their shores less than a century before. The very first club, established in 1882 in Brookline, Massachusetts, was about twenty minutes from my childhood home, and was called—drum roll for originality here—The Country Club. Although its members rarely associated with our family's nouveau-riche club, Indian Hill, everyone knew that to get in, not only did you have to be recommended by a longtime member whose family went back at least two generations, but the waiting list was several years long, and most vacancies occurred when someone died.

Out of self-defense, and in the true spirit of equal exclusivity, blacks, Jews and even blue-collar workers formed their own clubs. In the 1920s, crime allegedly organized the Mount Prospect Country Club near Chicago, which held what was (very quietly) said to be the

"Mafia Open" golf tournament (Did the losers end up waking up next to a decapitated horse's head? Or did they even wake up at all?). Before joining New Wellington, Shelia and Todd had belonged to Winding Hollow, Columbus's solely Jewish country club. Todd's father, a former president, told him you could always tell a club's ethnicity by looking at the chits—Jews spent more money on food than alcohol, whereas with WASPS it was the other way around. And of course no one ever handed you the receipt after the meal; you either gave them your member number or discreetly signed it and received a bill at the end of the month. If you had to ask or worry about it, you couldn't afford it.

"Whatever you want, Tish. I'll do anything you ask." Brian's voice interrupted my mental meanderings. Why was I thinking about this now, when our lives were falling apart? I started to tell him that the country club wasn't the real issue here, that we should resign because it would help ease the financial strain, but he continued. "I do love you, Tish. I will make it up to you, I promise. Starting now." He reached for me. "Why don't we go upstairs?"

Neither of us had used that line in years—since we'd moved into this house that actually had an upstairs. But I could feel myself relenting. Perhaps a stronger or more savvy woman would have walked away, or stood her ground, but the truth was, I loved Brian. And we'd been happy for many years...surely we could get that back if we both tried. And who was I to criticize? I would have gone to bed with Nick if he'd allowed it. I now understood the lure of an extramarital affair, or so I thought.

Seeing my troubled expression, Brian backed off. "OK, I can tell you're not in the mood. That's certainly understandable. But let's try again. Please forgive me. I made a mistake and I'll make it right...I mean it." Then his shoulders slumped, as if the burden of the night's events had finally caught up with him.

Then he said, "Listen, honey, I have to go to bed. I have a 7AM meeting—I'll make sure Evan's up before I leave so you can sleep a bit before work." Normally we took turns blasting Evan out of bed, threatening him every few minutes until he got up, pulled on whatever clothes he'd thrown on the floor the day before, and made a dash for the "Cheesemobile" that picked him up at 6:45. No wonder high school kids were cranky; they were sleep-deprived. They'd been allowed to slumber until 8 A.M. or so as children. Now, in adolescence, when they needed lots of rest for their rapidly growing minds and bodies and also were at their most nocturnal, they were forced to get up at the crack of dawn.

"We'll talk more tomorrow," he continued, leaning over and kissing me tenderly. "I love you. Oh and by the way, Mom and Dad think the lawsuit's a worker's compensation issue—so please don't tell them."

For a while I remained in that kitchen, wondering why I hadn't said anything about Nick. We'd had what might be called an emotional affair, or at least I had. Other than nonverbal cues like touching me during conversation and giving me what we used to call "the look" during dinner, Nick had said nothing untoward or even overtly flirtatious. Yet I intuited that he cared for and was attracted to me. And I also sensed he was unhappy about certain aspects of his life, although he never mentioned anything directly. It was more what he didn't say—rarely if ever discussing his wife or the things they did together.

But to be fair, to level the field, I should have disclosed my relationship with Nick, because an emotional affair can be almost as devastating to a marriage as a physical one. And I had intended to, until Brian let slip that he'd been having sex with Amber. Between my anger at uncovering that fact and Brian's barrage of clichés, I hadn't had a chance to express what I was really thinking.

But perhaps it was for the best... I told myself that I was protecting my husband's feelings, that two wrongs didn't make a right. But on a deeper level, one that I wouldn't yet acknowledge, I was protecting myself. I needed to appear virtuous, the wronged woman. If I'd confessed to Brian about Nick, it might come back to haunt me in ways I couldn't begin to comprehend.

Finally, exhaustion and the emotional upheaval caught up with me and the tears came. Once I started crying, I couldn't stop. So I went downstairs into our finished basement, where no one could hear my sobs. How could I explain them to Brian, and especially Evan? They were tears for myself, for lost opportunities and love I would probably never have.

By the time I slipped into bed next to Brian, it was an hour before Evan was due to get up. But I heard him moving about, unprompted for once by either me or Brian. Then my husband awoke and quietly shaved, showered, and dressed, stopping to kiss me before he left, something else he hadn't done in years.

After they had gone, I lay there and thought: about my life, about what I would do if I lost everything, about myself as a woman. While I came to no clear conclusions, for the first time since I could remember, the endless internal seminar of fears, concerns and replayed conversations that always seemed to fill my head had stopped.

The silence was bliss. It was like I'd dug through a pit of emotions and reached the bottom—inner peace.

Now I understood why people went into yoga and transcendental meditation. Sometimes it's just enough to be, to sit quietly and let the answers reveal themselves. Or not, because the mind works on its own timetable. When you have kids or a family it's easy to lose that mental compass, because you're always doing something or worrying about the next activity or thing.

*****

I called in sick at the clinic. I wanted to think, to really think about my life, but I also needed to talk to someone who knew me, someone I could trust. So I phoned my big sister Lisa. Of my four siblings, she was the closest to me since our father passed away.

Like me, she hadn't had many dealings with our two younger sisters, especially after our family drifted apart after Mom's death. The last time all five of us had been together had been for Daddy's funeral; before then, it had been years.

The combination of death, money and property can bring out greed and true personalities, especially when large assets are involved. What happened between Lisa and her "Irish twin" Caroline,

13 months her junior, was a perfect example. Because Caroline's conception had been unplanned, my earliest memories of her were of her complaining that she had been unwanted and tormenting me because my birth three years later had been met with great joy (obviously Mom and Dad wanted a large family, a point flaky but book-smart Caroline somehow missed).

Caroline's hippy-dippy lifestyle, as well as her longtime companion—who had no visible means of employment and looked like a cross between a refugee from the Summer of Love and a Hell's Angel—had been a source of amusement until we discovered that Mom's jewelry—which was to be evenly divided between the five of us upon Dad's death—and other valuable works of art had suddenly disappeared. Lisa, never one to avoid an issue, came right out and asked Caroline if she had seen the stuff. Caroline immediately took offense and a huge row ensued. We ended up calling the police, who investigated the home healthcare workers who'd attended to Daddy during his final months. Sure enough, about half of the missing items turned up. The rest were never recovered.

After that, things deteriorated between Caroline and Lisa. As we helped close up the house where Daddy spent his declining years, Caroline came out and stated that she was donating her entire inheritance to the commune or "intentional community" as she called it, where she resided in Oregon.

Lisa said something along the lines of "Are you nuts? To that cult?" and after that Caroline left in a fury with her insignificant other, and has since refused to speak to Lisa or anyone else in the family. As far as I know, Caroline still lives in Eugene, tending the land and cooking and cleaning, which is expected of the women in her "back to nature" movement. It was almost like being Amish, only with light bulbs and indoor plumbing. I decided that if I ever was really bad in this life, my punishment would be reincarnation as a Plain Person.

The situation with Cassie and Robin, the two youngest girls, was different, but with similar results. Like many country club women, they made a career out of being trophy wives and acted as if they didn't need the inheritance, stating they'd spend it on trips and cars and whatever else they fancied. Most of their conversation revolved around what Shelia had jokingly referred to as the "three rules" of endless money and perfect husbands and kids. But once the will was read and they knew the check was in the mail, they left.

Which left me alone with Lisa. Most of the packing was done anyway and it gave us a chance to get reacquainted. Although her husband Nate was an investment banker and wealthy in his own right, now that their kids were almost grown, she had decided to go back to school and get another degree. And it wasn't just any old sheepskin; she was accepted at Harvard and graduated with honors from the MBA program. Granted, Nate's money enabled her to afford it, but considering the competition, that was a pretty amazing feat for a woman who had just turned 42. She worked on Wall Street for a while, then opened her own boutique consulting firm.

Lisa got up early to exercise before going to her office, but the minute she heard my voice, she knew something was wrong.

"So are you going to divorce Brian?" she asked after listening to my tale, the recounting of which took nearly an hour.

"Of course not," I was horrified at the thought. "Both Brian and I made a mistake—that's no reason to end a marriage."

"But Brian acted upon his," she pointed out.

"And I would have, had Nick been willing," wondering why I suddenly felt so defensive of Brian.

"At the least, you guys should go for counseling."

"Look, we sat up and talked most of the night. We both want this to work so we're going to make it happen." And we can't afford marriage counseling, I didn't tell my sister, although I knew she'd offer to help pay for it. Even if the insurance covered it, Brian's family would notice, and questions would be asked. Jack would mention it to Mable and she'd probe until she got an answer.

"Tish, I'm worried about you," Lisa said as we wound down the marathon conversation. "It sounds like you're not taking care of yourself, spreading yourself too thin. Take some time just to think about things, some 'me' time, is what they call it."

"I'm beginning to see that." Yet it was exactly what I'd been avoiding for...how long? Several months? A few years? I was so busy running around, doing this, accomplishing that, that I could not remember when I last sat down and simply reflected upon my life and where it was headed. Worries over Brian, money, my job, Evan, Nick, and the animal shelter had all crowded my mind like a cacophony of voices that simply would not shut up.

*****

A month later, Brian and I were getting ready to leave for Cincinnati for the weekend. We'd agreed that the best way to rekindle our marriage was to spend some time by ourselves without the encumbrance of family or business. On the surface, Brian seemed to have reverted to the man I married—considerate, kind, and affectionate. Yet inside, I held my breath and tried very hard not to do anything that would set him off. It was like that Annie Lennox song, "Walking on Broken Glass," tiptoeing through the shards so as not to make a mistake and get cut again.

We planned to take in a Reds game and have a leisurely dinner at the Montgomery Inn. Brian had made the arrangements and seemed to be looking forward to it, raving about how he couldn't wait to dig into a plate of their ribs. A newly subdued and grounded-for-life—or at least the next six weeks—Evan agreed to stay with his grandparents.

We did have to go Downtown to see the judge and the prosecutor. Each of the boys was arraigned differently and since Evan had no prior charges, it was hoped that the prosecutor would be lenient. But I wasn't taking any chances; a few minutes before we were due in Juvenile Court, I took my son on an informal tour of the facilities. "Meet your potential cellmates," I said, pointing to a locked room with a small, plate glass window. Several rough-looking, disgruntled young men sat on benches. "Who knows, maybe one will ask you out on a date!" I almost said, "Ask you to be his bitch," but thought, even though Evan can use rough language, I don't have to. The point was made.

"I'll kick their ass," Evan threatened. "Those wimps don't scare me." I could practically hear the unspoken word "pussies" but he was returning the favor by toning down his own verbiage.

Evan was the perfect gentleman in court, appearing properly remorseful and very polite. He got off with community service and making reparations to the store for the stolen CDs. The judge also recommended family counseling, so it looked like we were going to see a therapist after all. Maybe it would help—I was willing to try anything to mend my frayed and tattered family. We did not want to end up like Brett and CeCe, although I was nothing like her. I still believed things would get back to the way they'd been during the early years of our marriage, when Evan was a wild but adorable toddler and Duke a cute, frisky young dog. Hey, maybe we could even get a puppy!

Evan's charm and ease under duress reminded me of Brian. Hopefully he was being truthful, but unlike the teenage girls of my friends who were more blatant and openly hostile in their rebellions, boys were much harder to read. After all, they were becoming men, those inward and tough-acting creatures who are mysteries, even to their own mothers.

I'd called Nick several times to apologize for my behavior. I also wanted to reassure him that the situation would not be repeated and in fact the crisis had strengthened my commitment to my marriage. And, in spite of everything that was going on in our lives, I wanted to move forward with the animal shelter.

But when he finally did phone me back, he was—not unlike my son—obdurate, with only a few terse words. "We don't need to discuss this, Tish," he said, when I tried to explain that the problem had been mine, and had nothing to do with him.

"But we do, if we're going to work on the shelter."

Silence. Then, "I was going to tell you, Tish, that I've decided not to pursue this project. Between my family and the practice, I just don't have the time."

Now it was my turn to be obstinate. "And when were you going to inform me of that?" I demanded, my voice harsher than it probably should have been. "You certainly were enthusiastic at dinner." In more ways than one, I wanted to add, but didn't.

"It had been a concern before then, but after that night I realized it was too much." Nick's caramel voice had crystallized into a Heath bar, hard and brittle.

I didn't believe him. "You mean, after I told you how I felt... Really Nick, that should have nothing to do with the shelter."

"Tish, I have to go. I'll mail you a list of vets who might make a good replacement." Then he hung up.

I was furious. How dare he not accept my explanation! Who did he think he was to abandon a wonderful project that could help dozens of homeless animals? And what about our friendship? Did it mean so little that he summarily rejected me when I told him how I felt? Had I really listened to what he'd been saying, I might have reacted differently. But I was still too absorbed in my own dramas to pay much attention to anyone else's.

"Brian, will you get the phone?" I said now as I shoved Nick out of my mind, furiously stuffing a negligee into my suitcase. It hadn't been worn in a while, but I planned on spraying it with perfume to eliminate any musty smell. I'd also purchased vaginal cream and condoms in anticipation of the big event. I'd stopped taking birth control pills years ago...where was that diaphragm? But it was probably dried out and full of holes. Besides, my forty-something-year-old eggs were surely as lethargic as I often felt. The condoms would be fine.

I heard a shout from the other room, then the word, "funeral." Something has happened to Mable or Jack, I thought as I raced downstairs in time to hear Brian say, "We'll be right over."

"Omigod Brian, I'm so sorry," I went over to embrace my husband as Mable walked in the door. She was smiling, a rare occurrence for a woman constantly plagued by one ailment or another.

"Your father's in the car...can't you two wait until I get Evan before you start that stuff?" There were times when I actually liked my mother-in-law.

Brian was stiff in my arms. But if not Jack or Mable, then who?

Brett, who in his mid-to-late 40s had taken up the jackass sports of snowboarding and bungee jumping? He was hardly my favorite person but to lose him at such a young age would be a tragedy. "That was Gary's brother...Gary's dead," Brain stated flatly. "They found him in the doctor's lounge at University Hospital—he was supposed to be in surgery. They think it might have been a heart attack." Then he burst into tears and laid his head on my chest, sobbing.

Chapter 8 - Joker's Wild

You don't really think much about death when your kids are little and you're trying to establish yourself professionally. After all, you've got a house to build, friends to impress, and creditors to keep happy. And isn't it all worth it when you show up at a soccer game or a golf or tennis match and there's everyone in your group, healthy and happy and their lives are going just great? Why can't you be more like them?

Like bad breath and taxes, loss is something country club people rarely discuss among themselves. At least, if it affects someone in their own circle. It's OK if it happens to an acquaintance—along with divorce, plastic surgery and money problems, anything remotely scandalous is fodder for the gossip mill. After all it's their problem, not yours, and most likely their fault anyway.

But no one wants to be the source of that material, and many will go to great lengths to avoid it. The husband in a couple who'd been friendly with Shelia and Todd had recently died of pancreatic cancer. During the entire six months after his illness had been diagnosed, his wife pretended like nothing was wrong. The man literally wasted away in front of his friends, who also ignored his condition. It was an irony, considering that particular clique at The Club was among the most competitive and materialistic. Of course when the poor man finally passed, there had to be a funeral. But could the woman have embalmed him and dragged him around with her, acting as if everything was perfect and money was no object, she would have done it. After all, she had to uphold the three rules.

Such was not the case with Gary, of course. He was the real deal, as the kids would say. Susan had mentioned he'd been excessively tired lately and had scheduled an appointment for him at the Cleveland Clinic. But doctors can be notoriously neglectful of their own health, and Gary was no exception. His free time was limited and precious and he wanted to spend it with his family, playing golf, and drinking, in that order.

Country Club Wives

If the man had taken a few hours for a checkup, everyone would have been spared much pain and Gary would likely still be with us. And I might still be married, although not likely—there were plenty of rich widows to be found, especially as we edged towards our 50s. If detected early enough, many heart problems can be treated. This is true on a spiritual level as well, but as with the physical ailment, many times no one wants to deal with it within themselves.

So, instead of going to Cincinnati, we went to Susan's, helping her prepare for Gary's funeral. The thing was, they didn't really need us there. Their McMansion already overflowed with relatives, their friends and those of their almost grown teenagers, Amanda and Justin. Amanda, a domestic goddess in her own right, had planned on going to Kansas State to matriculate in their world-class nutritional science program, which was known back in my day as Home Ec. (or home eech, as we used to call it). But now she was thinking of getting her undergraduate degree at Ohio State instead, so she could be near her now-widowed mother. Justin, sixteen, had two more years left at Columbus Academy. Between answering the phone and the constantly ringing doorbell, Susan kept insisting that Amanda not change her plans, that Justin would be around to keep her company.

And their labradoodle, named Thomas Edison in a satirical acknowledgement of his notorious lack of smarts, kept dashing outside every time the door opened, so someone had to run after him and drag him back, which he thought was great fun and at least provided some comic relief. Still, it was a madhouse and I felt we added to it with our mere presence.

But Brian insisted on staying and was on the phone, making funeral arrangements, even setting up an appointment so Susan could pick out the casket. No one else seemed to be doing much of anything. They just brought food and sat around talking about how terrible it was; in this setting, even genteel country club folk could not ignore the topic. Finally I gave up and went home, catching a ride with my neighbor Ann, who had recently moved from London— England, not Ohio—with her three kids and husband, yet another newly imported executive of the ever-expanding Katz empire.

On our way out the door, I encountered Shelia, whom I hadn't seen in nearly six months. She looked even thinner than usual, pale, and almost angry. She'd changed her hair style, from its short mop of natural red curls to perpendicular bob almost perfect enough to be a wig. As a person who has always had boring hair I wondered why anyone would straighten their locks when curls were much more interesting. Despite the situation, I was glad to see a fellow Drama Queen, whose life seemed untouched by the shit that had affected the rest of us. I broke into a smile, momentarily forgetting the circumstances. "Shelia! How are you? It's been ages!"

"Not very well, considering what just happened." Her stern reaction stopped me cold.

"I didn't mean it like that, Shelia," I stammered, and taken off balance even more, dug in even deeper, blurting "Geez, I haven't even seen your new house."

"We don't have much time to entertain," Shelia snapped. "I've been busy. I'm up at Ohio State all the time and that precludes sitting around at The Club and playing tennis. " Before I had a chance to ask her what she was studying, she went inside.

"Chuffing cow," remarked Ann in her plummy, upper-crust British accent. "That's fucking bitch, in Yank-speak." I chuckled, in spite of my sadness over Gary and my now hurt feelings. "She acts like she should charge admission. And her place is nowhere near as posh as the Katz's party house." It seemed as if everyone but me had not only seen Shelia's but had at least been in outbuildings of the oh-so-subtly named Briarcliff Cottage.

Like many inhabitants of New Wellington, especially those who came from other cultures or big cities, Ann had a much more sophisticated worldview than your average born-and-raised Columbusite. This included even those with money, inherited or nouveau riche, and had been a pleasant surprise. For the first time since we'd moved to Ohio, I felt at home among these women who, like me, had grown up and lived elsewhere. They saw a life outside Columbus and Ohio State football; many remained successful in their own right after marrying and having kids, rather than hanging their identities upon their extended family and a tight childhood circle of friends. They kept their careers and in some cases their maiden names, and traveled extensively, with and without their husbands. As a sister-in-law to a former linebacker, I got awfully tired of hearing about the Buckeyes. Even Brian went on and on, especially when he was around Gary and Susan, who were avid fans and had fifty-yard-line tickets.

Poor Gary, I thought, he would never see his beloved Bucks play again. And what would become of those prized seats?

*****

Movies and television shows often depict funerals as glamorous events, filled with tension and drama. The most unexpected people show up—rich, poor, and in-between. Gary's funeral was like that, down to the local TV reporters and their video cams covering tonight's big story on the interment of one of the city's top docs. Brian peremptorily went up to Susan and asked if she wanted them escorted off the property. I saw Susan shake her head "no" and wondered—not for the first time—what my husband's motives were. Brian rarely did anything without a reason—what did he have to gain here? Things between us seemed fine; just last night he'd told me he valued our marriage more than ever, that Gary's death made him appreciate what we had together. And then he proceeded to make love to me, just as he'd promised to do during our canceled trip to Cincinnati.

It was so crowded that Brian and I became separated at the cemetery. What seemed like hundreds of people milled about and I couldn't see him anywhere. Mable was having another one of her "spells" so she and Jack stayed home. And I wasn't about to seek out Shelia again, not after the nasty way she treated me. I'd glimpsed CeCe's bright coif huddled next to a Middle Eastern looking guy, but that was another scene I wished to avoid. So I wandered from cluster to cluster, looking for my husband's lightly graying blonde pate, with no luck whatsoever.

I was about as far away from the burial site as you can get—which was a relief, since I couldn't even bring myself to look at

Gary's dead body during the viewing, much less see him being put into the ground—when I nearly ran headlong into a pretty, classily dressed woman surrounded by a bevy of small children. They were well-behaved, too. If I hadn't heard the oldest—who seemed to be eight or so—say, "Watch out for the lady, Mom," I would have also mowed down their golden retriever puppy. My first thought was, how odd. People never brought dogs to funerals, unless it was for another dog. My second thought was, where can I get a puppy just like that one?

The woman smiled in apology. "My kids loved Dr. Gary. He delivered them all—but they were worried about Nigella here—we just brought her home yesterday. So I told them we could come and bring Nigella but we needed to stay to the side so we wouldn't disturb anyone."

"Oh, that's fine. She's so cute." I fall in love with practically every animal I meet, except for lizards and snakes which we fortunately don't see many of at the Banford Veterinary Clinic. "What breeder did you get her from?" Our office manager was the president of a group called Golden Endings which helped place retrievers who'd lost their homes. She worked closely with breeders and I knew most of them. Maybe we could get a discount...Evan would be so excited!

"Oh, no," the woman shook her head. "We adopted Nigella from the pound off of Alum Creek Rd. Although it's wasn't easy—we sat for 45 minutes in crazy traffic and then once you get there, the atmosphere is so depressing. It was hard on the kids too—all those dogs we couldn't take home and you know what happens to most of them."

"Yes," I sighed, thinking, damn Nick and his bailing out on Paws That Refresh. Before I knew it, I was telling this lovely woman about the research I'd done on establishing animal shelters in middle-class suburbs and she listened intently, with growing enthusiasm.

"That's a great idea! You could start with animals from the Humane Society and distribute them to different areas. I could help you fund-raise..." Then I noticed what looked like Secret Service men—guys in sunglasses wearing earpieces—bearing down on us. What the hell?

"Is this woman bothering you, Mrs. Katz?" demanded the biggest one, who resembled a low-rent Arnold Schwarzenegger.

"Absolutely not," retorted Janice Katz, ignoring my open-mouthed reaction. And then I thought, omigod, Nigella…Nigella Lawson, the British food maven whose show is sponsored by Katz Enterprises. How could I have missed that? Come to think of it, she looked familiar, which was probably why I felt so comfortable talking to her. The question that had slowly been percolating on the edge of my awareness was to ask her where we'd met before. I had seen pictures of her and Eli, who was now also coming towards us, a worried look on his face.

"The rest of the troops have arrived…" Janice pulled a paper and pen from her diaper bag-cum-purse, a clever combination, I now noticed, from Louis Vuitton that probably cost at least a thousand dollars. "Why don't you give me your name and number and I'll give you my private line and we'll talk further? I think you've got something here, and I want to help." She was scribbling furiously and when I looked up again, I saw the news media heading towards us.

A quote from Eli would provide the perfect sound bite appetizer for the main event. "Let's go Janice, before they catch up with us" said Eli, with a polite but brisk nod, acknowledging me. Janice handed me the paper, and they and their kids disappeared into the crowd, thanks to the expert maneuvering of the bodyguards.

I'd never even introduced myself or had a chance to provide her the information she requested. If I did call her, would she remember me? After all, no one had seen or heard our conversation, except for her kids, who were small. If a tree falls in the forest does it make a sound? Still, I took the information and stuck it in my wallet, and went to look for Brian.

*****

But the day was not over. Back at Gary and Susan's—I was having a hard time thinking about it as just Susan's—there was even more excitement. And this time, it involved CeCe.

She and her new husband Ahmet—that was his name, Ahmet Al-Sharif, he was Turkish, I found out—had opened a catering business, something to keep CeCe away from the delectable personal trainers and tennis pros, I suppose. From what I'd overheard at Susan's, Ahmet had left Soaps 'N Scents for an early leap into that golden parachute known as executive retirement. Although only a few years older than us, he was set for life—or so they said.

Unprompted, CeCe and Ahmet had decided to supply the food for the after-funeral gathering. Only the problem was, there was too much to begin with—casseroles and salads and cakes and cookies and pre-heated meals to last for weeks. And now this, an enormous banquet of Middle Eastern fare—hummus and stuffed grape leaves and shish kebab and falafel, spread all over the long granite countertops that were already overflowing.

I had found Brian and he'd been anxiously seeking me out as well, wanting us to be the first on hand for the after-funeral gathering. We'd arrived even before the new widow.

When Susan walked in and saw the spread, she exploded. "Where the fuck did this come from?" I stared, shocked, at a woman whose strongest epithet had been "darn," and that was once, years ago, in reference to a burst pipe that caused $10,000 worth of damage to her living room of their old house in Gahanna, shortly before they finalized the sale.

"Mr. and Mrs. Al-Sharif had this delivered," a kitchen worker said in an apologetic voice. She was pushing things around in the refrigerator, struggling to find room in a space already stuffed to the gills. She looked familiar. Had I met her somewhere before, maybe at one of Brian's softball games which I infrequently attended? He didn't acknowledge her so maybe I was wrong.

"Why?" Susan shrieked. "Can't they figure out we have too much food? That gold-digging bimbo and her damn Arab are just trying to bribe their way in…" Here was a woman who'd practically come from poverty herself, condemning someone else's act of kindness as a method of social-climbing. I detested CeCe for what she'd done to our family, but even I respected an attempt to help, although to use Evan's vernacular, her timing sucked.

Which was how I found myself defending CeCe. "Oh, c'mon Susan, it's a nice gesture. You're just overwhelmed, understandably so."

"Thank you, Tish." I knew that sarcastic-but-deeply injured tone anywhere but refused to turn around and face CeCe directly. I felt Brian go tense next to me and wondered if later, there would be shards of glass in my feet from my attempt at fairness. "And my husband's Turkish, not Arab. Get your Middle Eastern countries straight, Susan. Or as your precious son Justin would say, your sand niggers. I believe it was he who taught that term to my two girls."

For a moment, there was dead silence. The epithet hung in the air like a bomb about to explode. And then the front door opened and Thomas Edison, the not-so-bright labradoodle burst into the kitchen in yet another attempt to go outside, running into the worker and CeCe and knocking over a very large chocolate cake. It landed on his head with a plop, turning what had been an essentially beige animal into a black-and-white canine confection.

The shocked look on the dog's face was so priceless I had to giggle. Talk about integration... My sense of the absurd kicked in and I broke into a variation of "Ebony and Ivory" which caused everyone, including Susan, to laugh. It also helped that the dog began to howl as well, because I can't sing worth a damn. At least he was smart enough to try to cover up the sound. And then time moved on, the ugly, horrible moment glossed over because people were coming in and offering their condolences to Susan. Silently CeCe began to gather up her food, avoiding eye contact.

After wiping down Thomas Edison, the kitchen worker started to help CeCe and Ahmet. "Let's get this to the Open Shelter," she said. "That way, it won't go to waste. My truck broke down again. Can we use your car, Brian?" She turned to my husband, her warm smile revealing a missing molar. Then I remembered her name, Sally. We had spoken briefly at a pizza and a beer party held for the softball team and their spouses a few months ago. And she was divorced.

My husband looked as if he'd gotten his hand caught in the cookie jar. "Uh, yeah, sure," he mumbled. "Tell you what, I'll take it down myself. I'll get the car." He left, jangling his keys, something he did when nervous or annoyed.

Two things went through my mind. The first was that Brian had slept with this woman. Although she lacked dental intervention, she was kind of cute. I wanted to kill my husband, and I fully intended on getting the facts about his relationship with Sally as soon as we got home.

The second, which is by far more irrelevant and was probably my way of controlling my fury, was that you could tell who was the help and who were the landed gentry by their cars. If you saw a beater in the driveway during the day, it was probably the nanny, landscaper or cleaning crew. It was not unusual for these vehicles to have yellow-and-red license plates, the scarlet letter of those caught driving under the influence of alcohol or drugs (some feel this is hardly punishment, that DUIs should be making license plates, rather than driving cars with them). And although the monied set drank and drove at least as much as their lesser brethren why didn't *their* cars ever get branded with the scarlet plates?

Homeowners have either foreign rides like Beamers, Mercedes, Lexii, or SUVs, the most extreme of which is the Hummer. Why a vice-president of pillows and bedspreads needed an assault vehicle used to deploy troops in combat zones was beyond me. But you never know. I supposed they wanted to be ready for any contingency except for the tripling of gas prices, which given the economy and current President seemed inevitable anyway. And the way I felt, I was ready to take up battle myself.

CeCe's husband Ahmet came into the kitchen. He was a handsome man, with striking, prominent features and glossy, dark hair with only tinges of grey. Seeing his wife's distress, he began to help. They touched constantly, their bodies in perfect sync as they wrapped the various dishes, talking so quietly that no one else could hear. CeCe's shoulders were shaking so I knew she was in or near tears.

Nevertheless I felt sick with envy. I would never have that closeness, never know that kind of love. So I said, "Too bad you didn't include a dish with squash," referring to the grocery-store comparison she'd once made between Susan's sagging breasts and her own pert rack. "It would have made for a much better comeback. More politically correct, too." There. I'd scored points against her happiness, which she didn't deserve, that conniving bitch.

But rather than lashing out at me, CeCe looked at me with wet eyes. "Not you, too, Tish," she said wearily. "Well, I guess I understand...I'd feel that way myself if I were in your situation."

What did she mean by that? Did she, too, know about Brian's extracurricular activities? But Evan rushed in before I had a chance to ask. "Dad's got the car and he wants to go...now." Having just turned fifteen-and-a-half, Evan had gotten his temps—which he'd passed with a perfect score. Although he barely maintained a C minus average, whenever Evan set his mind to do something, he shone. The trick for him was to find an outlet that was at the very least, legal. Driving was his latest passion and if there was a remote opportunity that Brian or I was planning to use the car, Evan somehow always found out about it and begged us to let him operate the vehicle. So our days of going anyplace alone were temporarily suspended. Maybe a good thing, considering what was I was thinking right now.

"Well, thanks Ev," CeCe reverted to the nickname we used when he was a little boy. "Would you mind giving us a hand with this stuff?"

"Sure, Aunt CeCe," Evan seemed happy to help and his smile included Ahmet. Young people were much more accepting than adults, I thought. We could learn a lot from them.

*****

As it turned out, Sally had just gotten engaged. After Brian and Evan came back from dropping off the meal at the Open Shelter, and as we left Susan's, I saw her kissing a heavyset, bearded guy whom she'd obviously arranged to pick her up as soon as the wake was over.

I felt a great sense of relief—here I was, desperately trying to save our marriage and thinking he'd cheated again. When I asked

Brian about why he reacted as he did, he explained that he didn't want our country club friends to know about our social activities with the softball group. "You know how they can be, Tish," he said in the pleading, smarmy tone that seemed to permeate so much of our conversation these days. "You and I aren't snobbish like that, but they can be. I'd rather not bring it to their attention."

"But who would even notice?" I wondered aloud. "People were pretty upset, between Gary's death and Susan's outburst."

"You didn't help things any," Brian retorted. "That little concert you gave, Tish, was pretty damn inappropriate."

"Oh, please," I could feel myself getting angry all over again. "It broke the tension. People laughed."

"Would you two chill?" demanded Evan from the back seat. "It's bad enough you wouldn't let me drive home, but I'd rather you not bring whatever you're fighting about to my attention," he mimicked Brian perfectly, and I turned my head to hide the grin that was forcing itself to the surface even though I struggled to disguise it.

Brian glared into the rear view mirror. "One more comment like that, young man, and you can forget about driving for a week."

But Evan saw my expression and a frisson of understanding passed between us. Brian failed to notice the sarcasm underneath Evan's "Yes, sir." He was too busy planning a future that had nothing to do with us, something everyone but me was beginning to realize.

*****

Gary's death provided me with a glimpse of my own mortality, and I decided to forge ahead with the animal shelter on my own. The first thing I did was call Janice Katz.

"Mrs. Katz's office," the male voice answering the phone was young, snippy, and slightly effete. Of course she wouldn't answer her own phone. Of course she had an assistant.

But how not to sound like another charitable cause asking for a handout? Perhaps the direct approach would be best. "May I speak to her please?" I asked in my most polished tones. Months of dealing with sick animals (called "patients" by the vet staff) and their owners (known to us as "clients") had given me the sense that even if I didn't have the upper hand, I should act as if I did. "I met her a few weeks ago and she gave me this number."

The thing was, it worked more often with patients than with clients. "Whom may I say is calling?" He sounded like a "Queer Eye" wannabe, the kind who tries to score points by poking at others' foibles. What's humorous on TV is far less amusing when you're the target.

Annoyed at his officiousness, I was tempted to respond with something like "Ronald McDonald" or "Hillary Clinton" but instead offered up "Tish McLean" with enough of a sigh to give him an opening.

"This is Vaughn Monroe. How may I help you?" Even his name sounded pretentious.

So I ended up relaying my encounter with Janice and his silence grew more skeptical with every sentence. I could practically hear the wheels in his head turning, figuring out how to rid of yet another supplicant who'd come to beg at the altar of Katz Enterprises.

"Well, I will be glad to pass along the information to Mrs. Katz. It is Tish, correct?" As if calling me "Mrs. McLean" was too much of a sign of respect. That would put me on an equal footing with Janice and this stuck-up manlet couldn't have that. Surely his lack of height had to be only one of the many issues that made his job such a great compensation for what surely must be a deep-seated lack of self-esteem. He probably only wore size seven shoes.

I'd had enough of being nice. "You know, Janice Katz and I had quite an involved conversation about this project. She expressed a great deal of interest. I'm sure if you put me through she'd talk to me."

"And what would you tell her? That you've raised the funds and have backers and a board of directors? That you've found a space and have obtained all the necessary licenses and tax clearances? Mrs. Katz gets a dozen calls every week from people like you. She's a kindhearted lady and it's my job to screen callers, especially if they haven't developed a business plan."

But my hearing stopped at "people like you" and I failed to

process the last two words, a phrase necessary for the success of any undertaking, nonprofit or otherwise. "Well, you do a great job, Mr. Meader, I mean Mr. Monroe" unintentionally referring to Vaughn Meader, a different kind of poseur whose career had hinged upon his imitation of John F. Kennedy. Not that he would get the reference anyway, the arrogant pup. "I wonder how many 'people like me' Mrs. Katz would like to talk to that she doesn't get to, thanks to your so-called efficiency."

"Ma'am, I am just being upfront. There is no need to be rude." Along with being condescending, he made me feel out of date, like the world was being overtaken by young Turks who knew all the answers and were just waiting for us Baby Boomers to pack up and retire. What they didn't yet realize was that they too, would eventually be replaced by an eager posse of hungrier honchos, with even sharper teeth.

"Like I said, the projects that Mrs. Katz considers have reached a certain stage of development. And while your idea is solid, it's still that…Just an idea."

"So what am I supposed to do? Come up with a building and a check for a million dollars?" My anger had morphed into frustration and I struggled to hide the tears in my voice. Not only had I failed to reach Janice Katz, but I still had only a vague idea about the actual machinations needed to make the shelter a reality. Although Nick and I had talked in general terms about locations and setting up the workflow, I hadn't a clue as to how to actually go about getting the money for all this. It looked like my dream was too much to do on my own. It hurt, and even more so to hear it from someone who sounded only a few years older than my son.

Unexpectedly, he softened. "You really don't understand about nonprofits, do you? What you need are several backers—including Mrs. Katz, whom you say is interested—and a two-year business plan. It's a lot of leg work…Going to various places, doing the research, talking with people who've done it before." Then his voice changed, and although it still contained that fussy snideness, he seemed to have switched from hostile gatekeeper to a potential ally.

"Look, I know a lady who manages the shop at the James for women who have cancer. She was like you—she had no idea of how these things run. If you give me a minute I'll dig out her number. She's a sweetheart and I'm pretty sure she'll be happy to help."

Well, I thought. Just when you're about to give up, a little miracle happens. Nothing major, but enough to give you hope. When he came back on the line with the name and number, I found myself apologizing. "You know that thing you said about the business plan, that made a lot of sense. For a while I was working with a local veterinarian and he had a good grasp of those kinds of details. Frankly, I don't."

"Well, find someone with a head for business and study a bunch of different plans." Vaughn suggested. "The library has tons of books and examples and there are lots of online resources. Donna—the woman whose number I gave you—only had a degree in chemistry, so she networked liked hell." He paused, as if marshalling his thoughts. "Once you've got a crew on board, come up with a workable division of labor. Someone to do the fund-raising, another to deal with the accounting end, and whatever else is needed to get the shelter up and running. Then when you've got a plan, come talk to me and I'll put you through to Janice."

Now it was "Janice"…Hallelujah! This actually might happen. It wouldn't be easy—other privately-run shelters had failed due to everything from mismanagement to embezzlement of funds to the neglect of the very animals they were trying to protect. But I was determined to avoid these pitfalls. And if it meant visiting a dozen successful, similar enterprises—even if they were in other cities—to see what worked and what didn't, so be it. Still, where I would get the money for all this was beyond me. But one thing at a time…my first stop was to call Donna Wyman at the James Cancer Center.

"Oh and by the way, I wanted to tell you, I was named after Vaughn Meader," he continued. "My parents were big JFK fans and since they didn't like the name "John" or "Jack" Vaughn it was."

"Are you from Boston by chance?" Most people who named their offspring after one or more of the Kennedys usually hailed from the area. As it turned out, he'd grown up in Connecticut and spent summers in Hyannisport, where a favorite childhood pastime had been stalking the by-then-mostly-uneventful Kennedy compound. Still, there had been occasional sightings of Teddy and even Jackie and her kids.

We talked for a few more minutes and I hung up, feeling more lighthearted and happier than I had in a long time. Although I had no idea of where I was going to get help, I had the sense that if I started to build it, it just might come together. It never occurred to me to turn to the one person who supposedly had a keen nose for business—my own husband.

Chapter 9 - With a Little Help

"Welcome to Endless Possibilities. I'm Donna Wyman." The woman greeting me was not what I expected. She'd had a big phone presence—as confident and hearty as any successful businessperson—but in reality was at least six inches shorter than I, barely five feet. She had CeCe's nails, flawless, obviously fake, with white tips and was dressed in a tailored white shirt, khaki Capris and black sandals, the uniform favored by New Wellington women in the late 1990s. She appeared no different than the country club wives I'd encountered on and off the tennis court. Mable would have loved her.

Like its founder, this place was nothing like the picture in my mind. I'd thought it would be bare and clinical, with wigs and mastectomy prostheses hanging unadorned on metal hooks. But it was more upscale boutique, similar to Publik Commons, New Wellington's frou-frou refurbished shopping area, which, with its Starbucks and overpriced stores, was only user-friendly to the monied inhabitants. The natives still hung out at the feed store, which with its mini-silo and tractor display, was deemed "quaint" by the pilgrims, sort of like a mini-reservation in the middle of white occupied territory. And eventually, like its Native American counterpart, it would be replaced by more red brick Georgian gingerbread.

Even its name gave no clue, although it could hardly be called the Cancer Warehouse. Books, beauty care products and knick-knacks of all types lined the shelves. Sexy lingerie shared wall space with perfumes and jewelry. It even lacked the hospital smell, although it was adjacent to The James, one of the most prestigious cancer research facilities in the country. The odor usually permeated every hospital's gift shop; I'd been there often enough as a young teenager, buying presents for Mom, in the hopes that if I gave her enough, she'd get better.

Actually, it had taken considerable courage for me to even come here. Although I was used to a medical environment, anything to do with cancer scared the hell out of me. I was afraid I'd catch it, as if by osmosis. Ridiculous, I know, but when your mother dies of ovarian cancer at an age which you are rapidly approaching, all logic goes out the window. The weeks before my annual gynecologic checkup were always filled with dread, and I worried every time I felt bloated or tired. My mother had been diagnosed with Stage III ovarian cancer when she'd gone to see why her periods had become so heavy and irregular. It was supposed to be routine; we'd thought her symptoms were due to approaching menopause. You just never knew when the fucker was going to sneak up on you and steal your life. It was like avoiding a crime-infested area. If you didn't go there in the first place, you might not get mugged.

"I'd like to start with the tour, if that's OK," Donna was saying. "Everything we do here is designed to give our customers a sense of peace and calm, to make them feel that things are normal, even if only during the short time of their visit. All the products are helpful to them in some way..." She went on to explain the uses for the various lotions and creams, how they were specially formulated to either ease the effects of chemo and other treatments or made with carcinogen-free ingredients. The books were mostly practical guides on dealing with cancer or were inspirational.

"And these are the dressing rooms." She knocked on a door and when no one answered, opened it to reveal an elegantly decorated cubicle with a Louis XIV settee. Where did she get the money for all this? I wondered. She pointed to a slim stack of mirrors on wheels. "Sometimes the ladies—believe or not, we get some men too—want to see what they look like and other times they'd rather not. So we had these specially made, so we could give them a choice." In answer to my unspoken question, she added, "Katz Enterprises donated many of the furnishings and Ohio Designer Craftsman came up with the mirror design." Even hearing an oblique reference to Janice added to my small but rapidly growing stockpile of hope.

Another dressing room door opened, and out walked Shelia. She was carrying a thick bra. Her hair was exactly the same as it had been at Gary's funeral and I realized with shock that she'd been wearing a wig after all. It was to cover the effects of chemo. Shelia had cancer.

For a moment, we stared at each other, dumbfounded. Then we both began talking at once.

I put my hand over my mouth, indicating I wanted her to speak first. After all, she was the victim—I mean, patient. "Omigod Tish, I'm so sorry," Shelia blurted. "I was so rude to you and here you are. I'd just had my left breast removed and then Gary died so suddenly... I was mad at the world. I wanted to hurt anybody and you were in the right place at the wrong time. But I've just come from the doctor's and they're almost positive they got it all. So I'm feeling so much better these days. Can you forgive me? What about you?" Donna stood by, silent.

I knew that I should explain my presence but somehow, in the face of Shelia's own tragedy, it seemed inappropriate and trivial. And she'd been such a bitch to me which, considering the circumstances, was understandable. But she could have told me...I thought we were friends, fellow Drama Queens. And it wasn't like I ever had anything more than she did; we were hardly a threat to her and Todd as they climbed the social ladder of the New Wellington elite. So maybe that was it. I wasn't good enough for her to confide in. Well, I would return the favor. So I said nothing.

"If you don't want to talk about it, that's OK." Shelia said hastily, obviously embarrassed at what was construed as prying. "But if you ever want to, please call or come over. Any time—I'm usually at home. And again I'm really, really sorry." Then she was gone, bra in hand.

"It's complicated," I said in reply to Donna's curious look. My whole life was built on deceit and unspoken thoughts and not fitting in and suddenly, ridiculously I felt like crying. "My mother died of cancer and this is difficult." At least that was the truth.

"I understand," Donna replied, and I sensed that she truly did. A cancer survivor herself, she must have gone through more than I could even begin to imagine. Vaughn told me Donna's mother and sister had both died of the disease but she never gave up, continuing with experimental drugs until she found a treatment that worked.

She radiated such empathy that I had to fight the impulse to spill my guts to her. Instead I swallowed my emotions—what was going on with me these days that required the need of personal advice from strangers?—and asked her about how she went about establishing the boutique. So we headed back to her office and spent a couple of hours pouring over business plans, while I took notes and got ideas for establishing contacts and fundraising.

*****

I told myself the reason I hadn't said anything to Brian about the animal shelter was because Mable was sick, this time for real. Her kidneys were failing and she was not a candidate for a transplant. The doctor cited her poor health and age—although at 68, technically she had two more years before being ineligible. I also believed that a lifetime of physical inactivity—save for a weekly round or two of golf—her obsession with her family and appearances, and her lack of outside interests were other contributing factors. After years of fretting about her health and thinking she might die, it looked like it was going to finally happen.

Of course, we all go sometimes, but the goal—at least in my case and hopefully that of Evan—was not to fixate on why or when. Mable, however, appeared to be in her element, planning for her funeral, down to the type of casket and the food that would be served afterwards. I'd never seen anything like it. Perhaps she believed in the afterlife and was looking forward to hanging around and seeing what everyone said and how they acted. Didn't she realize they called it death for a reason?

Because Brett had relocated to Florida, Brian was saddled with the responsibility of taking care of all the arrangements. Brett now sold real estate in Palm Beach, and by all accounts, was doing well. Jack and Mable had been his first customers, having purchased a condo there several months ago, where Brett now lived rent-free.

Brian made it clear he expected more from me, but I wasn't about to spend my few free hours tending to Mable because Jack was too cheap to hire full-time care. I had my work at the Banford Clinic and Evan to look after. Even though he was 16, he still needed minding. Perhaps now more than when he'd been younger, although since the shoplifting fiasco, he'd gone back to his pre-thug friends, the middle-class white boys who, although while fluent in Ebonics, dressing 'hood, and blaring rap music on the streets of New Wellington, locked their doors upon seeing a person of color, just like their moms and dads. Evan had even gotten a part-time job, and as a reward Brian purchased him a bright green Geo Tracker, promptly named the Hoopdee, which caused me endless hours of worry because it was little more than a tin can driven by a walking hormone.

And now I was faced with a conundrum. I'd finally developed a business plan, culled from several books I'd gotten at the library. But I had no idea who to approach or even if it would be viable to those from whom I sought money. Donna Wyman had generously shared her proposal with me, but the people she contacted had been professional associates and friends—she'd been in pharmaceutical sales before opening her shop—and it had been for a totally different cause. And in addition to Janice Katz, I would be seeking support from local veterinarians, pet and animal supply stores, and private nonprofit foundations like Maddie's Fund, whose purpose was to create no-kill programs for adoptable shelter dogs and cats.

I'd even come up with a motto "In Your Own Backyard" and had a vague idea for a fund-raiser, possibly at The Club. I'd become friendly with Kevin, the head maître d'—he took his Shih Tzus to the Banford Clinic. He'd offered to work with me, once I finalized things for Paws That Refresh.

But I needed another pair of eyes, both in terms of how to approach potential donors and in refining the plan. A good way to get sponsors was to ask them to serve on an advisory board and use their names on publicity materials and informational brochures. But this was new to me and I was uncomfortable with it.

So I decided to talk to Nick. We hadn't spoken for months and in fact he'd never sent me the list of veterinarian contacts he'd promised. Rather than calling, which might be misinterpreted as pestering—he'd probably not return my calls, anyway—I decided to attend a meeting of the Columbus Veterinary Society in hopes that Nick might be there. It had been a long time since I'd gone, simply because my life had gotten so busy. If I was going to stalk him, at least I'd be doing it in a public place.

The solar system must have been in alignment, because Nick was sitting in his usual spot towards the back. He didn't look particularly happy to see me, turning his shaggy head quickly when I walked in a few minutes late. But the other members seemed glad, asking about my progress on the animal shelter after the meeting was over. I sensed an imminent departure from Nick, and moved swiftly towards him as he edged towards the door.

"You didn't think you could leave without saying hello?" I gave him a big smile. Nick was sweating and wiped his forehead with his hand, for a moment widening the gap in his collar and revealing dark, curly chest hair. Damn.

"I just got a call from a client—his dog's having puppies and there seem to be complications," Nick's reply was terse. Too late I realized, shit, he thinks I'm flirting with him.

Well, I suppose I was in a way, but my purpose for cornering him was all business. "Look, Nick, I know you're busy, but I need your help. I want to go forward with the shelter but I need you to look over what I've come up with. I've taken it as far as I can."

"I have to go," I'd never seen Nick so nervous. In the past, his calm and even-temperedness served as a soothing counterpoint to Brian's unpredictable reactions.

Yet his vulnerability gave me the courage to persist. "Can't you just put aside the past and help me with this? I need your advice—you of all people know best what's required. I trust your judgment. I don't know what I'm doing really... I want this to work more than anything." I stood rooted to the spot, and the phrase about not being moved from the old protest song "We shall overcome" ran through my mind.

"God, Tish, it's just that so much is going on in my life right now..." Nick rubbed his face and I could feel him falter. Then my cell phone rang.

"Not again..." I said and in spite of everything, we both smiled. "Does there seem to be a pattern here?" I flipped it open, glad for the comic relief but also dreading what might be on the other end.

"Hey, Tish, it's me," Brian sounded cheerful. "Can you stop off at Kroger's on your way home? They're having a buy one-get-one free sale on Coke and Diet Coke. We need about 20 two-liters."

"Twenty two-liter bottles of soda? Why? We never drink that stuff," Nick was watching me in that intent male way of his and I felt myself flush.

"It's for Dad. He needs it for the wake. And the sale ends tomorrow."

"The funeral?" I was dumbfounded. Mable wasn't even dead yet! Although she was mostly bedridden, the doctor said she might live for six months or more. "Well, what is he going to do if all that Coke expires before she does?" Nick's sparkling eyes widened and he started to laugh.

"Tish, this isn't funny," Brian turned stern. "I don't ask that much of you. Why can't you do something for once without questioning it? And where are you, anyway?"

Nick and I smiled at each other and the magic was there, all over again. "I'm at a meeting of the Veterinary Society. I'm just getting ready to leave. And if you want me to get the Coke, I will."

"You're not there about that dog shelter, are you? It's a bad idea, I told you from the start."

Just as quickly, my happiness evaporated. "Can we talk about this later? I didn't want to bother you with it, Brian, because so much has been going on lately."

"You better believe we will. Come straight home – forget about the pop," he said, using the Midwestern reference for soft drinks instead of the East Coast one I'd grown up with. Evan had been showing me how to navigate the Internet and we'd come across a survey by a college professor who was compiling data on geographical preferences for common names. Obviously the professor had a lot of time on his hands and who would want to know anyway, I'd wondered, not realizing that in a few short years the World Wide Web would become the Niagara Falls of information, useless and otherwise. "I'll be waiting for you." Brian said and hung up.

If only our differences were as clear-cut as soda vs. pop, I thought, as the sick feeling returned to my stomach. What was I thinking that I could do this on my own without the support of my husband? If I went ahead with the shelter, Brian might leave me. And divorce wasn't an option in my family or even a consideration. Besides, Brian and I had been through so much. Now that Evan was almost grown and Brett was away from McLean's, things could only get easier...

Yet I couldn't meet Nick's gaze. "Never mind... Forget I even mentioned it. It was a pipe dream, anyway."

"Look, Tish, it's none of my business regarding what's going on in your life," said Nick. "It doesn't sound much better than mine, these days. Elena is at work so much and the kids need someone to take them here and there and spend time with them. And it all falls on me.... But my point is, if you want to do something, do it. Paws That Refresh is a great concept. Don't let anything stop you, whether it's my not having the time to help or the negativity of others." He was being honest, I realized, not just making up an excuse.

The truth in his words touched me in a place I didn't want to go. I didn't know how to reply, but I had to get out of there, before I burst into tears and made a complete ass out of myself in front of Nick this time, rather just than a partial one. So without saying good-bye to Nick or a word to anyone else, I hurried from the basement of the church, ignoring the curious glances of my colleagues and coworkers. If God was listening, He surely must be laughing at this nasty joke.

*****

I could have purchased the two-liter bottles and saved $10; Mable passed away within the month. She waned steadily, along with my hope for Paws That Refresh. Brian made it icily clear that any and all extra time was to be spent at work or with family. He accused me of being selfish and not for the first time I wondered, what is wrong with having a dream and pursuing it? What is the matter with doing something that makes you happy?

Yet it was not the McLean way, which involved focusing on earning money and doing the "right" thing. Anyone who deviated—

whether it be showing too much cleavage at a country club dance, being overly friendly with another's spouse, or chucking a high-paying job for lesser work was the object of gossip and condemnation.

But to be fair, my parents had been somewhat materialistic as well. I remembered them arguing with my oldest sister Lisa when she was in high school and wanted to become an artist. They insisted that she do something "practical" like teaching or nursing, the usual careers for women in the late 1960s. Never mind that Daddy had been a closet painter himself and quite accomplished.

I suppose it had to do with the mindset of the generation that came of age in the 1930s, growing up with very little and saving every penny. Forced to be sensible during what would normally be their most carefree years and sacrificing everything so the family could survive. Yet several of Daddy's siblings—the family had come from Sicily in the early 1900s—had pursued their own dreams and goals, managing to get degrees in medicine and law. In spite of the fact that they'd been first-generation Italians in Boston, where minorities—especially "spics, Micks, wops and kikes" (not to mention the "n-word")—were discriminated against. And even though some of them were women, adding even more strikes.

Most of my inheritance had been spent and I was just beginning to realize how vulnerable I was. I couldn't imagine surviving without Brian and his protection. I'd heard stories at The Club about women whose husbands left them. They slipped away into social oblivion, bitter and lonely, fighting over the few available men. They were occasionally sighted on their own at the mall or eating a solo meal in a restaurant. Only those who remarried—like CeCe—or snagged a clubbable significant other were accepted back into the fold.

What I didn't understand at the time is that what seemed like a desolate existence in the mindset of one group might actually be enjoyable to the individuals in question. The freedom that comes with being your own person can come at a high cost, but it also can have rewards beyond a fat bank account, a group of superficial friends, or knowledge that you'll have a "date" every Saturday night with aforementioned friends and bored spouse.

Yet life seemed so much more difficult for my coworkers at the clinic, who lacked the cushion of a husband, ex or otherwise. Many were single parents on fixed incomes who could barely manage their bills. Their former spouses neglected to pay child support or left no forwarding address.

OK, so it was the late 1990s, but we were talking about an exclusive enclave here, in the middle of the conservative Midwest, not some sitcom, where available (and attractive and age-appropriate) single men lurked around every corner. Maybe being a middle-aged, divorced woman was quite different in the big cities, if movies and TV were to be believed. But the thought of picking up and starting all over again at age 45 in a strange place filled me with fatigue and fear. And as my mother was fond of pointing out, you take yourself with you wherever you go. So what would be the purpose of moving to a city to meet new people? How different could one place be from another in terms of finding a mate?

But my last real encounter with Mable derailed this train of thought, who as she lay dying, requested my presence. Because she required dialysis at least four hours a day, we had no choice but to move her to a healthcare facility. Although it was one of the nicer ones in the city, and far from the institutional shabbiness of a nursing home, the transfer seemed to hasten her decline.

Out of respect, I obliged her. Although I'm good with animals, both sick and well, I'm not nearly as skilled with their two-legged counterparts. It's difficult for me to express deep emotions and deal with another's suffering. Both my mother and father understood this, so they asked little of me when they were dying. They knew how much it hurt me to see them go and why I kept my distance. Mable, on the other hand, seemed to cry out for a daughter she'd never had. So I sucked it up and became a frequent visitor to that awful room, with its tubes and monitors and smell of sickness and impending death that no amount of disinfectant and cleaning could wash away.

Mable wanted to discuss her past, something she'd never really done before. As the only child of a wealthy store owner, she had been immersed in the world of etiquette from an early age. "We had a position to maintain in the community, so it fell upon me to behave properly at all times," she recalled in her wavering voice. Her parents had other motives as well: "Father was disappointed that I was a girl, so their big hope was that I marry a man who could carry on the family business." Regularly quizzed on each chapter of Emily Post, she received a stern reprimand (and even an occasional spanking) if she dipped the spoon away from herself while eating soup or held her bread in the flat of her palm and buttered it in the air. At my puzzled expression, she explained, "Mrs. Post had rules for everything—it's the only civilized way to live—and although I rebelled at one point, I learned to appreciate the importance of such things." More like post-traumatic stress syndrome, I thought. Or brainwashing.

She met Jack during her mutinous period. "I was 18 and stage-struck. I grew up watching Joan Crawford and Bette Davis and hearing about girls being discovered in the booth at Schwab's drugstore. And I'd always had the lead in school plays and thought I was the cat's meow, so to speak." She exhaled, a bitter, cackling laugh. "So I went to New York to make it big on Broadway. Well, it was a good thing Mother insisted I graduate from steno school beforehand and that it was during World War II. There were plenty of jobs for secretaries—all the other girls were busy being Rosie the Riveter or jumping onto the casting couch so they could be actresses too." I could not imagine Mable doing either, even as a teenager.

She encountered Jack at a USO canteen a few days before he was to be shipped off to France. "He was handsome and presentable and I knew he'd always take care of me," she crowed triumphantly. Unlike Mable, Jack came from a large and friendly Irish family who had immigrated to Paterson, New Jersey. "We had big plans for when he was going to return—he wanted to open up a Chevy dealership in Newark with a GI loan. But then Father became ill and we had to come back to Columbus." The story had a creepily familiar ring and I realized that it was almost exactly parallel to what had happened to Brian and me after we'd met.

Until very recently their sex life had been active, much to

Mable's annoyance during the times she wasn't feeling well. "But you have to make a man happy, or he'll stray," she told me and once again I wondered if there was something wrong with me to make Brian so disinterested.

She also talked about CeCe for whom, much to my surprise, she expressed a grudging respect. "Brett never amounted to much," she admitted. "He showed such great promise during his youth and I suppose we spoiled him and made it too easy. CeCe was a smart cookie. She saw a better opportunity and went for it."

I was so shocked by this that I blurted, "You didn't think it was wrong that she left him without warning and tried to take Britney and Whitney away?" Not to mention costing the family and the business nearly half a million dollars. As it was, the girls only saw Brett during the summer, and if nothing else, he was a loving and attentive dad.

To me, grounds for divorce meant that someone was abusing you or the children or was an alcoholic or drug addict or defaulting on bills, or the two of you fought constantly and couldn't stand the sight of each other. "Her actions were unwarranted, not to mention self-indulgent and sneaky." In spite of instructing myself to mostly listen —after all, Mable was in bad shape—the words tumbled out.

"But Brett made her unhappy," Mable stated in that bland tone of voice I'd come to recognize as a hiding a reprimand or barb. "It used to be the woman's responsibility to make a man happy but thanks to women's lib, now it works both ways. But still, when a man is unhappy he's more likely to leave than a woman." With an appalling flash of insight, I realized she was really talking about Brian and me. However obliquely, she was condoning his prerogative to walk out, simply because I brought him down.

The sheer arrogance of her statement took my breath away. If she hadn't been so ill and Evan's grandmother, I would have told her to go fuck herself. A few more words from her and I might have done it anyway, except that she suddenly cried, "Oh my God, Tish, I can't breathe. Quick, run and get the nurse!" Then she slumped back onto the pillow and closed her eyes as if to pass out. When I returned with the aide she was sleeping peacefully, ostensibly worn out from the ordeal of warning me that my marriage was on the brink of destruction.

An exhausting day's work even for someone engaged in the lifelong pursuit of meddling. Now having accomplished her mission, she felt entitled to a rest, hopefully her final one, I reflected spitefully. But nooo…she'd need to save her strength for tomorrow, for the next chance to interfere. And then I felt guilty for having such vindictive thoughts.

So Mable also knew what it was like to see dreams shoved aside for the supposed good of the family. Yet she willingly perpetuated the same pattern in her own son. How could she be so selfish? I despised her for destroying the youthful Brian, the sweet boy I fell in love with, with his ambitions of becoming a pro golfer or a country club coach. No wonder our marriage had festered in the same petri dish of circumstances.

My world, the world that Brian and I lived in, was filled with people like Mable. They mouthed words to each other and went through the motions of living in a polite and civilized manner. But you never knew what they were thinking. These country club people, they can spend years and years together and not have a clue about the truth of each other's lives. Because money and "things" are their religion and all that really matter to many of them.

I remember reading a book about Africa. About how in the poorest regions, where AIDs and starvation are rampant, people are the most generous, the most willing to share. They will even go hungry, it said, so that others can eat. And they'll be insulted if you don't partake of their meager fare because, after all, they are offering you the best of themselves.

I hadn't been raised on the shallow surface. Nor had our lives been that way until we had moved to Columbus. Somehow, amid this serpentine bramble of pretentiousness and deceit, there had to be a better path.

*****

I never really talked to Mable after that. But our last conversation and Brian's accusation of selfishness gave me pause.

Was it necessary to sacrifice personal happiness and the essence of who you are to maintain a relationship? Did you have to become a different person—or pretend to—to make someone else happy, to save your marriage?

It wasn't until years later that I realized that, like love, selfishness comes in many forms. There's the kind where you pursue something no matter what, because you love it, and because you think you can make a difference. And the other type, where you think you can get more than what you have and if others are hurt in the process, so be it. And still another, where you only think about yourself, with no regard to those around you. We are all self-absorbed, in varying degrees. But those who claim to be the most concerned with others' welfare—in the name of "right"—are often the most selfish. Like Mable.

The last few times I visited my mother-in-law, Evan went with me, which made it more bearable. He loved his grandmother, and it broke his heart to see her fade away. Many teenagers would avoid the situation, but not Evan, who took after his father in this way, handling the pending loss with equilibrium and grace.

Jack and Brian were in and out, making arrangements and closing up the elder McLean's house. Jack planned on retiring permanently and moving down to Palm Beach with Brett. Mable finally slipped away at 4 am on a Thursday, a few hours after we'd gone home. How like her to want us to be with her until the very end, then die when we weren't around. It was as if she wanted us to feel guilty up until the last moment… "If only we'd stayed a little longer," Brian wept. "I had a feeling she wasn't going to last the night…but I was just so beat…"

"It wasn't your fault," Now I was in the position of comforting him, and it felt good. "Between work and helping Dad and visiting Mom, you've been running yourself ragged. What good would it do to ruin your own health?" I reached up and stroked his arm.

Brian pulled away. "You don't have to pet me like one of your sick animals, Tish. I'm upset enough as it is."

"Sorry," I withdrew, thinking, once this is over, we'll talk about why he's so irritable.

The funeral itself was a revelation. For one thing, it was an open casket, something my family never did. Both my parents believed that it was best to remember the person from when they were alive. As children, we never attended the funeral of friends or relatives if there was a viewing. So essentially I'd lived for nearly forty-six years and never even seen the dead body of anyone I'd known.

As in life, Mable was perfectly appointed, her grey hair coiffed into an iron helmet, her face still and composed, her pantsuit tailored and impeccable. Although the McLeans and their friends seemed comfortable in her presence, I found it morbid, as did Evan, who used any excuse to get away, even offering to dump the trash in the funeral home. But as immediate family, we had to sit in front during the ceremony and be present at the viewing at all times. Although Brian was grieving, it was obvious that in a way, he too, relished the drama and the attention.

But the real surprise was Jack. He greeted all comers with smile and a handshake. I'd never seen him so sprightly, even though he'd been battling heart problems for years. "How come he seems so happy?" I asked Brian.

"Oh, that's just Dad. He's mourning but he won't show it."

"Well, he doesn't look upset to me," I watched as Jack gave Susan a friendlier-than-necessary squeeze around her voluptuous waist as she leaned over to offer her condolences. I found myself wondering which "casserole lady" would get to him first. Or maybe he'd sample all of their offerings, and I wasn't talking about their recipes.

I hadn't seen much of the Drama Queens during the past few months, giving myself the "no time" excuse when in reality I didn't want to be around them at all. I didn't want them to see how Brian was treating me, or how badly I felt about myself these days. The only things going for me were my job at the Banford Clinic—which by now had become routine to the point of almost-boring—and Evan, who was going to graduate in a year-and-a-half and was already talking about moving out of the house and joining the Army. Once we got our debt situation straightened out and our marriage back on track, I'd have them over for dinner. Except CeCe, of course.

But they were all here—Shelia, Susan, even CeCe. Like Brian when Gary died, Susan became an almost-fixture around our house, helping corral the flowers and donations and schedule the brought-in dinners. For a while, I thought maybe she and Brett might start dating.

Susan had expressed an interest in purchasing a condo in Boca Raton and Brett went out of his way to find her best deal possible, locating a penthouse being sold for a fraction of a cost due to the owner's pending bankruptcy. Delighted, Susan jumped at the deal and made a point of being nice to Brett whenever he was in town, which during Mable's final illness was fairly often. But after the closing, Susan suddenly declared that she had no interest in Brett, or in anyone for that matter. "I'll probably be alone for the rest of my life," she sighed. "When you've been married to the best, it's hard to settle."

I was surprised. "But I thought you really liked Brett. You guys always have such a good time whenever you're together." He took her to dinner at the nicest places, insisting on paying despite her declarations that they were "just friends." And he even appeared to have his gambling under control, betting only on an occasional Dolphins game or Hialeah greyhound race.

And I thought Susan, who hated being alone, would have found someone by now. She was having a tough time adjusting to her emptying nest: daughter Amanda had her own nuptials in six months and Justin had been accepted into Yale in the fall. Soon the only one left would be Edison, the IQ-impaired labradoodle, and even he was getting up in years.

"Well, frankly, after what happened with CeCe and the scandal with McLean's, he's got a lot of baggage," confided Susan. "Besides, I'm not one to mess with anyone's husband, even if it's an ex-husband of a formerly close friend. It's too much like pooping in your own backyard if you know what I mean."

Actually, I didn't. CeCe and Brett had been divorced for years and she was happily remarried, and probably could care less. I mean, Brett was single and Susan was single, so what was the big deal?

Chapter 10 - Cashing Out

"Good bye, Mable," called Jack as they lowered her casket into the ground. His tone was casual, almost as if he was dropping her off at the mall or her weekly bridge club. Evan and I exchanged glances, my seventeen-year-old son's far more perplexed than mine. So I felt compelled to parrot Brian's explanation: "Grandpa doesn't like to show his feelings" while hoping that Evan didn't remember the sobs and shaking of my dad's "significant other" when he'd been buried a few years ago. Although the woman only received a few thousand dollars, having money of her own and knowing Daddy's estate was to be divided equally among his five daughters.

In fact except for her two sons and the grandchildren, hardly anyone seemed upset. The mourners stood around politely, listening to the pastor's speech about what a good wife and mother Mable had been. And how, as the only offspring of prominent citizen George K. Smith, she had upheld the upstanding name of what had been one of Upper Arlington's oldest and most respected families through her work with the PTA and various clubs. "You could count on Mable to always say and do the right thing," opined the reverend. "Not only that, but she had the shiniest silver in Franklin County!" This drew a half-hearted chuckle from the gathered mourners. How unlike Gary's funeral with its tears and heartfelt reminisces about his work among poor women in the city to encourage them to practice birth control and how, no matter what the time of day or night, he had always been there for his patients. But then Gary had been a doctor, cut down shockingly in early middle age. Yet still...

The brief service over, the mourners hurried back to their cars. It was cold and rainy, and as it was also almost Christmas, they had lots to do. Plus, who was going to the country-club bash this weekend? Apparently most of Mable and Jack's friends, from the snippets of conversations I'd overheard.

Part of it was denial, this turning away from the inevitable and towards the mundane. The older you got, the harder these things must be, especially as they encroached upon your family and friends. But still…

But still. I realized that, like so many of her peers and even ours, Mable had done nothing outstanding and never gone out of her way to really help anyone, other than the expected charity work. In all fairness to her, considering what she'd told me about her upbringing, any creativity and sense of adventure had been tamped down, then stomped on by her failed acting dreams and her family's insistence that she and Jack return to Columbus.

Granted she hadn't broken the law, nor had she hurt anyone—at least not physically. But where was the common thread, the underlying passion that gave substance to her life? Wife, mother, pillar of the community, champion of gleaming flatware, serving dishes and platters…like that old song, a whiny number from the '60s that I found incredibly annoying, was that all there was?

Yet, for some people hardship and discouragement only fueled their resolve. I thought about my own parents. About how, despite her blue-blood, WASP background, my mother had a strong sense of social injustice and tried to correct any inequities she encountered, even if they were minor. Like paying our cleaning lady Nancy more than the going rate for "colored maids" because Nancy was college-educated and helped us with our homework, while serving as an intelligent sounding board for the controversial social issues of the day.

It was tough being a teenager in the early '70s when pot-smoking and casual sex were common, even among freshman and sophomores. Having gone to high school a few years earlier, my two older sisters had at least been reined in by dress codes and dances with curfews and strict chaperones who weren't caught up in their own extramarital key parties—at least not obviously.

And how, even though he didn't have a penny, my father managed to finish medical school, by working several odd jobs and walking to his classes, rather than paying for the "T." Not to mention my parents' devotion to each other despite their vast differences in backgrounds, which as an adult, I'd come to recognize as a rare and beautiful thing. And something I would probably never experience, an emptiness that made me both sad and angry.

I was surrounded by people whose sole purpose in life, it seemed, was to make and spend money, to enjoy themselves and impress others. And it didn't make sense why my own husband and his family should condemn me for trying to start something that could benefit the greater good…

"Tish. Tish." Shelia stood before me, a concerned look on her elfin face. Her hair had grown back, a darker red threaded with grey, but just as curly. "Why are you standing out here in the rain alone? Everyone's leaving." As soon as the pastor had finished, Evan had gone off to talk to what he called his minions, friends who thought enough of him to attend his grandmother's funeral. Evan seemed to inspire that kind of loyalty, which would probably make him successful in the Army, even though I begged him to reconsider his decision not to go to college. After all, it was paid for, with the last remainder of my inheritance. And Brian…Well, where *was* my husband? During the funeral, he'd been standing close to me, holding my hand, an act of solidarity and comfort. Like Evan, he'd disappeared from my side as soon as the formalities were over. Accepting condolences, I supposed.

"Tish, you're getting soaked," Shelia said now. "Come stand under my umbrella. If I'm not mistaken, the limo has already pulled away. I can't believe they left you here…Are you all right?"

"Can you take me back to my house?" During the funeral, Brett had been talking to CeCe, who had attended by herself. They'd walked toward the limo together and perhaps everyone thought it was me… After all, CeCe and I resembled each other, or had at one time and since it was almost dark…who knew? I felt numb.

"Of course," said Shelia. "I'm sure you must be terribly upset by Mable's death. Although it was expected, it's still traumatic. I still can't believe they drove off without you…"

"Maybe they thought I went with Evan and his buddies. They like me, you know." Unlike the rest of the McLeans, they always laughed at my jokes and silly antics. Besides why were we even discussing this? What difference did it make?

"Tish, I know something's wrong," Shelia said as we got into her late-model BMW 750li, fully loaded, with a newfangled navigation system, something called GPS. I remembered Todd telling Brian how it could give you directions no matter where you were, and if the car broke down or got stolen, its location could be pinpointed by satellite, a vehicular homing pigeon. "Do you want to talk about it?"

I ignored the question. "Oh goody, I get to ride in your new car. Can you show me how the route thingy works?"

But Shelia was insistent. "Tish, I talked to Donna at Endless Possibilities. I was happy to hear you're OK."

"Thanks," I inhaled deeply. "Don't you just love that new car smell?"

"I was really worried about you so I kept after her until she finally told me why you were there. Not that it's a secret, nor should it be. What's happening with the animal shelter?"

I knew she'd had cancer, and I knew I was supposed to be polite, but she was beginning to piss me off. "Nothing," I replied sullenly. "Nothing is going on. Brian said I can't have it, so I'm not doing it. I have to respect his wishes."

"Oh, that's bullshit," Shelia retorted. "Why is Brian against it? It's not like it's his money or anything. And from what Donna said, and what I heard through the grapevine, you were making good progress."

Now I was mad. "What do you mean? What grapevine? Are people talking about me? Do they make fun of me? Because that's exactly what Brian said would happen…"

"Of course not. Everyone thinks it's a great idea. It's just that they were wondering why you were going great guns on it and then suddenly you stopped…"

So Brian had been right. They—whoever "they" were, I had no idea—were waiting for me to fail. "I don't know why you care, Shelia, or why you even bother to ask. I mean, aren't you in with the Katzes now? I just saw your picture in the paper next to Janice for some United Jewish Fund benefit."

"You know Tish, if I hadn't been so sick, I would be really offended and hurt. And in all honesty, there was a time in my life when those sorts of things mattered. But not any more…you need to understand that."

"I'm tired of people telling me I'm wrong," the moisture on my face was tears, not remnants of rain. "I'm tired of people telling me what to do. I look at a person like Mable, who spent her entire life conforming, and my own husband too and what did they have to show for it, Shelia? What?"

"I can't answer that, Tish. That's something you might want to ask Brian." We arrived in front to my house just as the limo was pulling away. Susan's Lexus was in my driveway, although it looked as if everyone else had left.

I reached for the shiny door handle, but Shelia grabbed my arm. "I don't know what's going on with you Tish, but it doesn't sound good. I want you to call me if you need to talk to someone. I want you to promise." I remained silent, and she continued, "Tell me you'll promise, because if I know nothing else about you, Tish, you keep your word. You'd rather not say anything at all than lie, which in itself can be a fib of course." Despite her gentle phrasing, the reprimand stung. I had lied by omission at Endless Possibilities that day, leading Shelia to believe I had cancer. Talk about cursing your own karma.

"I will, Shelia, although there's nothing anyone can do and no point in discussing it."

"And one more thing, Patricia," I looked at her in shock—No one called me that except for my parents when they'd gotten angry with me, and Nick, when he wanted to get a rise out of me because he knew I disliked my formal name. My indignant reaction always made him laugh.

"CeCe and I have been talking. She came to see me a lot when I was sick, which was much more than the few people who actually knew about my cancer did. Somehow, she found out and it showed me who my friends were, I'll tell you that. I don't know how much you know about what's going on with McLean's, but if I were you I'd be putting some money away. You still have your inheritance, right?"

Now my anger turned to fear, a cold chill that seemed to erupt from the base of my gut and snake all the way through my insides. "Brian takes care of all the money. What are you saying? That McLean's is going bankrupt? Jesus, Shelia, are you rumor central or something? Why do you even listen to that dumb bitch?" Even now, with her perfect life and rich husband, CeCe was still causing trouble.

Susan and Brian came out of the front of the house, partially obscured by the encroaching misty darkness. Brian went around to the driver's side of her Lexus and opened the door for her, something he hadn't done for me in years.

A sick rage choked my stomach. If I hadn't known better, I would have thought they were intimate, which was ridiculous. If nothing more, at least Susan had scruples and high morals. Of my own husband, I wasn't sure.

Shelia saw, too, and narrowed her eyes. "CeCe's not the dumb bitch I'd worry about, if I were you."

"Susan? Oh, please. She has more money than even you, thanks to Gary's investments. And she wasn't even interested in Brett, who's single and very cute. She refuses to go out with him because she said she'd never date a friend's ex-husband, even though CeCe's not loyal to anyone but herself."

"Well CeCe's a friend to me, and I'd take her over Susan any day," Shelia replied.

In spite of myself, and in spite of my doubts, I felt compelled to defend Susan, who, although she wasn't the sharpest tack on the bulletin board, had proven to be a steadfast and consistent presence in our lives despite our troubles. "And I feel that way about Susan, especially after Mable got so sick," I retorted. "She's been helping us out—I don't know how we would have gotten through without her, because Brett sure didn't do much."

"Whatever...But Tish, I meant what I said about calling me."

I thought of Bette Davis and the movie "Dark Victory." About the scene when, having just learned that she had an inoperable brain tumor, her character insists on going to a country club dance. "I want to show the gentry I still have it," she'd said. Well, that's how I felt about Shelia and the women at The Club. They pretended to be worried, to show they cared, but did they really? They fed on other's misfortunes to make themselves feel superior. I knew, because I had been party to so many of those conversations. No way in hell was I going to be this week's carrion.

"OK, Shelia I get your point," I said stiffly. "I appreciate your concern."

Susan pulled out of the driveway and waved when she saw us. Brian noticed us as well and hurried towards us, a worried look on his face.

"You know my number."

I nodded, avoiding Shelia's probing gaze. "Thanks for driving me, Shelia. Great ride, by the way." Flippant was good, and mentally I thanked Evan for his generation's ever-evolving, glib vernacular. Yet despite everything, I found myself wondering if she was sincere. What if she knew something I didn't?

I got out of the car and practically fell into Brian's arms. He looked genuinely upset. "My God, Tish, what happened? I came back to the house and you weren't there. I thought you'd caught a ride with Evan or Susan and when they showed up without you, we didn't know what to think! We were getting ready to call the police!"

Shelia rolled down her window. "You need to pay more attention to your wife, Brian. If I hadn't found her, she'd still be at the cemetery!" Her words were jocular, with an undertone of grimness.

OK so maybe she cared…a little. "Thanks so much for bringing her back, Shelia. I am so sorry Tish! God, you're soaked!" Brian slipped his arm around my waist, hugging me. The full-body contact felt wonderful. How long had it been since he'd touched me with any kind of enthusiasm?

"The others are still in the house," Brian said as Shelia drove off. I presumed he meant Brett, Jack, Evan, and whatever minions my son had corralled into staying. So much for Shelia's insinuations about Susan's designs on my husband. "Although they're a pain in the ass, we really need those damn little phones." The battery in my cell had gone bad a few days ago and I hadn't had a chance to get a replacement.

"I didn't mean to upset you, Brian," I turned towards my husband and grabbed his other hand, holding him tightly. "But before we go inside, you've got to tell me something." I felt him tense. "Is McLean's going bankrupt?"

"Don't be absurd, Tish! Where did you hear that?" Brian's reaction left no doubt that this was news to him as well. "I mean we've had some financial trouble lately, but nothing I haven't told you about." Oddly he looked almost relieved.

"Shelia mentioned it…And she also asked me if anything was left of my inheritance."

"Well, considering your spending habits, we know the answer to that question," Now Brian was back to his old confident self. "I wouldn't listen to her and that bullshit gossip at The Club. You know what those people are like."

I was almost giddy with relief. "I know. That's exactly what I told her."

"Besides, Tish, you know I'll always take care of you, no matter how difficult things get. You can count on me. I love you."

We kissed and I said, "I love you, too" but somehow the words felt hollow. Sort of like Nixon's reassurances just after the Watergate break-in.

*****

I wish that I could say things improved between us after Mable died. That they went back to they way they'd been when we first got married, or at least before I inherited and then lost all that money. Then Evan might have had a decent senior year in high school, his last few months before leaving home. He might even have reconsidered going to college instead of joining the Army, which although it was peacetime, terrified me. There was Kosovo, Afghanistan, and elsewhere in the Middle East, and God knew where else trouble could erupt in the world. But no…Brian quickly returned to his hypercritical self, and McLean's closed two more stores. Which left only one, the flagship salesroom in Upper Arlington and the warehouse. A few weeks after the funeral, Jack moved to Palm Beach, which left me alone with Brian, who was rarely home. He was either working, practicing with or running the softball league which he claimed took a lot of his time, even during the cold months, or doing some long-distance errand for Jack.

I was constantly afraid. I went to bed with a knot of fear and I woke up with it. I took it to work with me and it sat next to me when I ate. It never left me, and when I went in for my annual gynecological exam, the doctor took one look at me and ordered a complete physical. I had lost ten pounds and couldn't explain why. When he went to examine me, I almost jumped off the table. I was convinced that, like my mother, I was dying of ovarian cancer. But it was only because I hadn't had sex in a very long time, was a mess of nerves, and it hurt like hell.

When I think back on that period in my life, just after Mable died, I can't remember much. Only the fear, which never left me. And I don't even know exactly when Brian started talking about wanting more space, or suggesting that we separate. But I went through life like an automaton, performing my job, spending time with my son, and thinking, well, if Brian leaves me, I'll be destitute. How can I keep up with all the bills, while living on a salary of $21,500 a year?

We were neck-deep in debt, with a second mortgage, the payout of which I couldn't explain. I didn't know where the money went, and still don't. Brian said he needed it to keep us in the lifestyle to which Evan and I were accustomed. But Evan was working now and rarely asked for money. Brian wanted to put our house up for sale immediately, even if it meant that the move take place before our son's graduation. He glossed over Evan's sorrow about losing his childhood home as: "You'll be gone soon. What difference does it make?" And this from a man who had devoted his whole life to his parents' whims. Who at one point had even considered purchasing his childhood home from Mable and Jack, before Mable got sick and we decided upon New Wellington. Like the shoemaker's children gone barefoot, his only offspring's desires seemed not to matter at all.

When the gynecologist asked me why I was so tense, I told him I hadn't played tennis in over a year. He suggested I get out and exercise. Or do something I really enjoy. Like what? I thought to myself.

Then Brian started coming and going at odd hours, and taking phone calls on his cell and hurrying from the room. Although deep down inside, I knew what was happening, I didn't want to admit it to myself. So I accepted his excuses and rationalizations about private business conversations and not wanting to bore me with details of managing the softball league, of which he'd recently been elected president. After his admission of the affair d'Amber, I'd forgiven him, telling myself that everyone was entitled to a mistake—I would have slept with Nick, if he'd let me. Was it unrealistic to expect complete faithfulness for an entire lifetime…as long as your marriage strengthened and you grew together as a couple afterwards? In fact we'd cheated almost concurrently, so each canceled the other out. Or so I told myself, glossing over the detail that Brian had actually consummated his desires. No matter what the so-called experts say about emotional infidelity, once you cross the line into actual sex, there's a world of difference. But we'd been through terrible times before, and we'd been together 21 years, so surely this would pass. And he was still mourning the loss of his mother. As I knew so well, grief did strange things to people, skewering their judgment and perspective.

Brian was flying down to Palm Beach to finalize some financial arrangements with Jack. I was supposed to take him to the airport, and had left work early on Friday to get home on time. But he wasn't there when I arrived. Evan was spending the weekend with his friend Daniel, a freshman at Bowling Green State University. I encouraged him to go, even lending him my Beamer, so he'd have a safe ride on the highway, still snowy even though it was getting toward March. Perhaps exposure to actual campus life would guide Evan towards the path of higher learning.

The house, once my haven of relaxation and security, felt cold and empty. With his littermate Freddy recently departed, a victim of a quick and painless stroke, my cat Teddy also was at a loss, wandering around, meowing aimlessly. I didn't dare ask Brian for a replacement; given the slightest provocation, he might have insisted that Teddy be put down as well, despite the twelve-year-old feline's stubborn good health. He'd see Teddy's incessant vocalizing as the first symptom of his decline—why spend the extra money on vet bills when you were just delaying the inevitable?

So I sat in the living room, whose cozy, chintz-and-dark wood furniture was once the height of style in the early 1990s, when cocooning in front of the fireplace (or more realistically, the big-screen TV) was the next big thing. Back then, it was no big deal to replace the various rooms in our house with whatever seemed to be the trend. If we grew tired of it, we could always get something new. But since McLean's economic troubles had worsened, this was no longer an option. And I never much cared for the homey, flowery look. But I was stuck, in more ways than one.

Finally I heard the garage door's opening rattle, and Brian walked in. He looked uncommonly happy, and eerily like the young man I'd fallen in love with at the University of Virginia. But something was off—the light in his eyes, the smile on his face, had nothing to do with me.

"Did Dad call?" he said.

"No, was he supposed to?" And then the phone rang.

Brian laughed. "Talk about timing… Tell him I'm not here—I have to go up and pack."

I was confused. "Why? What's the difference?"

"Well, he called me on the cell, and I said I was at the store getting some paperwork. But I was over at the League working on the schedules…Just do it, would you please, Tish?" He headed up the stairs.

He was getting some all right, I realized with a sudden shock, but it was hardly paperwork. The small deceit seemed to make no sense until you looked at the big picture and saw it for what it really was -- a fissure over a canyon, a blemish that hid an all-encompassing rot. I stared at my husband and with a rush of horror, understood with shocking clarity just how much he enjoyed the intrigue, however minute. Obviously he'd been with a woman, probably the flirty, shapely 40-something divorcee whose son he claimed to be coaching these days. The kid supposedly had a wicked pitch and curveball, and Brian was helping him harness it. Undoubtedly he was providing the same services in a different capacity for the mother as well.

Who was this man? What happened to the kind and considerate college student I fell in love with, the rescuer of all things needy and supporter of dreams? He had been replaced by a stranger, someone I didn't know at all. Someone I hadn't known for a very long time. I stood, rooted to the spot.

"OK, well don't answer the phone," Brian's voice floated down the stairs. He always reprimanded Evan and me about talking to him from a different room, claiming it was rude. But like most of his rules, it didn't apply to him. "But be ready to leave in a few minutes. And have you thought any more about putting the house up? Tish, we need to talk more about a separation... I need my space—and it's more than just a weekend or a few days away. Maybe we should go to a lawyer and see about making this official."

As if a separation were nothing more than a golf outing, or going to a movie. As if it weren't a prelude to the divorce he was really planning. My brain reeled. Well, he could go fuck himself. "You know, Brian, you're going to have to find your own way to the airport," I responded loudly, struggling to match his casual tone. "I know...Why don't you have your girlfriend take you?" I walked into the garage, for a moment disoriented because my car was gone. Then I remembered...Evan had my BMW. Well, I'd take his Tracker or better yet, Brian's Explorer, a relatively new model with four-wheel drive. But fuck it, what difference did it make if I slid into a ditch or flipped over in my son's tin can, better me than him anyway I thought as I turned off my cell phone so as not to get Brian's calls. At that point, I didn't care whether I lived or died.

*****

We always remember the momentous things in our lives, whether it be a historical event or personal trauma. We can usually recall exactly what we were thinking or doing at the precise moment it happened. Who hasn't swapped stories about the day JFK was assassinated or the Challenger space shuttle exploded or the much more recent horror of September 11? Although my tragedy was minute in comparison, it was indeed memorable. It was as if someone had opened a door in my mind and I'd stepped through it, never to return. Like Alice in Wonderland, having tasted the mushroom, I'd grown too big to slip back through the opening of the lie that had become my marriage. Or like the bird that slammed against the window just before CeCe and Brett had split. I'd been deceived by what I'd thought was reality, but it took a sudden onrush into clarity — if only for second—to help me understand the truth before being knocked about by the events that were to follow. Yet at that moment, at the worst time of crisis, I began to hold fast to a tiny grain of reality that would eventually turn into a pearl and then become an anchor— to listen to my own heart and instincts, above all else.

I drove for hours, losing track of the time. The tin can remained obdurately on the road, refusing to even skid when I slammed on the brakes, having almost failed to notice a red light. (Taking myself out was one thing, but having somebody go with me was another entirely.) It also kept running, despite the fact that the gas gauge was below "E" for how long I didn't know. But it was the cold that got me; after dusk, the temperature dropped rapidly and I'd forgotten to take a coat. No bun warmers in this beater, and Evan had mentioned something about the heating coils needing replacing. So after gassing up, I headed back to...where? I had a home that wouldn't be mine much longer, no husband to speak of and a cat that refused to shut up.

I thought, briefly, of going to Nick's office—but what would I say? You were right about my life, buddy. It's total shit. Besides you have a wife, two young children, and being as you're actually a loyal husband, she's probably getting some regular action. Besides I didn't want his pity...or Shelia's either, although, she too had proven to be right about things as well.

But there was always Susan...loyal Susan who had nothing but time on her hands and was always available to talk. Susan who'd known her own pain and suffering and would surely understand. As I drove towards Susan's house, I thought, in a way, it makes sense that Brian wants to be single. First his brother Brett, now his father…as usual, he was following the in the family footsteps.

PART FOUR: QUEEN OF HEARTS

Chapter 11 - Hairball to the Throne

I honestly think that people going through a divorce—and probably for about a year afterwards—should be shipped to another country. Not to be cruel, but the process is so painful it might actually help them to be isolated for a while. Because like war, divorce is hell, especially for a naive and unsuspecting third-world nation such as myself.

How do you make the transition to singlehood after being married for over half your life? People look at you differently, offer all kinds of advice: "You need to look out for yourself now." "You'd better consult a lawyer," and the ultimately annoying: "Why don't you try that Internet dating service/singles dance/transitions social club at the church?" As if finding another warm body was the solution to all your problems, the ones that destroyed your marriage in the first place. Because if I have learned anything through this hellacious experience, it's that it takes two to tango, even if the enabler is a cheating son of a bitch. You can lie to yourself and keep going, which is what I did for many years, or you get the hell out and face the scary consequences of the unknown.

But no one can describe exactly how to transform yourself from a married entity to one who is self-sufficient. That can only be learned under fire, through battle.

In the beginning, I was a walking wound. I would talk to anyone who listened—convenience store clerks, gas station attendants, the cleaning crew in the building where I worked. Strangers were especially good, since I didn't have to be accountable for what I said and would likely never see them again. Friends were more difficult, although my coworkers were immediately sympathetic and my boss Jim Gladstone offered me a more responsible job which also meant a raise.

And what would I have done without Susan? When Brian told me that McLean's was filing for Chapter-11 bankruptcy which would likely prevent me from getting alimony—at least for a while—she listened to my hysterical sobs. When Brian presented me with a list of how to divide our assets, she was there for me, counseling me to be rational when listening to his suggestions. Although they were skewed towards his own self-interest, she pointed out, they were not totally unfair. I would get the proceeds from the house—from which I would have to pay our marital debts—and most of its contents while he would get his pension, uncannily prescient planning that I would question a few years later, since it was in no way tied to his business. Of course he would have to liquidate some of the funds to help pay for the bankruptcy, but just exactly how much was never made clear.

But as Susan reminded me that, even if he remarried, eventually I would also get a percentage of his Social Security. And I had my own job, with its small pension plan. Not much of a career path, but once I turned sixty-five I could retire and live on a fixed income. And maybe take a trip or two to Florida with the other old ladies, provided we shared a room and meals and they didn't get lucky and hook up with one of the geezers all the other Golden Girls were fighting over with their canes and walkers. Oh, what a grand future that would be. I could hardly wait.

But when Tammy Shepherd, a bimbo from the softball team called, and asked for Brian in her breathless, fuck-me voice, even Susan understood why I could go from a member of polite society to fishwife in 0 to 60. Apparently she couldn't reach him on his cell and Brian had told her it was OK to call the house since he and I were recently separated. "Some of these women would do anything for a man," she shook her tastefully highlighted head—a recent improvement thanks to my recommendation of my hairdresser—in disgust and indignation. "I am sure that Brian did not give her permission to call the house, in spite of what she told you." Having been single a few years herself, she was well acquainted with the lengths to which some women would go. "You can just smell their desperation...they swarm to dances and parties like they're on the hunt, and believe me, the guys run like scared deer!"

But the biggest surprise of all was Evan. He suddenly announced that he was applying to Ohio State. I was thrilled. It was easily affordable, since the tuition had been taken care of through the prepaid plan. He already had friends on campus to live with and always managed to find employment that would help pay rent and other expenses. He also seemed to accept our breakup and the pending loss of his childhood home with equanimity.

But a few weeks later, after Brian moved out and into the house so recently vacated by his parents—which supposedly was on the market but somehow oh-so-conveniently never sold, Evan took me aside. "Mom, I've got to tell you something," His face, a younger but finer-featured version's of Brian, was entirely too serious for someone whose biggest concern only a few years ago had been lobbying for the latest Nintendo game. "But you've got to promise not to say anything, especially to Dad."

"Why?" At that point, I was still shell-shocked and still considered Brian my husband, confidante and partner, especially regarding all things Evan. "Are you in some kind of trouble?"

"Now, c'mon Mom, that's so old-school, back in the day when the five most dreaded words in the English language were…"

"Mrs. McLean, your son Evan…" I finished with a smile. Like Nick, Evan could always make me laugh.

My son turned serious, his green eyes, so like my soon-to-be ex's, darkening with intensity. He had inherited my father's height and had shot up to 6'1," making me feel almost petite. "I'm not going to Ohio State—at least not right away. I'm enlisting in the Army. I've already met with the recruiter."

"But I thought…" I began and he held up his hand. "Oh Evan, you can't do this. You promised you'd talk to me about it first."

"C'mon Mom, I'm seventeen. I'll be eighteen in two months, and graduating in three. Legally you could stop me now, but you won't be able to soon." In June, he planned to move into an apartment on campus, which was probably for the best, especially since there seemed to be a regular exodus of buyers interested in a "discount"

New Wellington home priced to sell! (exclamation point courtesy of the Realtor). I hadn't even begun to figure out where to live myself although Susan, bless her, had said that if necessary I could stay at her house for a few weeks until I found a place, since she'd been spending quite a bit of time in at her condo in Boca Raton.

Still, I was puzzled by the request for confidentiality. "But why the secrecy, Evan? Dad was OK with you going into the service." Of course he would be—he'd get half Evan's college tuition back, because I wasn't savvy enough to tell the lawyer that it came from my inheritance and was rightfully mine. Besides, both Jack and Mable approved of anything to do with the Armed Forces. According to Jack, even Vietnam could have been won had the U.S. had the guts to turn Southeast Asia into a parking lot. "So what's the problem?"

"Jesus, Mom, you don't know? Think about it." My son shook his head. "What have you been fantasizing about all these years?"

Nick, I thought wildly, my son knows about Nick? I never told anyone, not the Drama Queens, not even my other sisters. Only Lisa knew and she wouldn't say anything to her own nephew…Not about that… Yes, Nick had been figuring more and more in my thoughts these days although of course I'd done nothing about it. And, being as he was happily married, would continue do nothing.

"The shelter, Mom, the animal shelter," Evan's insistent voice cut through my mental haze. "You've been talking about it forever, and with the money you get back from my college tuition, you'll be able to set it up."

I shook my head. "Oh, no Evan. Absolutely not. No way would I use your college money for Paws That Refresh." It only seemed like yesterday that a 14-going-on 4-year-old adolescent bubbled over with excitement at coming up with such a clever name. "It's not going to happen. You need that degree."

"Mom, I don't even know what I want out of life. But I do know I'm sure as hell not ready for college." My son looked disappointed and angry. "I'm going to join the Army no matter what. If you want to be stupid and tell Dad so he can get half the money, do it. But if you keep quiet until after the divorce, you'll get all of it. It's up to you. I'm leaving." He pulled out his Beavis and Butthead keychain and headed towards the door.

I reached over and drew him back. "Evan, please think about this...it's your future."

"No Mom, *you* think about it," my son shot back, sounding more like the teenager he really was, the rebellious kid I knew, pre-divorce. "All these years you've done what Dad's wanted and kissed his ass. Never what you thought was right, or what you needed to do. And where did it get you, Mom, where?" His voice cracked, and he pulled away. "I've got to go. Clay is waiting for me." He slammed the door, the sound echoing through the house.

For a long time I sat in the kitchen as dusk slowly turned to dark. I smelled the cigarette smoke from my departed son's clothing—he'd started in eighth grade, quit at fifteen after the shoplifting fiasco and had recently begun again, although I said nothing about it. He had enough to deal with.

I tried to look into my future and saw...nothing. More years at the Banford Clinic. Living on a fixed income? Or a new start with the animal shelter? Something of my own making, something, as Evan so accurately pointed out, that I'd dreamed of for so long. Out of the mouth of babes...during my increasingly frequent nocturnal excursions into late-night TV, I remembered hearing some celebrity—Paris Hilton? Kirstie Alley, who, given her size, had reason to talk?—commenting about how a woman can be sexy no matter what her size or appearance, as long as she felt desirable and attractive from the inside. OK, so she probably got the idea from watching "Oprah" but couldn't the same principle apply to career success as well?

Even my son was more proactive than me. Although he claimed otherwise, he knew what he wanted, at least for now. And he was going after it. Even though he had little to no experience with so-called "real" life. Was I, who supposedly had so much more, ever going to do the same?

*****

I did solve one problem, however. A few weeks after Brian

moved out, a female Himalayan kitten was left at the doorstep of the clinic. We promptly named her Trump, as the fur on her head grew sideways, oddly resembling The Donald's comb-over. I fell in love and brought her home that night, hoping to cure Teddy of his incessant crying.

To be anatomically correct, we should have called her Ivana, but like her namesake, Trump had a gigantic sense of self-worth. She was unintimidated by Teddy, who was at least twice her size. So after a few threatening growls from Teddy—whereupon Trump promptly walked in front of him and stuck her tail in his face as if daring him to make something of it—the two settled into an uneasy truce. Which eventually grew into a mutually beneficial relationship in which they constantly double-teamed me for food, treats, and attention—when they weren't chasing each other around, eventually bringing their conflicts to me like quarrelling children who expect the parent to resolve a standoff. But along with being quieter, Teddy was much happier, as was I, with this small scrap of life to nurture and cherish.

Shortly after my dissolution became final—I'd agreed to a dissolution rather than a divorce, it was less of a legal hassle and I was hardly the type to fight to keep someone in a relationship they didn't want—I encountered Nick. In my ultimate humiliation and embarrassment over being abandoned by my husband, Nick was the last person I wanted to see. First he'd rejected me—although logic told me he'd done the right thing, given both of our circumstances—and now Brian had followed suit, pegging me in my current emotional state as the ultimate loser. Except for my co-workers at the clinic and of course Susan, I avoided the few friends Brian and I had made during our years together in Columbus. I somehow felt that they thought I was getting what I deserved. I hadn't played the game of being socially adept, of being the penultimate country club wife like Mable.

Even CeCe, as much as I despised her, had managed to make the system work in her favor, parlaying a hefty settlement from Brett and snagging a rich, handsome second husband a few months later. Would I end up a nonentity, a bitter, lonely bottom feeder scrounging the social scene for leftover men, worrying about every penny on my fixed income? Or could I transform my life into something better?

Occasional tiny slivers of hope sustained me. Much of the time, I felt that I might end up a financial horror story whose life takes a downward turn and who ends up living in their car, or worse, a homeless shelter. After all I'd had a quarter of a million dollars and was left with less than a tenth, which could be mine as long as I kept my mouth shut. As it was, I'd have to pay a stiff penalty to cash it out.

And yet, I told myself, if I'm careful with money and smart, I might be OK, even though I'd been so foolish in the past. My sister Lisa and her husband Nate had taken me aside and helped me work out a budget, which although it was a pain in the ass to follow, was doable financially. They also "loaned" me several thousand dollars to pay off several high-interest credit cards, monies which I fully intended to reimburse although I couldn't say how or when.

And as a now-experienced vet tech I definitely had a marketable skill, as evidenced by my recent promotion and high marks on my annual performance review. Sometimes I felt almost uplifted, as if I'd been given a second chance and was almost (but not quite) exhilarated by the challenge. What if I actually could open the shelter? Now there was nothing to stop me from at least trying.... The life that I dreamed of could be mine, as long as I made the right decisions. But having relied on Brian and his family for so long, my intuition was rusty and I was just so afraid.

I was in an unhappy, black place when I went to the March meeting of the Columbus Veterinary Society. I hadn't attended in months; one thing or another always interfered, problems with the divorce or getting the house ready to sell or my simply being exhausted from the day itself. Some mornings, it took all my fortitude to drag my ass out of bed, not to mention getting dressed and going to work. But with my only social friend Susan having taken off to her condo in Florida, and Evan being gone with his senior class for their spring break graduation trip, I'd been alone for several nights running and was desperate to see faces other than my coworkers or strangers at the grocery store.

Even Brian was spending the week with his dad and Brett, and although exchanges between us were usually hostile, he managed to call or stop by every few days, with one excuse or another. And he was either overly solicitous ("How are you doing, Tish? Is everything OK?") or hostile to the point of near-paranoia ("You'd better make sure the heat's turned down! I'm still paying the electric bill. I'm coming over to check and make sure the house is spotless—we need to sell immediately!") And so on. Oddly enough I hadn't heard from him, although that was a relief.

But this meeting was a special event, a dinner at my boss Jim Gladstone's Muirfield home. He'd made a point of stopping me in the hallway earlier that day and eliciting a promise that I would at least make an appearance. His wife Cynthia was a gourmet cook, although everyone else was to bring a dish. "But don't you worry about that, Tish," he reassured me. "You just bring yourself and have a nice meal. We miss your presence and your ideas."

If I'd bothered to read the Society's newsletter I would have learned that officers were being elected and that Nick was running for president. And I most probably would have stayed away, inventing a sudden onset of stomach flu or whatever. But Evan had planted a seed with his generous offer; although I wasn't quite yet sure how to tend it, I sensed that the answer lay with my colleagues, tireless volunteers and like myself, advocates of homeless animals.

I'd been peppered from all sides about my weight; I was too thin, I wasn't eating enough. Well, who could think of food at a time like this....But when I saw the Cornish hen, grilled salmon, and pasta with its selection of four sauces at Cynthia's elegantly set table not to mention several other yummy-looking side dishes, I found myself actually hungry for the first time in weeks. And as I loaded up my plate and located a corner where I could sit down and dig in, Nick entered the room. And then my appetite was gone...again.

If I'd been paying attention, I would have noticed the dark circles under his eyes, and that his long, rapidly graying brown hair was even more in need of a trim than usual. That there was a tightness around his normally genial mouth. But I was only aware that he looked gorgeous, as usual.

He spotted me and rather than avoiding me as he had during our last encounters, came right over. "Where have you been?" he demanded in his creamy voice, plucking a tiny drumstick from my plate.

The nerve…"How did you know I didn't want that?" I spluttered, completely taken off guard. It was as if someone had rewound a time machine back to our easy empathy, before my humiliating revelation, before I'd told him how I felt.

"Well, you weren't eating so I figured that rather than wait in line, I'd help myself. I'm hungry. Any more you're willing to share?" He peered at the rest of my plate.

"Nick, get away from her." Cynthia, a slightly plump, perpetually cheerful woman came up to us, chiding him. "Can't you see that Tish needs every calorie?" She looked at me and sighed. "I wish I had your problem, honey. Thin *and* beautiful."

How I loved her for saying that at that particular moment! I felt better than, well, I couldn't remember when exactly.

Nick looked at me, his face as unreadable as the color of his eyes, which always seemed to shift between grey and brown. If someone had stuck a gun to my head and demanded that I identify their hue, they'd have to pull the trigger. Nick and I had spent hours looking at each other and talking, and I could only tell that they usually sparkled and were expressive.

"OK, but first I have to go out and corral some votes." His glance shifted to Cynthia. "Cindy, would you be an angel and please fix me a plate? Just more of what Tish is having. I'll talk to you later, Tish."

"Sure, honey. I'll bring it around." At Nick's departing back, she remarked. "What a hunk. Too bad his wife's never there to take care of him. If he was mine I wouldn't let him out of my sight."

Et tu, Brutus, a cheating heart? "You mean he screws around on Elena, too?" Her name tasted like ashes in my mouth.

"Oh hell no. If anything, it might be the other way around. She's what we used to call a ball-buster in college and has no problem using her sex appeal to get what she wants. So it's hard to tell what she's really thinking. Nick on the other hand, is totally real—what you see is what you get. Not all men are bastards..." And at that moment I knew that everyone in that room, Nick included, had heard about my divorce. And although it was unsettling, it was also intensely reassuring to know that at least some people still liked me and were my friends, in spite of Brian's desertion. Even Nick, whom I would have thought would have hightailed in the opposite direction once he found out I was unhinged—not just mentally, but now maritally.

*****

But the evening wasn't over yet. Shortly after Nick was elected president of the Columbus Veterinary Society by a landslide, he said, "As my first official act, I would like to make a request. Tish..." He looked directly at me, and I felt myself go stiff in my chair. After he'd walked away earlier, my appetite had come back and I ate with gusto, even returning for seconds. But my stomach, which had shrunk, was beginning to complain about being overfull. And now it was clenching with anxiety as well. There was nothing I hated worse than throwing up, but all of a sudden, that seemed like a distinct possibility.

And here was Nick, asking me to talk about Paws That Refresh, saying that I had done a lot of the initial leg work and was looking for some additional help in getting it started. Instead of being angry or annoyed, here I was standing up in front of all these people, including some of the most prominent in the community, who would not normally even attend a meeting of the Veterinary Society but were friends of my boss. And explaining the concept, the vision, and the research I'd done, as if public speaking was an everyday occurrence to me. Which it most certainly was not. Yet somehow it didn't matter; because it felt like the right thing to do, I felt at ease.

After the meeting broke up, several people came up to me, peppering me with questions and compliments. I was deluged with business cards, offers of help, and suggestions, the most useful of which included the idea for a fund-raiser to get the ball rolling. "It's like house-breaking a puppy," Jim Gladstone told me. "Make it an annual event, and people will be conditioned to expect it and look forward to it. It's got to be a hell of a party, though." Immediately I thought of The Club, and my Shih Tzu-loving maitre d' friend who had offered his assistance. Talk about the ideal setting. Especially if the shelter was going to be in New Wellington anyway.

By the time I got out of there it was well past 11:30 and Nick was long gone. And I had a ton of ideas and leads, including one from a land developer who offered me a great deal on a storefront in a strip mall in New Wellington that was in the process of being built. Apparently he'd been doing so well with commercial real estate in the area, he could afford to be generous... It would be several months before it was ready, but that would give me plenty of time to get things organized and gather a board of directors, as well as the necessary benefactors and permits. And best of all, I finally felt confident enough to call Janice Katz. Once I had everything down on paper of course.

Hopefully her snippy but ultimately helpful personal assistant Vaughn was still there. And hopefully Janice even remembered our brief encounter of almost two years ago. It was too bad that Nick had already left; I really wanted to thank him. Solely from one professional to another, of course. Although I couldn't help secretly fantasizing what might happen between us if his marriage ended. After all, he and Elena seemed so different—if what Cindy said was true.

I was on such a high—really happy for the first time in months—that I called Susan in Florida from my cell while driving home. She sounded a little strained when I announced that it was me, but also surprisingly awake, considering the lateness of the hour. I chattered on for several minutes about the meeting and how excited I was about the project, then realized that I was talking into a dead phone. When I called her back, I got her voice mail. Oh, well, I'd probably bore her to sleep; as someone who had unlimited funds she might have a hard time relating to not only the achievement of a vision but finding a career that I loved that might actually support me.

The next day she called back, apologized, and invited me to stay for a week at her condo in Boca out of the blue. She even offered to pay my airfare, which of course I declined. I wasn't that poor, and besides I had the leftover ticket from when Brian and I had abruptly canceled a visit to Brett, ostensibly because too much was going on at home and (yet again) Mable was so ill. At the time I thought nothing of Susan's unexpectedly generous offer, but then nothing improves blurry vision like hindsight.

Chapter 12 - Paper Cuts from Pushing the Envelope

But God, Buddha, Jesus, or Mohammed or whatever higher power ultimately guides our lives had other plans and he, she or it wasn't laughing. I did indeed get to Boca for a well-needed vacation. Except for Susan's uncharacteristic obsession with lightening her hair (again, thanks to my hairdresser, it never looked better—or blonder), spending hours by the pool tanning, and watching everything she put into her mouth, it was enjoyable…by my standards back then. As it was my first vacation without my hypercritical ex-husband and his family, no wonder I thought Boca was almost heaven; but then, so is West Virginia, according to the late John Denver.

In the country club universe or any place where appearances are #1, such as, say, the glossy pages of Mable's favorite publication *Town and Country* magazine, you can never be too rich or too thin. And while Susan never had to worry about the former, her voluptuous proportions were the occasional subject of the sly, well-placed jibe. All the Drama Queens except for Susan had what were considered "good" figures, despite our disparity in shapes and height. And the older generation in particular—those women past menopause who didn't seem to have to worry so much—took especial delight in monitoring the weight of the younger members, especially the new mothers with baby pounds to shed. The men, as usual, were mostly exempt from such observations.

Shortly before the final episode of Mable's ailments—too bad reality TV hadn't yet become ubiquitous, the McLean family drama might have made a great show—she, Jack, Brian and I went to the Club for dinner for Jack's birthday. It happened to coincide with the Fourth of July buffet, so tout le monde was out and about, en famille, to put together my own smorgasbord of clichés, which come to think of it, pretty much describes country club life, anyway. Mable and Brian spent a pleasurable (for them) evening dissecting who had "put on a few" and who had slimmed down, an observation which was usually met with a big smile and a "You look great!" if you happened to encounter the individual face-to-face.

Should you be on the chunky side or—horrors!—if you'd gone up a couple of dress sizes, people approached you with concern—"Are you feeling all right?" Or they didn't say anything at all but you could feel their eyes burning holes into your larger ass and/or additional roll(s). I only know this because my sister Lisa had always battled her weight and refused to go to our childhood club when she was on the dark side of 140 pounds. Over the past several years, however, she'd pulled a successful Oprah with a personal trainer and cook who helped her keep her healthy and trim. Now she no longer flinched when I introduced her as my "big" sister.

Done dissecting all the available bodies, Mable—who also rambled on about her never-changing weight as she chowed down the scalloped potatoes and chocolate mousse from the buffet—turned her wisdom to our circle of friends of whom Susan was the most obvious target. She began with "such a pretty face" as the opening course and was about to launch into the main menu of Susan's ample bosom and slightly flabby arms when Brian suddenly cut her off with, "Enough Mother!" in that tone of voice that McLean men use when their women are getting just a little bit too self-important. Jack, who had zoned out (apparently relieved for the moment at not being the object of Mable's critical eye) brightened and echoed the sentiment, in the exact same pitch.

Suitably chastised, Mable switched her laser beam to the beaded dreadlocks and skimpy sundress of the wife of the president of Shoe Corp. "I know they just got back from Jamaica, but that doesn't mean they have to bring back the habits of the natives..." The hairstyle wasn't the only thing she'd exported. I'd never tell Mable what I'd heard: That the lady in question had also smuggled some ganja up her va-jay-jay.

Susan loved to shop, and was never happier than when, for instance, while in Boca, I bought one dress at the same pricey boutique where she'd purchased several outfits of similar style. It seemed like she got a kick out of the fact that she could afford more and I could not. Susan also loved to do crafty things and visit flea markets so we spent hours wandering from one store or stall to the next. She'd also made a new "BFF," a ditzy blonde who at first reminded me of CeCe, although she was Czechoslovakian, several inches shorter, and had been married and divorced three times. Maruska constantly complained about her lack of money and lousy luck, although I was beginning to suspect her predicament had more to do with personal choice than external factors. And if CeCe was nothing more than an appendage, she was at least successful at it and seemed content. I had to give her that.

Maruska was also sexually active, openly dissecting the performances of her "friends with benefits" and one-night stands, much to my great discomfort. I'd always believed such things were private and since I'd only had sex with two men (and almost a third, if Nick had only...), it fueled my insecurity. Sensing my unease, Susan would shrug and say, "You Eastern European women are so different from us Americans. Tish and I are just so conservative..." She'd sigh, a sound that never failed to elicit sympathy, while I laughed, which probably appeared rude. A lifelong square peg, I found it amusing to be grouped with the conventional Susan.

And I was beginning to notice other things. For the past several months, Susan had an "off-and-on platonic friendship" (her words) with a widower named Keith, a dental hygienist who appeared quite taken with her although it seemed that she was leading him on so she could have a Saturday night dinner companion. "Thank goodness he likes movies, plays and concerts because talking with him can be like pulling the teeth that he spends all day cleaning!" But what did I know, since I hadn't dated in, oh, something like twenty-two years?

I also noticed how Susan would never go anywhere by herself. When we'd all been couples together, such neediness hadn't been apparent. If we weren't with our spouses, we were with our kids, and our lives were always busy. Who had time back then to worry about being alone? And the only one of us whose husband traveled occasionally was Shelia—but she had her big house with live-in servants and her extended family. I'd grown up in a large family and relished any solitude I could find, whether in a quiet corner in my father's den or among the trees at a nearby park. Brian had been like me in that way—he enjoyed what he called his "space" even during the happy times.

But since Gary died, Susan always seemed to need to be around people. It was especially difficult for her after the initial shock and sympathy had worn off and her Club friends abandoned her, claiming other commitments and "forgetting" to include her in their couples outings. Yeah, right... For a while it seemed as if Brian and I were her only social outlet, even though her daughter Amanda opted to remain at home while attending Ohio State and her son had only left for Harvard last fall. Later Susan found companionship among her church group; and what she called her "sewing circle," non-Club women she'd become friendly with when she and Gary were just starting out.

Occasionally, during the daytime, one of her former tennis buddies would deign to meet her for lunch. "But as an extra woman, I feel like a social outcast," Susan told me more than once. How well I thought I understood. I was considerably less sympathetic when all those "friends" suddenly had room on their calendars after she and Brian became a couple.

Like Susan, I had had a lifetime of being surrounded by others and being told what to do. Raising a child and going back to school, first in business and later to become a vet tech, had kept me busy, and the problems and drama generated by my ex-husband and his family had really topped things off. So I'd never had much chance to contemplate anything else.

Yet, although I felt rudderless and often at a loss, I was beginning to grasp the importance of quiet. So much so that I'd purchased several books on meditation and had signed up for a class in beginning yoga, planning to start shortly after I returned home.

Being alone also gave me a chance to think, to observe, and perhaps most vital of all, to really listen, something I realized I hadn't done in years. Everyone has so much to say, but who among us actually hears what others are communicating? Look at my own marriage, with Brian telling me one thing and then doing something entirely different.

Like opening Paws That Refresh, which I was beginning to realize could actually become a reality, if only it could be accomplished the right way. From everything I'd read and heard, the people whose businesses succeeded had only done so because they'd made the right choices and considered all angles and possible pitfalls (and also pit bulls, Rottweilers and mastiffs, often unfairly unpopular and therefore difficult breeds to adopt).

But I said none of this to Maruska and Susan, who were preoccupied with shopping, manipulating their children so they'd spend the holidays with them, and the general bastardliness of men, the exceptions being the late, great Gary and any other male who appeared to be happily married.

The last night of my vacation, we went to South Beach and stayed overnight at the Catalina Club. I should have been in an upbeat mood—here I was, footloose and available (and somewhat naturally blonde and very thin, as Susan constantly reminded me in an envious tone) in one of the most glamorous places on earth, having dinner and drinks at a fabulous Art Deco restaurant facing pristine sand. The sunset cast multicolored, pastel waves over the shimmering sea and later we planned to hit the bars and listen to music, either reggae or salsa, the merits of which Susan and her friend were currently debating. Maruska was leaning towards the latter on the basis of available men, while Susan campaigned for reggae. Brian had always enjoyed Bob Marley too, although he never let his parents know, fearing their reaction. I was miserable and bored.

Perhaps Maruska just grated on my nerves—she'd been with us most of the time, regaling us with tales of one catastrophe and/or sexploit after another. Or maybe it was the fact that Susan seemed to need constant looking-after. The woman just couldn't do anything on her own, not even go to 7-11 for a bag of tortilla chips. Why hadn't she remarried, anyway? She was attractive in a cushiony, comforting way that I would never be. And certainly sexy-looking now that she was almost Marilyn-Monroe blonde. Whenever we went out, I noticed men eyeing her, although Susan seemed oblivious to their interest.

I dragged behind them, from bar to bar, my feet hurting in the new, expensive "fuck me" heels they had talked me into purchasing. Like I needed the extra height and what was this fetish with Jimmy Choos, anyway? At least they matched the overpriced dress that I wasn't sure I liked to begin with.

I felt like an imposter. I just wanted to go home, even if it was to what had become the big empty house we were trying so desperately to sell, a white elephant of black memories.

All manner of humankind—gay, straight, Botoxed, and bouffant—can be seen on any given night in South Beach. Normally such an array would be vastly entertaining, but I was tired, and getting progressively grumpier. Who were these people, anyway? And why the hell did they feel they had to be out here, dressed to the nines (or barely at all), practically in the middle of the night, showing off and shoving each other aside just to gain entry into yet another noisy, jam-packed club? The jockeying for position reminded me of New Wellington, although it was much more crowded and definitely a lot weirder. "This place is like a country club for freaks," I muttered, not quite realizing how loudly I had vocalized my discontent.

"Excuse me?" Susan stopped short, looking at me in the gently accusing way that worked so well with her kids and Gary, when he was alive. "Do you want to go home?"

I'd had enough. "Actually I do. These heels are damned uncomfortable and it's really crowded. What is the purpose of this, anyway? It's not like we're going to meet Mr. Right." More like Mr. Goodbar, I thought but had the sense not to say.

"Really, Tish, you need to stop being so negative," Maruska reprimanded in her clipped accent. "Susan has gone out of her way this week to make you feel at home. We both know you've had a hard time, and feel very sorry for your troubles, but being so down on things will get you nowhere." Susan, too tactful to add anything, nodded.

Fuck this shit, I thought, what the hell do these two know?

Maruska's three marriages totaled all of maybe, oh, nine years and Susan had the best guy in the world who set her up for life. "I'm going back to the hotel. I'll see you in the morning." I walked away quickly, before they could see the inevitable explosion of tears. God, I hated how at times, my emotions just spilled over. Why couldn't I hide my feelings like other people?

Fortunately, we were staying in a mini-suite, and I had the living room to myself so I could agonize in relative privacy. I pretended to be asleep when they came in later that night. Maruska apologized the next day, although it was obvious they were glad to see me board that airplane. As was I. Even though Susan was the only one in my social circle who seemed to stick by me during the divorce, I was glad to get away from her. She was my only friend, yet I needed room to breathe.

*****

Shortly after my return, things began to improve. For one, we sold the house for more than initially anticipated. A last-minute bidding war unexpectedly resulted in several thousand dollars additional profit. Not that my pocket would ever see it, but it meant that I was leaving the marriage almost debt-free. Although the realtor tried to talk me into purchasing a condo, I wasn't ready for such a commitment. What if I decided to open the shelter and it failed? Or, worst case scenario, what if I lost my job? Or got sick? I could never afford that and a condo fee, not to mention taxes, mortgage, and insurance.

No, I opted for an apartment on the north side of town, close to the clinic. Although I was assured it was quite spacious by the rental agent, once I moved in and saw how oversized my furniture looked, I started to feel like I'd come down in the world… Then I told myself, fuck this, I can make it better if I want to.

Evan graduated high school and now finally seemed to be seriously considering Ohio State; he'd been accepted for Winter Quarter, having taken the fall off and moved into an apartment with some friends. So I held onto his college tuition fund, which had grown into an almost-princely sum of nearly $30,000, in hopes that he'd come to his senses and not enlist. And, although I had made inquiries about Paws That Refresh—even gaining Vaughn's assurance that I would get Janice Katz's ear once I got things organized—without some initial capital or seed money, it looked like it was going nowhere. At least not for now. I was beginning to understand there was so much more to learn about operating an animal shelter than even Nick realized when we were doing the initial research, from figuring out the architectural design to screening potential adopters to motivating and organizing volunteers. It definitely required the efforts of more than one person. The trick was picking a team and Board of Directors I could rely on.

And actually, I was doing a lot. I visited several animal shelters throughout the state to see what designs worked and what didn't. Along with the aesthetic importance of light, airiness, and space, the shelter needed lots of drainage so cages and other areas could be easily cleaned and a good air filtration system to prevent the spread of disease. Not to mention green space for kennels and an exercise area. And a cheerful lobby with user-friendly, private visitation rooms so adopters could get to know their potential pets without the distraction of other animals and humans.

The most impressive shelter, I found, was practically in my own back yard. If that could be said of the suburb of Hilliard, some 25 miles away. Unlike my native Boston, Columbus is pretty spread out. But I'd lived here long enough to appreciate the relative perspective.

Built in the early 1990s, the Capital Area Humane Society practically screamed "New Wellington" with its impressive exterior, high ceilings, and white-painted wood. Although the CAHS was somewhat confusing when I first walked in—a long hallway led to several closed doors which housed the dogs and cats, so most first-time visitors probably weren't sure where to find what they were looking for—it really seemed to be all about the animals.

For one thing, each dog area contained six large cages, giving them plenty of space and light. And unlike many shelters, there were several "get acquainted rooms" and a large park-like spot out back to take prospective canine companions for a test walk (human driver's licenses had to be left in the office). The kitties were housed in smaller cages, with the older, sicker cats in one room and the younger ones and kittens in another. An occasional random bunny or guinea pig was thrown in for good measure—variety being the spice and all that, although how could you tell whether rabbit adopters were looking for a pet or a little something different for their next meal?

Each section contained a limited number of animals, and the breeds never saw or heard each other, making it much less stressful for them. No one likes being put in a cage. Especially if you're being incarcerated against your will, which is about 99.99 percent of the time. What creature, animal or human, eagerly anticipates being confined to a small space with bars?

Of course visitors weren't allowed access to what went on upstairs at the CAHS, on the second floor. But if it had to be there, the place of death and destruction needed to be as far away from the animals as possible. Depending on the situation, animals can react to their impending demise in vastly different ways. If they are pets and very ill and the owner takes them to the vet to be "put to sleep," the passing is usually peaceful. Generally they are given two injections, one a tranquilizer or sedative to put them in a deep state of unconsciousness, and the next, an overdose of barbiturates to stop their heart and respiration. Either way, it is relatively painless, except for the owner, who needs to decide whether to be present or not and must deal with the loss of one of the best friends she ever had.

When my cocker spaniel Duke died, I ended up staying with him during his last moments, although initially I'd planned to leave just before he was to be injected. Although Evan was only twelve at the time, he insisted on being present, so how could I not? Surprisingly, it provided a sense of comfort for all three of us, and closure for Evan and me, and made me a lot less apprehensive and fearful when my vet tech training took me to the euthanasia room. And although I would never in a million years have admitted it back then, it offered a secondary opportunity to get to know the handsome Dr. Nick Fairchild a little better. With my cat Freddy, because he was unconscious from the stroke and I was so stressed from the divorce, I let my boss Jim Gladstone take care of the matter. I knew Freddy was in good hands and beyond suffering. However, Evan and I gave Freddy a good send-off, burying his ashes in the back yard and holding a mini-wake in the kitchen with Tostitos and bologna (Freddy's favorite treats) and plenty of catnip for Teddy.

But when an animal is abandoned by his keepers (or runs away) and is dropped off at a shelter, it is an entirely different matter. Whenever the subject of lost and/or discarded pets comes up, Emily, my coworker and friend, goes into full rant mode. Before coming to Banford, she'd worked for several shelters, including the now-defunct chains run by the slimeball Arnie Freeman, the same jerk who tried to shut me up when I was just beginning to voice my ideas about Paws That Refresh.

"As soon as the pet hits the shelter, it has, oh about three days max to find a new family or else," she pulls her finger across her neck, an ominous gesture. "That is, if the cages aren't too full and it stays healthy…One sniffle and it's off to the gas chamber. So here's Rover or Fluffy confined to a small run or kennel with dozens of other barking and meowing strangers and he's scared as hell and wondering where his people went and why he's being punished. He has to shit where he eats and cries constantly, hoping to see a familiar face – who wouldn't? The only attention and human contact he usually gets is a bowl of food slid under the door or a high powered hose used to spray waste out of his pen. And if he's lucky enough to be kept around longer because he's sweet, gentle, and cute and if his owners don't locate him or he's not adopted, eventually he'll turn territorial and aggressive and end up being destroyed anyway.

"Then sooner or later—usually sooner—along comes someone holding a leash. Rover especially gets excited and starts wagging his tail thinking, oh yes! Finally my people have found me or at the very least I get to go outside for a walk. Even the most diva of felines—the ones who regard all humans as subordinates—is by this time humble and eternally grateful for any attention.

"But nine times out of ten, it's a ticket to a different kind of eternity. Instead of going toward the sunlight, they head the other way…and the minute they get near that room, they start freaking out.

I don't know if they smell death or sense the poor desperate souls who have passed before them but they fight like hell and sometimes it takes 1-2 people to subdue them. And if they don't calm down enough for the vet or tech to find a vein, then the needle tears into their paw and blood spurts everywhere and they die in an agony of pain, screaming, and fear." At this point, I usually tell her to stop. I already know that if the euthanization is done improperly, the poor creature will hang onto life for several agonizing minutes, defecating itself, gasping for air and struggling. And then afterwards—hopefully by then the animal is truly dead—stacked like cordwood in a freezer in the back waiting to be picked up with the garbage or rendered into pet food. "After all it's just an animal," Emily concludes bitterly. "So what if it runs away or you get tired of it and it seems like too much effort to try to find it or work with it to adjust its behavior. You can always get another one, right?" When it comes to this matter, Emily always has to have the last word, not that I blame her.

It made me want to cry just to even think about it and all the more determined to make sure that every dog and cat taken into Paws That Refresh would find a good home and be spared an untimely death, supposedly painless or otherwise.

My last stop at the CAHS was the administrative area. I found it almost by accident, on my way back from the rest room. The place was so sprawling, it was easy to get turned around, or that would be my excuse if a worker asked why I was hanging around (real answer: being nosy). Suddenly there I was, in a hallway with glass doors that said "Director", "Administrative Services", and the like. If Paws That Refresh became a reality, I would be the director, the one in charge. I would be responsible for the place, the go-to person when things needed to be taken care of. It was both scary and thrilling, an awesome responsibility. It gave me goose bumps.

That visit helped me realize that while I appreciated the offer from the strip mall builder, it wasn't going to work. A small storefront lacked the room and green space necessary to make a shelter comfortable and habitable for its four-legged occupants. So now it was back to square one... Although there was still plenty of available land, the New Wellington Company owned most commercial developments, making it out of my price range. There was the option of less expensive Columbus properties which bordered New Wellington, but reasonably-priced office space in such a desirable area was limited. I hated to say "no" to something that was practically free but my ability to make decisions without consulting anyone—slightly rusty from over 20 years of disuse—was slowly starting to emerge. So I needed to turn the guy down, even if it meant taking a risk and waiting until the right space came along, which might be never.

I also went for "ride-alongs" with humane control officers, a task that I dreaded. It was horrible to see what people did to animals, beating them and tying them up and starving them and leaving them alone to die. Even, I found, in so-called respectable neighborhoods. I would return from these sessions in tears, throwing myself on my bed, too exhausted and drained to do anything else. Yet I felt that I needed to understand that part of it, that if I saw cruelty firsthand, I would hopefully be more perceptive is sussing it out in potential adopters.

But as the officers themselves told me, preventative efforts were often in vain; you could rarely tell what evil people were up to, unless a neighbor reported a disturbance or smelled something, or an escaped, abused pet was identified as belonging to someone. And then you had to prove that the animal was abused, which was difficult if not impossible, since they obviously couldn't speak for themselves.

In many ways, animal abuse cases were similar to the human justice system; the laws seemed to favor the criminal and punishment for certain crimes was ridiculously minimal, although legislators were working to increase penalties and allow pets of domestic violence victims to be included in protection orders. I didn't quite make a connection with the last point, until one of the ride-along officers told me about a case involving a man, intent on avenging his ex-girlfriend, who nailed her pet parakeets to the wall of her home. Although the man was charged with a misdemeanor and fined only a couple hundred dollars, if the bills in the Ohio House passed, then that and other types of abuse, including dog and cock fighting would be upgraded to higher-level felonies with stiffer fines and possible jail time.

What if someone came into Paws That Refresh with an animal that had obviously been abused? Would I have the mental fortitude and strength to not only deal with the situation but track down the perpetrator of the crime? And what about possible lawsuits if I was wrong?

Then two events distracted me from my goal of opening the shelter. Claiming to be inspired by the tragedy of September 11, Evan joined the Army. It should have come as no surprise, given our earlier conversations and the constant presence of recruiters who buzzed around him his senior year like vultures circling fresh roadkill. I did everything I could to keep them apart, from "forgetting" to give their messages to Evan to "accidentally" erasing same on our voicemail to transposing the numbers when they asked for his cell. But they got to him anyway, with their promises of glamorous jobs in exciting locales and cash incentives. The President had been talking about invading Iraq for reasons I couldn't fathom, yet Evan and many of his peers totally supported that. Evan was buying into the whole weapons-of-mass-destruction thing, although I was convinced that the only "destruction" taking place was the Pottery Barn theory of invasion. That is, if we barge in and break it, we have to buy it, to the tune of billions of dollars and thousands of American lives lost, not to mention those of many, many more innocent civilians.

As hard as it was for me to believe at the time—I mean, what could possibly be worse than seeing my 18-year-old jump feet first into a combat zone?—the second development was even more traumatic. In spite of us having been divorced several months, Brian still checked in from time to time. So when the phone rang and his number showed up on my caller ID, I thought he was calling about Evan's sudden enlistment; perhaps he could still dissuade him. When Brian said, "Susan and I are seeing each other," I didn't quite get it. So what? I thought. We've all known each other for years.

I'd been so preoccupied with figuring out the hows and whys of the shelter, and now this thing with Evan, that I hadn't thought much about Susan. Except for an occasional dinner out, we hadn't spent much time together since that ill-fated vacation in Boca. "So how's she been?" I asked. "She hasn't been around much lately."

Come to think of it, when I called her shortly after our return from Florida to see if she wanted to meet for brunch, she put me off, saying she had to get ready to go to a concert that evening. I had assumed it was with the perpetually unexciting Keith. And she couldn't spare time for a meal nine hours before the event? This from a woman who could barely stand to be alone for more than fifteen minutes?

"Yes, well there's a reason for that, Tish," Brian said now, his voice laced with impatience and the all-too-familiar arsenic of conniving smoothness that made the hair on my neck prickle. "We haven't had sex yet. We've just started going out."

For a moment I was silent, as my brain started processing the information. As in…dating? Brian was dating *Susan*? Who swore she'd never go out with a friend's long-divorced brother-in-law, not to mention that same friend's ex-husband? I couldn't believe it, not that Brian wasn't capable of such perfidy, but of Susan. "Say something, Tish," Brian's voice broke through my haze of confusion and blooming anger.

Had Susan switched brains with Thomas Edison, her not-so-bright, ancient labradoodle? "What do you want me to say? I just spoke with Susan the other day and she didn't bother to mention that little factoid, although I thought it was odd that she was too busy to meet me for breakfast because she had to get ready for something much later that night…and it was an Eagles concert. I mean, who dresses up for an Eagles concert?" I realized that I was rambling and then stopped because I became aware, in the dim recesses of my still-numb mind that Brian was talking, and talking fast.

"You need to understand that this didn't happen until months after you and I were divorced. Susan and I weren't involved while we were still married. You need to realize that…Plus you yourself encouraged me to invite her out to dinner because she seemed so lonely…"

Had I said that? Well, maybe. But if Brian were to be believed—and there was no doubt that Susan and others might accept this as true—I was responsible for bringing them together. Which was bullshit and we both knew it. "Listen, Brian, I'd really like to hear more about your trading up," I had found my rage and was going with it. The fucker would have to pay for stealing my only friend, even if she was a shithead. "But here's the thing. If you marry Susan, you'll have to pay me alimony. Your financial situation will have changed and the McLean's bankruptcy will no longer render you exempt. So let me know the date, and I'll call my lawyer and set it up." I slammed down the phone.

My ex-husband hated catfish. If he did marry Susan—and if given the chance no doubt he would because it was to his advantage monetarily and hers socially—I would make sure that catfish would somehow be served at his wedding, dead or alive and stinking to high heaven. Even if I had to deliver it myself.

The situation was straight out of the ninth circle of Hell, the one reserved for treachery. Yet when I stepped back and looked at it objectively, it made perfect sense, a marriage between a man facing financial bankruptcy to a woman who considered being alone equivalent to an emotional one. My hands were shaking as I picked the phone back up and punched in the number of Shelia, the one Drama Queen who I hoped was still truly my friend.

Chapter 13 - Off with His Head!

In the late 1990s, the USA Network had a TV program called "La Femme Nikita." The opening credits showed a homeless, innocent young girl (tall and blonde, so I immediately identified with her) apparently a runaway, framed for a murder she did not commit. She is taken in by a secret counterterrorist organization and trained to be an assassin. At the end of the segment, she walks away from an exploding building that she herself has detonated. She does not even turn around and her expression is steely and relentless.

Like Nikita, I plotted various revenge scenarios, including a recurring fantasy whereby I dressed up in camos, darkened my face and did surveillance in The Club's parking lot while waiting for Brian and Susan to leave so I could blow their heads off with an M-16 borrowed from Evan. Of course, soldiers today are issued M-4s and 9mm handguns, but it was my fantasy, dammit.

My Sniper Period was consistently interrupted by Evan, who took it upon himself to try to find a site for Paws That Refresh before he went into basic training. He must have phoned six times a day with various suggestions and updates. Of course he was trying to distract me, but I was too angry and bitter to care about anyone's feelings but my own.

Then as if things couldn't get any worse, I had that encounter with Brian and Susan at Reich's department store, freaked out, and was taken away in an ambulance. The happy couple saw the ambulance pull away and didn't realize it was me until a couple of days later when some country club snoop told them I'd had a fit while shopping there and had been sent to the Emergency Room. My few hours there, among the truly ill and traumatized, helped me realize that no one was worth compromising my physical and mental health over. I was angry, I would get even, but I would go on.

I also spoke with my lawyer, Timothy Harris—whose beagle, Abby, was one my favorite patients—about getting alimony. He looked into the matter and found that although McLean's had filed for bankruptcy, they hadn't completed the proceedings, due to a sudden infusion of cash that settled their debts. Timothy, who like his dog had an uncanny knack for picking up a scent, discovered that this been partially accomplished through the profitable sale of Jack and Mable's Upper Arlington home along with some help from Susan, a dumb bunny if there ever was one. In addition to being deceitful, she was even more ignorant and naive than I'd realized... The grapevine worked both ways, and I'd heard that Brian had proposed and she had accepted, and there wasn't going to even be a prenup!

Now the buildings and remaining assets were to be sold and I was entitled to a percentage of that money as alimony. It could either be a lump sum or an annuity. Timothy recommended the latter as I would be getting more in the long run based on the duration of our marriage. "I'll see if I can get Brian to pay taxes on it as well," he added.

It was no surprise to hear about their sudden engagement, knowing how much Brian and Susan (whom I started to call DB, short for dumb bitch—why insult something as cuddly and sweet as an innocent bunny?) cared about appearances. Yet in spite of everything, it was hard to believe that they had fooled around during their respective marriages. For one thing, even Susan wouldn't be stupid enough to cheat on Gary for someone as socially beneath her at the time as Brian. Although looking back on it I wondered if the reverse was ever true. A handsome, powerful, popular doctor was catnip to a certain kind of woman, even if he seemed happily married.

Yet when I did the math, I wondered if Brian had started seeing Susan shortly before or during my visit with her in Boca. Looking back on it, there had been a lot of terminated phone calls and silences whenever I came into the room. At the time I chalked it up to Maruska's manipulations and her attempts to hook Susan up with a variety of losers she'd met through her online dating connections.

I cashed out Evan's annuity now that he was in the Armed Services and his college would be taken care of. After taxes and penalties, it came to about $25,000, which I promptly put into a short-term CD. That and the retroactive alimony which was immediately

Country Club Wives

due to me could be the seed money for Paws That Refresh.

But as it turned out, I might not have even needed to use my own funds. Shelia indeed was still my friend, and after listening to me cry and moan and vent my rage over the Brian and Susan scenario—which she and apparently everyone else knew about before Brian deigned to inform me—she suggested a fund raiser for Paws That Refresh at The Club. As a member of the Club's Board of Directors, she could make it happen. "It will keep you busy and help you get through this," she told me. "I know it's hard right now but the trick is to keep moving forward." Knowing she had survived one of the worst and scariest diseases imaginable, I respected the truth of her words.

We met every Wednesday after I got off work to plan the event, usually at the Starbucks in Publik Square or the Publik House next door, a casual dining bistro popular with New Wellington power brokers and families with young children. In spite of being so supportive, Shelia was still weird about people—or at least me—coming to her home, although it would have no doubt been more convenient and private. I had no idea why, and didn't have time to give it much thought. Between juggling my job and organizing the shelter and trying not to think about Evan's pending deployment (please, please God or whatever higher power, send him to Germany or keep him in the US...I promise I'll only think about killing my husband and his fiancée twice a day instead of 50 times...) and my rage over Brian and the DB, I had enough to deal with. I wanted revenge, and was still working on a plan of action, although I now realized that "cancellation" a la Nikita was neither viable nor in my best interest, because the Big House I'd end up in would be nowhere near as nice as Shelia's. They would simply have to be placed in "abeyance;" that is, humiliated so much that they would never want to show their faces in New Wellington again.

This particular evening Shelia and I met at the Publik House to discuss who we could corral to help with the event, tentatively titled "The Fur Ball." It was hardly the most original of names, especially when I Googled it and learned it had been used by dozens of humane societies and animal shelters around the U.S., although none locally. I had taken out a couple thousand from my windfall and purchased a laptop so I could finally explore the Internet—after years of hearing others rave about it—as well as a few other new items, most notably a replacement for the bed Brian and I had shared for so many years. Maybe this new one would see more action than its predecessor. Or not, given the dismal state of my love life, although the cats certainly appreciated the additional space.

Actually, the old bed ended up perpetuating my first official act of revenge. Before he left for basic training, I asked Evan and his minions for their help in hauling it over to Susan's since there was no room for it in the dumpsters at my apartment complex. It seemed like an easy and convenient solution, I told the boys, since trash trucks picked up old furniture in suburbs all the time. Of course it would not do to drop it off in the daytime, since the nosy neighbors might complain. We didn't want to get Brian and Susan in trouble with them, right?

In a late-night covert operation that would have done Nikita proud, we borrowed Evan's roommate's truck, loaded the bed onto it and placed the mattress at the bottom of Susan's driveway before trash day. In a surprise retaliatory move shared with no one beforehand I pulled my wedding dress out of the trunk of my Taurus-- a practical and dependable replacement for the Beamer whose lease had run out months ago—and spread it (the dress, not the Taurus) on top of the mattress. I neglected to tell Evan—the operation was executed on a "need to know" basis—that the previous Monday had been a holiday and the garbage truck would not come around until a full day afterwards, which meant the montage would be out there for all the neighbors to see for at least 24 hours. Oops! Was that the sound of Mable rolling over in her grave?

Of course this resulted in a furious phone call from Brian. When I innocently offered up the same rationale given to Evan—no place to put mattress, forgot about change in trash pickup schedule—he snarled, "You can pull that crap on our son, but not me. Remember Tish, I can still take you to court over alimony," which I had just started receiving. How very like Brian to threaten me with that, even though he'd barely begun fulfilling what everyone agreed was his legal obligation. After all, I had sacrificed a promising career as a veterinarian to raise Evan and take care of the family so he could work for yeoman's wages at McLean's. He would have been paid at least twice as much had he been employed by an outside company.

I had wanted to call the fund-raiser "The Hair Ball" but Shelia advised against it. "I love your sense of humor Tish, but not everyone would appreciate the mental picture that conjures up. And the goal is to draw as many people as possible, even those with a stick up their butts. They write checks too." I had to agree, but an ad campaign featuring a feline hacking over a wad of hair-strewn dollar bills would certainly grab people's attention.

I had my own resources as well. "Kevin"—The Club's Shih Tzu-loving maitre d'—"wants to help, as does my boss Jim Gladstone. Not to mention the Columbus Veterinary Society." And Nick, I added silently.

"CeCe's volunteered too," Shelia continued. "She and Ahmet are willing to provide appetizers and desserts at cost. Before you say anything"—anticipating my sharp intake of breath—"try talking to her yourself and make your own judgment. The McLeans are no longer a part of your life. You are and always have been your own person, Tish."

Although anything even remotely related to my ex-in-laws raised my Wrath-O-Meter to a full "10,"—discounted food or not—Shelia's patronage was essential to the success of the project. So I kept my mouth shut and changed the subject. "Which leads us to the next question. Who should contact Janice Katz? I mean, you're friends with her, right? But I had told her assistant I'd call him when I had something."

"I will leave that up to you." Twin toddlers raced past our booth and Shelia slumped in her chair as if totally worn out by the mere sight of them. They were immediately followed by their equally frenetic but distinctly less carefree mother.

Her sudden onset of fatigue worried me. "Do you feel OK? Do you want to order something or share an appetizer?" That fucking disease and its history of recurrence.

"No thanks," Shelia shook her curly red head. "It's been a long day and I told Todd I'd wait for him for dinner."

"OK, as long as everything's all right."

Shelia's merry green eyes locked into mine. "It's been a while since I've gotten my period, and I was thinking, what if it's not menopause? I'm kidding, Tish!" She laughed at my shocked expression. "At least I think I am... Even though the kids are older and I have help with the house, it's always something. It seems that the more you have, the more it demands of you."

I had never really looked at it that way, but when I considered what could go wrong with a ginormous McMansion or extended family when elderly parents were still alive but as ill as Shelia's and Todd's, it could devour much time and energy. I was beginning to realize life was like that for just about everybody. As Gilda Radner said, it's always something. Except for the DB and Brian of course, who had it perfect. For now, anyway.

*****

A few days after my meeting with Shelia, CeCe phoned. I might have hung up on her, except I had just received a disturbing visit from my son who was leaving for Ft. Leonard Wood the next day. "Nice work, Mom," he reprimanded me. "Dad yelled at me for leaving that mattress in the driveway. I thought you'd cleared it with him." Even before his first day of basic training, my little boy was beginning to sound like a soldier.

I didn't know how to respond to that, hadn't actually considered the repercussions regarding Evan's role in the scenario. Of course Evan was furious with his father for taking up with Susan. But Brian was still his dad and Evan obviously still wanted his father's approval and love. And in all fairness, Brian had always been there for him, at least physically. I had unjustly and unwittingly placed Evan directly in the line of fire, to use his terminology. Maybe I should cut down on the Nikita reruns.

"Look, Evan, he shouldn't have gotten mad at you. I told him it was my idea, that I'd implied it was all right..."

"But you know Dad. Not that I care of course." A grin tugged at the corner of my handsome son's mouth. Even though his facial features resembled Brian, I could see my family in his coloring, intelligent expression and graceful moves. "Actually the guys thought it was pretty sick that you put out the wedding dress after we drove away." Sick as in cool, I realized, not mentally ill. My exposure to hip-hop and rap music began when Evan was in junior high, and I discovered I actually enjoyed the high energy and the beat of it, without the misogyny and cuss words, of course. Although, these days, I found myself sympathizing all too well with some of the violent lyrics.

I couldn't help but wonder, with more than a little malice how Susan's kids were reacting. Only a year or so older than Evan, Justin was no doubt getting an earful, even at Harvard.

"I'm glad your minions appreciate my retaliatory stylings. But I don't want you getting in trouble with Dad, and for that I am sorry. From now on, I'll keep you out of any future plans for revenge." With Evan being shipped off to God-knows-where, the last thing he needed was guilt or worry over a hostile relationship with his Dad. If only Brian could go in his place…

Evan shook his surfer-blonde, soon-to-be-shorn head. "Dude, you really shouldn't be thinking about that stuff anyway. You've got all these people who want to help you with Paws That Refresh and you haven't even found a place for it. Promise me you'll concentrate on that while I'm gone."

I reached over and hugged him, a six-foot lug-child faced with the adult realities of a bitter divorce and learning how to shoot to kill. "Listen dude, I really appreciate your concern. Promise me you won't worry about any of this. Just get yourself through basic training in one piece with all your appendages intact."

"As long as you swear you won't do anything stupid, like putting dog turds in a paper bag, setting it on fire, and then ringing Susan's doorbell. That's so eighth grade."

I had to smile myself. "I can tell you're speaking from experience." He eyed me distrustfully and I wiggled my fingers and toes, assuring him that nothing was crossed. "I will do nothing of the sort. Scout's honor." But that wouldn't, however, preclude me from indirect acts of revenge. Or enlisting the help of others to accomplish the same.

So when CeCe phoned and suggested we meet for lunch, I was much more receptive than I otherwise might have been. I readily agreed to her time and place of choice, which, given her busy schedule happened to be two weeks hence at The Club, where in addition to occasionally helping with the catering, she and Ahmet also supplied specific menu items for it and other high-end eateries around town. She'd been exceedingly sympathetic and supportive over the phone, calling Brian a "shithead" and Susan "that twat with sagging tits." Still, I didn't trust her; after all, she had deceived Brett and from where I stood never seemed to have any valid reason for doing so. Not that Brett was an angel himself, but surely she'd known that going into the marriage... I just didn't get these people who switched partners as easily as they replaced boxes of Kleenex....

I had to admit I kind of missed the place, although once I arrived, no doubt the Club Paradox would reassert itself. That is, while the idea of a country club might be immensely appealing, the reality was far less exciting. In fact, it could be downright uncomfortable, especially if one was no longer a member and might run into people whom they'd rather not see, now that they were divorced. Plus it could be really, really boring and one might find themselves wondering, "Remind me again why I paid so much money for this?"

But still, even if, God forbid, we encountered Susan and Brian, I had no more plans to freak out, at least not where anyone could see me. And I knew I could count on CeCe to turn any potentially awkward or embarrassing situation into a social touchdown. Look at Gary's funeral, when the most non-Drama Queen Susan exploded into a racist rant over her and Ahmet's generosity and CeCe turned it on its head, pointing out how Susan's son had picked up on her prejudice! Like her or despise her, CeCe was good to have on any team, tennis or otherwise, and if Heisman trophies were awarded for country club scrimmages she'd rival Archie Griffin. She also might also be amenable to a little menu intervention during the loving couple's nuptials, which would no doubt be held at The Club. Catfish Nikita, anyone?

Next on my hit list of nerve wracking phone calls was Vaughn, who immediately put me through to Janice Katz. When Janice came on the line, I took a deep breath and launched into what I hoped would be a calm and concise summation of the progress of Paws That Refresh. Janice was as warm and enthusiastic as she had been during our initial encounter at Gary's funeral. She agreed to be on the Advisory Board and had me promise to inform her as soon as we secured the date so she and Eli could put it on their calendar. "And let me know if you need any help," she said. "I have a whole slew of volunteers from New Wellington Day who would love to participate." Her annual domestic violence/children services fund-raiser, a polo tournament that drew players from all over the world, collected millions of dollars and was even covered by ESPN 2.

After we said good-bye, Vaughn came back on the line. "I have Janice's calendar here, honey. Do you want some suggestions for dates when she's available?" Did I want their presence engraved in stone? Absolutely!

Wow! I thought, my spirits soaring higher than they had in a very, very long time. Did it get any better than this? I mean, here I was, a supposed nobody, a recently divorced worker bee—who was grateful for her job, of course—and now I was organizing what was shaping up to be the event of the season, next to New Wellington Day, of course. Thanks to the involvement of Janice and Eli, the country club bitches would be panting like dogs to help raise funds for Paws That Refresh. When it came to social order in that pack, there was no such thing as a humane endeavor unless it had self-serving motives. Now all that was needed was a location for the shelter.

*****

Of course, that was easier said than done. With the date of the Fur Ball rapidly approaching, we needed something concrete in so many senses of the word. Without a physical plant and a roughed-out draft of what the shelter would look like, it would be very difficult to sell the concept to potential donors. One thing I'd learned from all those boring business books was that the more details you had, and the more specifics nailed down, the safer people felt about investing their money. So I not only had to find a building but also a design. As soon as I got the former, I could contact Nick about the latter. He'd mentioned that he knew several architects who might be interested in working something up at minimal cost, if not gratis. "Actually they're more friends of my wife's, but she's made boatloads of money for them, so they feel like they owe us," he said. Even after all this time, I still hated it whenever he mentioned his wife. I also noticed he seemed to do this whenever our conversations went on for too long or even remotely approached anything personal.

I had visited dozens of places and so far, nothing looked promising. It was either too expensive, inconveniently located, or lacked the proper facilities. And then finally, just as I was about ready to give up and contact Nick anyway about having the architects work up a minimal prospectus so we'd at least have something, Timothy my beagle-eagle lawyer sent me an e-mail. A local grocery was going bankrupt and was auctioning off its properties at a sheriff sale.

I'd shopped there many times when I first moved to New Wellington before the other big chains came in and undercut their prices. Although it was actually in Columbus which made it cheaper in terms of property and income tax, the location, at an easily accessible intersection on the outskirts of New Wellington near the large suburb of Westerville, was ideal. So we'd be close to three communities with a variety of demographics.

Not only it was a free-standing building with plenty of surrounding property that could be converted to kennels and green space for the animals, but the design, although a bit dated, was light, spacious, and airy. Of course we'd need to erect walls and partitions for the various rooms but that was doable, given the layout. "We could put the dogs and puppies in fresh produce and the kitties in the deli," I wrote back in enthusiastic response. "Where do we sign?"

Naturally it wasn't that simple. I had to go through the machinations of incorporating the business as a non-profit and get a loan from the bank. But I was able to use my CD as collateral on good faith that it would be replaced by our generous benefactors. Vaughn informed me on the down-low that the Katzes were usually good for at least $100 grand and Shelia told me that she and Todd were pledging $50,000 to start.

During our increasingly frequent email correspondences, Timothy offered to help me pro bono. "Pro bone?" I wrote, adding the "smiley face" icon.

"It's a nice change of pace from the divorces and if things start getting 'ruff,' I can always consult my partners," he responded. In addition to having a sense of humor, he was single and good-looking, resembling a more rugged-looking George Clooney. But he was 15 years my junior, and even if I did a Maruska-style sport fuck, knowing me, it would unnecessarily complicate things. Besides, there was only one man I fantasized about and he was taken. I'm talking about Nick of course; my fantasies of Brian were of a completely different nature.

Timothy would represent Paws That Refresh at the land auction. "The trick is not to appear too eager or it will just jack up the price and start a bidding war."

Since I was the world's worst poker player—one look at my face revealed exactly what kind of hand I'd been dealt—I authorized him to be my representative with a limit of $200,000 and gave him my cell phone number should things escalate. "We're guaranteed at least $175 thousand so we should be OK, don't you think?"

"Should be fine, but don't forget the start-up costs. You'll need to clear at least $250,000 at the fund-raiser, which should be no problem. From what I'm hearing, everyone has your back." Whoever declared a dead lawyer was a good start had never met Timothy Harris. His cool, Clooney-esque demeanor might get us the deal of the (new) century.

*****

The Saturday I was to meet CeCe for lunch was also the date of the building auction. I was a nervous wreck—what if we didn't get the property? I went for a long walk and cleaned the apartment—twice, since it wasn't very big—all in the interest of keeping occupied. The phone remained stubbornly silent. Also, why hadn't I heard anything from Evan? In the several weeks he'd been in basic training, I had sent him letters and e-mails, and he'd only sent brief notes twice. Everything was fine, he was adjusting well, he wrote in his typical male, uncommunicative way. It was hot there, the food and the guys were OK, he'd made a couple of good friends. But I wanted to know, how was he *doing?*

Then finally Timothy called with great news—he'd gotten the property for an amazing $80,000! The guy really was as smooth as George Clooney! After I got off the phone, I shouted for joy. It was really happening! Now, nothing could stop Paws That Refresh! We had an actual, great location, and the fund-raiser was coming along. It was going to be *real*. Then the phone rang again, and it was Evan, who finally had some down time and wanted to talk. He filled me in on life at boot camp: Up at 6; the drill sergeant in his face; carrying heavy loads for miles; dirt, dust, sweat, heat and absolutely no privacy. "I will never complain about home again, even if I have to sleep on your tiny couch," he said. I told him the good news about the shelter and naturally he was thrilled. "You haven't had any dealings with Dad have you?"

"No, I'm happy to report that I'm too busy…" I assured him. Although there might be further opportunities if CeCe were willing to "assist" with the catering for the wedding. Then I glanced at the clock: 12:30. I was supposed to meet her a half hour ago!

After reluctantly cutting short the conversation with Evan, I called The Club as I was running out the door. I would have tried CeCe's cell if I'd remembered where I'd put the piece of paper where I'd written it down. I left a message with the distracted-sounding maitre d'—the one who shared duties with Kevin whose name I could never remember. "Please tell CeCe that I'm really sorry – my son called from basic training—and I'll be there in 15."

In retrospect, it seemed odd that CeCe didn't leave a message on my land line or call my cell to find out where I was because she had both of my numbers. But I was in a huge rush and never even thought about it.

What I didn't know was that something had happened that would rock the world of everyone whose lives it touched. Its impact would be felt for years at every country club in the city.

Chapter 14 - Catfish Wedding Fantasy

The moment I walked into the door of the main clubhouse I knew something was terribly wrong. It had been several years since I'd been in the dining room—in fact, the last time I'd eaten there was when Brian and I were still members—but the place was basically the same, lots of windows, hardwood floors covered with expensive rugs, hoity-toity paintings of English hunting scenes adorning the walls. Still, by country club standards it was pretty avant-garde, decorated in the muted colors of orange, brown and beige with touches of green and Art Deco chairs and light fixtures. Although the concept was when worlds collide the reality was far more aesthetically pleasing.

But people were standing around in clusters, talking softly. Some were crying…had the terrorists struck again? There hadn't been anything on the car radio.

Then CeCe came up to me. Looks-wise, she hadn't changed much over the years. But in spite of the Botox, the constant exercising, and God knows what else she did to maintain that perfect figure, she looked older…perhaps it was a seriousness that played itself around her mouth and the deep concern in her eyes, despite her cosmetically unfurrowed brow.

But hell, weren't we all older? While still on the smallish side, my boobs and butt were dropping faster than the stock market after 9/11 and somehow my girlish curves had transformed into the more angular look favored by the women on my mother's side of the family. The ones who I used to call "the old bats." Well guess what… at age forty-eight I was rapidly approaching the bat cave myself.

"I guess you haven't heard, Tish." I must have looked bemused, or puzzled, or even happy, now that everything was coming together for the shelter and Evan seemed to be doing well.

"Not another attack…" I began, feeling my stomach sink. Thanks to the oxymoronic (emphasis on the latter three syllables) "Operation Iraqi Freedom," a lot of people in the Middle East and elsewhere around the world were pretty pissed off at the good old

U.S. of A. I mean, why not give them yet another reason to blow us up?

"No, no nothing like that. It's much closer to home. You'd better sit down." She repeated, motioning towards the table with a half-empty bottle of wine. Geez, she was starting a little early, wasn't she? Even if it was the weekend.

"You might want a drink..."

"No thanks, I've found alcohol and bad news don't mix..." Then a horrible thought popped into my brain. "Unless of course it's Shelia." She'd looked so washed out the other night, in spite of her heated denial. And I'd barely spoken to her since then. I'd been busy with the fund-raiser and figured she was back to her usual M.O. of what my college German teacher jokingly referred to as KKK—Kinder, Küche, Kirche—"children, kitchen, church," or in her case, synagogue.

Seeing my freaked-out expression, CeCe wrapped my cold hands in her warm ones. "No, no, thank God, it's no one at our Club. But the way that it happened was so gruesome and once the media gets hold of it. I mean with the economy being so shaky and with so many new clubs just getting started..." She shook her head, as if the fate of countryclubdom—which made up the bulk of her and Ahmet's clientele—was one step away from that of Darfur.

"Just spit it out, CeCe." What happened to the boldly go where no one else would dare chick, who flirted outrageously and flaunted her hot body, and said whatever she damn well pleased?

"You know Lakeview Country Club in Powell?" CeCe's eyes darted this way and that, anywhere but at my face. "Well, a few days ago they found a body on the golf course there." Now that I knew it wasn't Shelia or some horrible world event, I had to resist the impulse to repeat Gerald Ford's one-liner, "I know I am getting better at golf because I am hitting fewer spectators." I always liked that guy, because he could laugh at himself. Maybe someone's loud pants did the poor soul in. Clotheswise, golfers make rap stars look like FBI agents.

"At first they didn't know who it was," she continued. "Because the woman's head had been blown off." Oh yuck. So it wasn't some sixty-five-year-old white guy who keeled over with his cleats on. CeCe took a deep gulp. "It looked like a mob hit. But that wasn't what killed her. It was an overdose—a combination of halothane and sodium pentobarbital."

"You mean like what vets use to put animals to sleep?" I said incredulously. "Why would someone do a thing like that?"

"Here's the thing, Tish. It wasn't just anyone. The victim was Elena Fairchild."

For a moment, I sat speechless, stunned. Nick's wife? Who could want to murder Nick's wife? He was happily married, or so he had told me the night of our confrontation and had implied in more than one conversation since. Although I didn't entirely believe it, especially since I'd become more adept at reading what people meant, rather than what they actually said. Still, he'd been a perfect gentleman, albeit an occasionally aloof and often frazzled one. But who wouldn't be with all his responsibilities? Kids…a busy practice…a wife with a high-powered job…

"But why? Why would someone use euthanasia on Nick's wife? It doesn't make sense."

"Oh, but it does, Tish. Apparently Elena's been having an affair with one of the other members since her kids were little, and Nick found out. Rumor is that Nick was so furious he killed her himself and then hired someone to make it look like a hit. He and Elena are both from Youngstown, and I don't have to tell you how mobbed up that place is." Even I had heard about "Murder City, USA" and how the Meander Reservoir was used as a drop off point for bodies, not unlike the doggie doo baggies at the bottom of the duck pond in New Wellington. Not to mention the controversial trial of the area's U.S. Congressman, one James Traficant, accused of having ties with the Mafia and filing false tax returns among other corruptions. But still—Nick? Putting his own wife to sleep like a cancerous collie? It just didn't compute. And besides, I suddenly remembered, Nick had told me he'd grown up in Mentor, near Cleveland.

"I can't believe that Nick would be capable of something like

Country Club Wives

that..." I began, but then stopped. Couldn't he? Hadn't I myself been contemplating all forms of revenge as a result of the betrayal in my life? I had certainly wanted to kill Brian and Susan, especially when I first found out about them. Only the specter of incarceration and the actual physical mess caused by their deaths stopped me. I had seen enough hurt and morbidly wounded animals to understand that there was nothing neat and clean about dying. It was often a chaotic, painful and prolonged affair. And besides, it was so much more entertaining, not to mention legal, to come up with ways to torment and embarrass Brian and Susan. Plus, unlike Traficant, if convicted, I wouldn't be going to any Federal country club.

Still, the situation seemed so far-fetched as to be unreal, one of those "punk'd" things that Evan was always talking about. "I'm only telling you what I heard," CeCe's voice cut through my thoughts. "They've kept it out of the media so far, but now that Nick's been arraigned, it will be all over tonight's news. And if I were you, I'd disassociate myself from Nick Fairchild faster than Eli Katz fires an underperforming employee. That is, if you want to continue to get support for Paws That Refresh."

For the third time in nearly as many months, my world had been turned inside out. First, Evan enlisting, then Brian taking up with Susan, and now Nick murdering his wife. It was as if someone had taken my life, tossed it into the air, and turned it into the card game of 52 pick-up.

*****

Of course, the first thing I did when I got home was turn on Channel 6. And there it was, the top story: "Local Veterinarian Puts Wife to Sleep," with a shell-shocked-looking Nick being led into the Franklin County Courthouse surrounded by a half-dozen grim men. Who was watching his kids? I wondered. The whole thing just didn't make sense. If nothing else, Nick was an intelligent guy. If he really wanted to knock off his wife, he would have hired a hit man who would have tossed the body in a dumpster somewhere far away—not in the middle of the fucking golf course of his family's country club!

And—not to be self-absorbed or anything—but what was I going to do about the layout for Paws That Refresh? The first item on my agenda had been to phone Nick on Monday and have him put me in contact with his architect buddy. Now it looked like Nick himself was on the hook—permanently—unless they took calls on Death Row ("Vet Headed for Own Lethal Injection")... I didn't mean to be flippant, but the situation seemed just too absurd to take seriously.

No, there had to be another answer. And I knew that I had it somewhere, in the dim recesses of my overcrowded brain. Something someone had said about Nick's wife... And, oh damn, I'd meant to ask CeCe about Brian and Susan's nuptials. The Club being one of her major clients, I figured she might be able to "accidentally" substitute catfish for, say, Alaskan salmon or grilled tuna during the main course. Of course, in the ensuing upset, I had completely forgotten. But given Nick's predicament, that now seemed unimportant.

One of the things that I'd learned from reading the self-help books and doing yoga and meditation was that the solutions are often right in front of me. I just had to listen, and look, and wait and see what the universe would serve up (hopefully catfish at Brian and Susan's wedding, but then I thought, oh stop!). But to be honest, I didn't have that kind of time, not with the fund-raiser only a few weeks away. I needed to get that architect's rendering *now*. So I would call Shelia on Monday instead. She knew builders and realtors and was connected with the whole interior design community, although it would probably cost me close to what we saved on the building to get a rendering on such short notice. Even if it was for a good cause.

Another Saturday night, and I ain't got nobody. Just like the song, I thought as I firmly turned my mind away from self-pity. I allowed myself to cry and feel badly about the direction my life had taken but put the brakes on the whole "poor me" thing. Millions of children were orphaned in Africa because of genocide, poverty, and the fact that their parents lacked even rudimentary treatment for AIDS, so being by myself should be the least of my worries. Besides, as the saying went, there were vast differences between being alone and being lonely, as I had often been when married and surrounded by people who didn't particularly care about me. Rather, I needed to focus on exactly what the new building required for the architect or designer or whomever I could find, given the time constraints. I figured the more information I provided them, the less they might charge me. So I worked late into the night.

Of course, the memory surfaced at the most inconvenient time—at two-o'clock in the morning when I was taking a shower. I was so excited, I dropped the soap on the floor and practically fell on my ass in an attempt to pick it up. That would have been cute. I'd found a way to possibly exonerate Nick and almost ended up permanently unconscious or in a coma. I would finally have a chance to really play Nikita, minus the leather minis, sunglasses, or mission control. No, my job would be much more challenging—to convince the detective or whomever was investigating the murder of Elena Fairchild to start asking the right questions. Now that would require some real subterfuge – especially since I wanted—no, I *needed*—to remain anonymous. No way was Nick to ever, ever know that the help had come from me. He would think that I was moving in on him, like some desperate casserole lady. And he'd turned me down once—I wasn't taking a chance on that happening again.

*****

When Evan was in sixth grade, I was a homeroom mother. One of the programs we assisted with was a visit by McGruff the Crime Dog, who told us that the police went to great lengths to protect the anonymity of their informants. Of course they didn't phrase it that way, more like "it's safe to tell an adult if you think something's wrong." So I knew enough to start taking my personal bite out of crime by calling the main number of the Powell police station (dialing *67 to block their Caller ID, although I bet a week's paycheck that they could find out my number anyway), knowing of course that 911 was for life-and-death emergencies and those calls were for sure recorded. The situation was hardly that desperate, since Nick wasn't going anywhere, at least until he made bail.

When I said I had information that might be of interest in the

Elena Fairchild murder, the helpful person who answered the phone equally helpfully referred me to a Detective James Poller with the Columbus Police Department. Apparently they believed the murder had been committed in the City of Columbus and not actually on the golf course. Or maybe the Powell cops were more confident dealing with speeders and high school miscreants than euthanasia-wielding, decapitating veterinarians. Whatever.

Remembering Evan's dust-up with the Franklin County and Columbus legal system a few years ago, I was hardly thrilled to be dealing with them again. Even just getting through to the detective proved to be an exercise in frustration. Apparently the City of Columbus failed to train their receptionists properly or maybe they were too busy filing their nails or reading *Cosmo* to bother with the phones, which rang, and rang, and if they were eventually picked up, it was by an actual overworked law enforcement professional. But hey, I would be cranky too, if I was out there trying to catch criminals and murderers and had to answer my own fucking phone. Nevertheless after calling the main number and being given put through to several extensions, I finally got through to the Man himself, who answered with an abrupt, "Yeah? Poller here."

My first instinct was to launch into a lecture about how McGruff always encouraged people to speak up and the best way to do this was to be polite and approachable rather than intimidating. But better judgment prevailed and my now greatly expanded experience in dealing with all kinds of people—especially those who were overburdened and didn't really want to speak with me in the first place—was to be hesitant and polite and almost apologetic. And of course I never talked back or argued with anyone who carried a gun.

"Detective Poller, the people at the Powell Police Department gave me your name in regards to the Elena Fairchild murder…" I let my voice trail off, knowing instantly by his sudden silence that I now had his full attention.

"What can I help you with?" He sounded less annoyed by only a few degrees.

"Well, I've been a friend of Dr. Fairchild's for years and I can tell you that I'm positive he had nothing to do with this..." I was about to launch into the rest of my speech, when he interrupted me with, "Yeah, you're about the 50th person to call me about this. That's what they said about Ted Bundy. Tell me something I *don't* know."

Comparing Nick to Ted Bundy was a little too out there even for me, so I snapped, "Actually my ex-husband is more like Ted Bundy, if you'd care to investigate him. But then you'd have to transfer me to the fraud division. I do have information about Dr. Fairchild's wife that I'd like to share, if you'd let me finish." Firearms be damned, and he couldn't shoot me over the phone anyway.

"OK, ma'am, well, give me your name and the information and I'll make out a report and check it out." Now he sounded bored. But at least he was being polite, which if you were applying country club standards to this situation would be equivalent to being invited to send in your $15,000 deposit for consideration for membership.

"Look, I'd rather not give you the specifics over the phone. And I would like to request anonymity. I'm a law abiding citizen and pay my taxes..."

"I don't doubt that, ma'am, but if you're going to provide us with a tip then we need to know who it's from and make sure it's valid. If you like, I could arrange a meeting."

OK, well now maybe I was getting somewhere, like having my name engraved in a plaque on cubbyhole No. 219 in the ladies' locker room. "That would be fine. Where and when?"

He named a coffee shop downtown that none of my friends, whether associated with my past life or new four-legged career as organizer of Paws That Refresh, had ever heard of. And he didn't even ask for my name or phone number. So I agreed. Nikita would have been proud—this time possibly for real. But well, duh, she was a TV character—so how could she be? Maybe I needed to start playing tennis again. Or adopt a puppy, if Teddy, who had simmered down to a gentle, laid-back old age, and the upstart and angelic-but-only-to-me Trump, would tolerate it.

So what was the "intel" that I worked so hard to impart and protect? Actually, on its own, it wasn't much. It was more like a scrap of information, a memory of a conversation from a few years ago that had resurfaced in my mind. When I'd first begun working at the Banford Veterinary Clinic, and was still married to Brian, several women and I went out for drinks after work to celebrate my friend Emily's engagement.

Conversation turned to money gained and lost and the vicissitudes of marriage, and I mentioned that we were thinking of dropping out of The Club due to financial reasons. Keisha, a tall and particularly beautiful African-American tech, stated she used to waitress at Lakeview while training for her certification. "Those country club folks," she rolled her eyes. "They say black people act crazy…"

"Are you kidding?" I made a "pfft" sound with my lips. "People at New Wellington can be the most boring ever and they come from all over!" Somehow the green hue of money seemed to bleach out the colorful ethnicities of the rainbow coalition.

"Honey, you did not see it from where I was standing," Keisha responded in that authoritative tone common to some black women. It worked especially well with recalcitrant pet owners and in collecting money, although was less effective with four-legged clients, especially the influx of bearded dragons we'd been seeing lately, a big fad among junior high school boys. You could yell at the reptiles all you wanted, and all you got in return was a beady, blank stare. Come to think of it, you could say that about the kids, too. "I mean those folks at Lakeview knew how to swing, and I'm not talking about dancing!" Keisha took a swig of her margarita (her third?).

"Do you mean key parties?" This came from Linda, a heavyset older woman who'd been divorced for several years. "I remember those from the '70s! Not that I participated in them myself, of course," she added quickly. "I just heard about them…"

"Keys, hell! They didn't even bother with those!" Keisha exclaimed dramatically. "I mean they had all-out orgies in front of each other, and everyone screwed everyone else. Those who were involved with it, that was—that was the condition of their being part of it—you had to sleep with everyone else, same sex included. The ones who didn't know about it were the kids of course—and some of the spouses. Nice guys like Nick Fairchild, for instance, and high-profilers like Lisa Jones," a well-known local TV announcer.

"So are you saying, Nick's wife..." I began, wide-eyed. What an irony if Nick turned me down, unknowing that his wife was a charter member of the Central Ohio Swinger's Association, Lakeview branch! But I was drowned out by the other women who were far more interested in Lisa, a particularly irritating TV anchor with ginormous pert boobs, who was always preaching fitness although she herself looked a few less mouthfuls away from a concentration camp. Her husband Rich was a highly placed official in the Republican Party, and confidante of the current Governor.

Keisha drained the last of her margarita, and shrugged. "Hey, what did I know? I was a nineteen-year-old kid trying to avoid the dirty old golfers playing grab-ass behind the caddy shack. But everyone who worked there knew about the swapping. It happens in every country club, girlfriend. Even your hoity-toity New Wellington."

At the time I didn't believe it. I mean, those people had been my friends for years and I'd been around country clubs all my life. The occasional extramarital affair, sure, or fling with a tennis or golf pro. But outright bacchanals, as Keisha had implied? At the time, it seemed preposterous.

Maybe not...And it was certainly worth investigating, given the turn of recent events. If Elena had been involved in swinging, then certainly those in her group were capable of other types of foul play. Even Keisha, in her intoxicated state had pegged Nick as a straight shooter. Just as I had.

*****

I considered donning a wig, sunglasses, and raincoat for my meeting with Detective Poller, but decided against it. If I wanted the man to take me seriously, I'd have to be real, even if he found out who I was. Any cloak and dagger stuff might make me less credible and would hardly help Nick's cause.

So there I was, sitting at the grungy, smoky Tip Top coffee shop on the west side of town. The regulars eyed me suspiciously, a tall slender blonde woman just a little too well-dressed, even though I was wearing jeans and a T-shirt. OK, it said "Dior" in Swarovski crystals but I got it for ten bucks at the outlet store and it was the only halfway clean thing in my closet. And it was probably obvious that I felt nervous and out of place, which I did, very much.

And even more so when a tall, handsome African-American man in his 40s strode towards me. He more resembled a lawyer or stockbroker than the hardened, short-tempered detective I'd spoken to over the phone. I'd expected a balding, squat white guy with uneven teeth and fashion issues. This dude screamed "metrosexual" and his suit looked like it cost a month of my vet tech salary.

"Normally I work undercover in vice and narcotics," he said by way of an introduction and explanation. He was more pleasant in person also, in addition to being easy on the eyes. "But we've got a big caseload. It's been a good year for murder in Columbus," he said, watching me closely to gauge my reaction.

"I'm sorry to hear that," I replied in an equally even tone. "But I do have information that might be of help in the Fairchild case..." And then I proceeded to tell him Keisha's tale of spouse-swapping.

Poller listened impassively. "Well, Dr. Fairchild made bail this morning. It seems he has a lot of friends—even the judge didn't set the amount as high as he normally would."

"That's great!" I blurted out with a surge of relief. "Nick is a well-respected vet in the community and thank God his kids will have their father back..." I trailed off, suddenly noticing Poller watching me closely with either a half-smile or half-smirk, I couldn't figure out which.

"So what's your interest in this? What do you have to gain?" Poller was an acute student of human psychology, but then most cops probably had to be.

"Nothing. He's just a good friend," I could feel myself flushing and wished I'd put on just a little more makeup so he could attribute my red cheeks to an over application of blush. "I mean he's been helping me with this animal shelter I'm trying to get off the ground."

Oh damn, I just gave away my identity...It wouldn't take much for Det. Poller to find out who I was now. Damn, damn, damn.

"Look you don't have to worry about anyone finding out about our conversation," Poller reassured me, seeing how flustered I was becoming. "I do this all the time, and if the information you gave me is solid, the only consequence will be having helped an innocent man."

"That's good. I honestly don't believe Nick murdered his wife, even if what I told you was only a rumor." Was this man an idealist or a cynic? I wondered. Perhaps both.

"Well, as my girlfriend always says, look at both sides of the story and you'll find the truth somewhere in between." His BlackBerry buzzed and he glanced at the screen. "Got to take this call." He handed me a card. "This is the number I use for informants. If you can think of anything else or come up with more information, leave a message and I'll get back to you."

So this man was single too. Suddenly the world seemed full of unattached males. And now, Nick was one of them.

Chapter 15 - Gimme Shelter

As the saying goes, you make plans and God laughs. Well, he (she? them? it?) must have been busting a gut as I frantically rushed to finalize the details for the fundraiser for Paws That Refresh. Nothing was going right—it was in three weeks and I didn't even have a rough sketch of the facility. I couldn't get Shelia to call me back and there was no way I was going to bother Nick during his time of trouble. Even the invitations, which were supposed to have been printed and mailed a few days before Elena Fairchild's murder were never sent out, due to a computer glitch by the printer, who was supposed to be doing the job gratis.

Cliché #2: Sometimes you get what you pay for. Or don't get, in this case. And sometimes you just have to listen to what the universe is trying to tell you. If Brian or his parents had done so, then maybe McLean's Fine Furniture might still be Ohio's largest today. And I would still be married and living the "good life" in New Wellington, which I was slowly, by degrees, beginning to realize had not been all that great after all.

But past was past. And I needed my own Pause to Refresh, so with major reluctance I called The Club and Vaughn and postponed the date indefinitely. "We're just not ready," I struggled to keep the tears from my voice during the conversation with Vaughn. "The money and building are in place but we don't have drawings yet and the situation with Dr. Fairchild has really upset the community. I just don't think it's a good time."

"Not to worry, darling," He sounded like Carson Kressley in "Queer Eye for the Straight Guy." As if he was reassuring a clueless male that if he swaps the holey underwear and beer can end tables for tidy whities and Ikea, the love of his life will indeed head straight for the altar. "Eli and Janice are not going anywhere and I promise you we will make this work when the time is right."

Good to know, but I had even bigger worries. The war in Iraq was now official—as if any of us had a say so. So now my son Evan was being deployed overseas. He was thrilled; I was devastated.

"Maybe I'll get to guard Saddam Hussein's castle," he said, his voice crackling with excitement. "Did you see them topple over his statue during the fall of Baghdad? How cool is that?"

"Not at all, if you get blown up by insurgents," I struggled to keep negativity out of the conversation but couldn't help myself. There was no reason for this stupid fucking war and they sold these kids a line of bull, luring them with incentives of money and tales of false bravery. It was dirty, hot, unbelievably dangerous, and most of the people over there hated Americans, whether they had good reason to or not.

But I had nothing to say in the matter, not really. Evan was eighteen and officially an adult. I just had to step aside and pray that he wouldn't be maimed or killed.

"Really, Mom, it's not that dangerous. A bunch of us guys will be over there, rebuilding roads and bridges and the people really need our help."

Yada. Yada. Yada… More lies and brainwashing. I didn't want to hear it. Somehow they'd gotten to my son, and now I might lose him forever.

And I found out why I hadn't heard from Shelia. It was as I'd feared: her cancer had returned. She didn't tell me; she never even returned my many and increasingly frantic calls—first about finding an architect, and then inquiries about her health. It was CeCe who had heard it via The Club's grapevine, with which she still seemed so well-connected thanks to her catering business and inclusion into the world of couples, one which I was no longer privy to. Susan had been right about one thing—nothing cools off married friends faster than losing a husband.

I always hated how Shelia always disappeared whenever things got tough. It was as if she didn't need her friends at all and could seclude herself whenever she wished. Most people didn't have that luxury—few had the cushion of family and wealth that the Weintraubs enjoyed. So she could receive the best and most private care money could buy and have her every need catered to. None of this going out and doing errands in a bandanna or a wig between chemotherapy sessions like ordinary people. The rich are indeed different and it wasn't until I'd lost the money that had separated me from much of life's unpleasantness that I realized how badly it could suck for the rest of us.

I wasn't trying to be unsympathetic but I did resent the way Shelia pushed me aside whenever things got difficult or even challenging for her. First it was the showcase house that she and Todd spent all that time and money building—which I finally saw only a couple of months ago when I went to drop off some information about the shelter—and then as now, it was her illness. It was as if I was some sort of project that she picked up from time to time whenever it was convenient. Well, I wasn't a cause or a charity case. I was a friend and an equal, and wanted to be treated like one.

I considered tracking her down and telling her exactly where to stick her patronage but decided against it. After all she was truly sick, and who was I to add to her pain and suffering? Cancer was hell and it didn't give a shit how much money you had, so being rich hardly exempted her from that. I just wanted to be there for her in times of trouble, as she had been for me. No more of this reverse "friend in need" crap.

The only good news in the sometimes overwhelming clusterfuck of my life was that Elena Fairchild's real killer had been found. Of course it wasn't Nick. Apparently there had been some truth in the tales of sleeping around and infidelity at the Lakeview Country Club. It wasn't exactly spouse-swapping—several of the husbands and wives of the parties involved had no idea what was going on – but Elena had acquired a lover who, to use the 1950s vernacular, had ties with the underworld.

When this man Richard Samson—a big-time thug aka Rocco Santucci, the papers gleefully revealed—finally realized Elena wasn't going to leave Nick and the children, he arranged for a hit. The plan was to exact double revenge—killing Elena and framing Nick. Samson/Santucci was highly connected with drug and firearms trafficking as well as money laundering; the FBI had been trying to arrest him for years. He was now linked to Elena's murder, thanks to undercover detectives who had located the hired killer, a 20-year-old freshman hit man and dishonorably discharged Marine who favored Northeast Ohio bars, MD 20/20 and bragging about his various "accomplishments." It was only a matter of time before they got Samson for the rest. Anonymous tips were also cited as helping solve the case.

Was that partially due to me? I wondered with a little thrill. Was I the one whose information had helped saved Nick? Maybe I had talents I never realized, thanks to inspiration from the fictional TV character of Nikita. Assassination? Not so much. But accomplishing things that needed to be done? Well, just maybe. It was almost Zen how sometimes things fell together when I knew when to listen and how to ask.

And the shelter was an all-consuming behemoth that, as it evolved and became more of a reality, left me little time to wonder about Nick or even plot further revenge against Brian and Susan, culinary or otherwise. From a project that initially filled empty hours (and house) that had left me feeling like a piece of unwanted real estate, it had taken on a life of its own, growing into something that demanded every waking moment, even when I was supposed to be at my so-called "real job." I was lucky to have an understanding and supportive boss in Jim Gladstone.

Every time I figured something out—like when I finally got the Board of Directors in place—a dozen more things popped up. Like, how would I find, organize and train the dozens of volunteers so desperately needed to keep the shelter running? How many dog runs and cat cages should we make room for? Should there be a spay/neuter clinic built into the facility? What about a multipurpose room used for educational purposes, such as cruelty prevention and pet care? And what type of intake procedures and screening should be used for both homeless animals and their potential adopters? Obviously we couldn't take everyone; sadly some animals were unadoptable either through sickness or behavior problems, and the same things could be said for prospective human owners. And then there was the issue of euthanasia—sometimes it was inevitable, how would we outsource that? The list went on and on.

The Board of Directors proved to be a huge resource. Jim offered the veterinary services of the Banford Clinic gratis, at least for the first eighteen months after we opened. He also hooked me up with Vern McAllister, the dean of the school of veterinary medicine at Ohio State, who agreed to not only organize educational classes and seminars for the community at the shelter, but to have student clinics that would allow for free spaying and neutering. The timing was perfect; the veterinary school had just ended its relationship with another shelter due to claims of mismanagement and was looking for a venue where students could get field experience. Although most residents in New Wellington could pay for veterinary care, those in the surrounding rural and even urban areas could or would not but might be convinced to bring in their animals for the free service, helping control overpopulation.

Shelia had remained on the Board, and—finally—a representative of the Weintraub Family Foundation contacted me about working with an architect to get conceptual drawings, artist's renderings that would illustrate what the interior and exterior of the shelter would look like once it was renovated. These would attract and convince potential donors that Paws That Refresh would be a huge benefit to animals and the community.

And of course, the Katz presence served as a major magnet, pulling in the Mayor of New Wellington and City Council, which passed a resolution supporting the shelter, even though it was actually in Columbus. And somehow the Mayor and the Katzes convinced the city to annex the land to New Wellington, giving the shelter even better tax breaks and access to local services, not to mention the cachet of being a part of an exclusive community. The Women's Club of New Wellington contacted me as well, offering me access to their network of schools, businesses, and other social activities. I received emails and phone calls from the real housewives of New Wellington, once word got out that Janice was involved. Apparently Paws That Refresh had become the chic cause du jour and, and, as I'd initially hoped, the Fur Ball was shaping up to be the second most important event of the New Wellington season, behind Janice's polo tournament, of course.

I always seemed to be putting out a fire or trying to figure something out. How many rooms did we need for spaying and neutering? What kind of cost-effective sealant would make the floor easy to clean, something vital to any well-run shelter? The open-air design of the former grocery store wasn't always conductive to the shelter layout, so we needed to figure out how to keep separate quarantine areas for sick cats and dogs as far away from the lobby, classrooms, and adoption areas as possible. Air ventilation, drains for the waste system, reducing noise—all these needed to be addressed before the first dollar was spent. Between my job at the clinic and Paws That Refresh, I barely had time to grocery shop and play with my own pets.

Somehow, four months flew by, and when CeCe called me with a date from The Club, one that would work with Eli and Janice's schedule and that of all the other major contributors, I was grateful that just about everything was in place and ready to go. Evan would be in town, on leave before he was shipped off to the Middle East, so he would be present for the fund-raiser and fruition of my dream that he had encouraged and indirectly helped provide funds for. He'd spent the last several months at Camp Shelby, Mississippi, receiving training as a medic—he'd managed to convince his commanding officer that he would be better at that than construction. While there, he'd met a veterinarian who selected him as part of a team to provide care to the cows, sheep, goats and other four-legged casualties of the war. So now my only child would be put in peril over a lamb or a calf, instead of a bridge or military base. Although it didn't make it any less palatable, I was comforted with the hope that by tending the animals he might be farther from the actual fighting.

There may have been another reason for Evan's furlough, one I refused to concern myself with. I told myself I was too busy organizing the silent auction, the door prizes, and the entertainment, a pet fashion and talent show, which seemed to take on a life of its own.

R. Nixon and his Tricky Doggies, a staple at local birthday parties and company picnics, had generously volunteered to perform (The "R" stood for Roger, not Richard). Then Janice Katz, through her connections at her and Eli's namesake arts center, managed to arrange for an appearance by the Moscow Cats Theatre, whose limited U.S. run—so to speak—serendipitously coincided with the Fur Ball's new date. The Russian troupe, consisting of a husband, wife and over two dozen cats, were going to stage a scene from "Meow Side Story" in which shelter cats and purebreds competed for adoption, with the "57s" clawing their way into the hearts of kids Maria and Tony—symbolically, rather than physically, of course. It would be a huge draw. People were paying something like $35 a ticket to see just the Moscow Cats perform. Admission for the Fur Ball was $75 and included a meal, auction, fashion show, door prizes and was tax deductible. What a deal!

And even before all this had been set up, I'd invited "Jungle" Jack Hanna, director emeritus of the Columbus Zoo to appear with some of his more exotic friends. Although he couldn't make the first date, he was available for the second. With such a jam-packed schedule, I needed to figure out how to fit in a pet fashion show to help encourage local adoptions.

So if my son also planned on attending my asshole ex's wedding to my former best friend, I didn't want hear about it. I'd deal with it after the Fur Ball.

Chapter 16 - Who Let the Dogs Out?

Ah, karma. If I could bottle and sell it, I'd be the richest person in the world. But, like love, karma is elusive and comes when you least expect it—for better or worse.

Take the Drama Queens. For the past ten years, we'd been like a revolving door in each other's lives, so I guess I shouldn't have been surprised when CeCe immediately volunteered to step in and take on Shelia's role as my advisor once Shelia retired from polite society.

I've always wondered about that phrase, "polite society." What forms of social discourse might then become acceptable? Rude encounters at Wal-Mart? Screaming profanities at customer service voice-bots or overseas agents who spoke English as a second language? Giving the finger to tailgaters or people who cut you off in traffic? That stuff happened all the time, in everyday life. But what a great excuse! "I can murder or at least publicly humiliate Brian and Susan because I have officially severed my relationship with civilization."

Come to think of it, it could also be a genteel way of saying that you were incarcerated. Change of address postcards, with a full-color portrait of Cellblock D, could be engraved with the words "They threw away the keys! Send all future correspondence to: No. D3489023, PO Box 45699, Lucasville, Ohio 45699."

CeCe served as my liaison with The Club and the various vendors who'd volunteered to assist with the event, smoothing over any hurt feelings and inconveniences caused by the original cancellation and somehow (miraculously!) garnering pledges of support until we found a new date. I felt like I had come full circle: First CeCe when I was married, then Susan, when Gary died and I was first abandoned by Brian, and then Shelia in-between, when she wasn't struggling with her disease or bolstering her position in the community, and now, back to CeCe again. We Drama Queens were supposed to be friends with each other, but the only time we'd truly been a unit was when our marriages were intact. Everything changed when one or more became single. What did that say about women's relationships in this supposedly enlightened era of equality, especially when we were supposed to be kinder, more understanding and more supportive of each other than men? One thing I believed for certain: Thanks to Susan, the four of us would never be together again. But, as usual, I underestimated the power of karma.

Maybe it was the friends that I made and relationships that evolved as I got older and buffeted about by life. Through the years, I'd found my true friends to be people from work or high school, not country club wives. They had known me in good times and bad, through solvency and near-bankruptcy, through disappointments with kids, family, and spouses and all manner of illnesses. There was family of course, but when things got rough, I knew I could also call Patsy and Bob back in Milton and Emily and Felicia from the clinic and be assured of their support and confidentiality. And, under certain circumstances, also even Nick, before his life had been turned upside-down... I'd seen firsthand what money did to people, especially those who'd never had it before. They believed it made them impervious and protected from life's random cruelties. They avoided and shunned anyone perceived to be weak or unlucky—transmitting "loser cooties" as we used to say back in junior high—because, after all, misfortune was contagious, wasn't it? Karma, however, is an altogether different story.

Yet I couldn't completely turn away from the Drama Queens, except for Susan, of course. Even CeCe, considered by many to be the ultimate trophy wife, could be genuine underneath the Botox and silicone. In the course of our working together, I learned how Brett had abused and neglected her, just as Brian had with me. Rather than chasing women and rejecting her sexually, Brett had been running up debt and gambling, two vices well hidden from family and friends, at least for a while. "Maybe I didn't go about it the right way—I realize I must have looked like the ultimate gold digger—but honest to God, Tish, I didn't know how we were going to pay our next month's bills. Brett had a huge salary and he wanted all the best stuff, but where the fuck was the money for it?"

And Ahmet had conveniently come along just as CeCe was following through on her threats to leave, after several years of back-and-forth. "Like you, I'm part Catholic and my family doesn't believe in divorce. Stay in the marriage, if only for the kids, Mom used to tell me whenever I called to complain. And for me to take the initiative... I'd be lying to you if I didn't say Ahmet was instrumental in giving me the courage to walk away." She'd made her decision to get the hefty cash settlement from McLean's Fine Furniture before Ahmet became a permanent part of her life, however. "Unlike you, I never went to college. I worked as a model before I got married, and what money I made was spent on clothes and makeup and trips to New York in the hopes of getting better bookings there. But who was going to hire me once I got divorced? And, as my lawyer so astutely pointed out, I'd have to go back to school for training to get a decent job. And how was I going to pay for Britney and Whitney's education and my retirement? Not to mention his fat fee."

Unlike my genial, beagle-loving Timothy Harris, CeCe's lawyer had been a pit bull—Benjamin Bluestein, whose firm also specialized in defending miscreant CEOs, investment and securities bankers, and big corporations. Just recently, he and his equally nasty wife Rosanne had retired to Scottsdale, well before the minimum Social Security age of 62. In the insular world of The Club, he'd been known as Mr. Golf, and she, Mrs. Tennis. She organized informal Friday night mixed-doubles get-togethers but Brian and I were never invited, even though Shelia and Todd always were. It was well known I was the better player and everyone knew Brian as an outstanding athlete, even in sports he had little interest in, such as tennis. Apparently selection criteria had something to do with spending, rather than athletic, power. The Club's singles women's champions for six years running, Rosanne and her longtime partner Marcy easily annihilated newbies Shelia and I during our first season there, during the New Wellington Women's Day for a Good Cause, which also featured a fashion show and a (very) light lunch; that year, all proceeds went to combat hunger in Central Ohio, a seeming contradiction. Sizewise, country club wives looked more Third World than the ginormous shown on

TV and in the papers waiting for food stamps or meals at the Open Shelter. Only in America could poverty breed obesity.

And of course, there was the proverbial elephant in the living room that we could never really discuss when we were both married to her sons—Mable. "That woman," CeCe said now, shaking her flawless blonde head—how did she manage to get all her highlights symmetrical with absolutely no flyaway split ends? My hair was always such a mess, so I'd cut it chin length several years ago. Never, I swore, would I ever resort to Mable's style—first the monochromatic ash, then the gunmetal blue-grey "bubble head" so favored by her generation. "How could you put up with her for so many years? From what I heard she was even hell when she was dying... Most people have regrets or want to make amends but not Mable. She was too busy deciding who to invite to her funeral!"

I could hardly dispute that. Once in a while I'd catch a glimpse of her humanity, but then she'd say something so cruel and outrageous it destroyed whatever warmth I'd felt for her. But part of me (the very superstitious part, since my son was soon going to Iraq) resisted speaking ill of the dead. "Well, she did love her family. And she was loyal to them, no matter what."

"I'll give her that," CeCe admitted. "Brett and Brian would do anything for her, to the exclusion of everyone and everything else." She sighed. "I'm just happy when my girls call me once a week."

Britney and Whitney had been so upset with their mother after the divorce that they refused to have much to do with her for years, but now, as young adults, they were slowly coming around. "I figured it was better for them to hate me for a while, and still respect their father, then for me to go around spewing the truth. Divorce is tougher on kids than we think."

Which might explain why my own son decided to jump blindly into the hellhole of Iraq. Maybe if I hadn't been so angry and bitter, he might have decided to attend college in Ohio, like most of his friends. Perhaps I'd driven him away, inadvertently forced him to join the Army. More likely, it was Brian's fault for taking up with Susan. For a while their engagement had been the talk of New Wellington, although gossip had died down eventually, the collective eye turning to juicier tidbits, like the murder of Nick's wife Elena.

The difference between CeCe and me, which still seemed like an unbridgeable gap, was that she had had a choice and I hadn't, not really. Brett had begged her to stay, and Brian had done everything he could to manipulate me into giving him a divorce. CeCe had a man waiting in the background, and I had no one.

"At least you're starting to have a good relationship with your girls," I said now. "I know you'll never get those years back but at least you won't lose them permanently." I felt like bursting into tears, which fortunately seemed to be happening less frequently these days, thanks to my new non-native American Indian physician, who believed in taking soy and other natural ingredients for menopause instead of those nasty, breast-cancer-inducing hormones.

CeCe put her perfectly buffed and brightly polished hand on my arm. "Don't go down that road, Tish. Evan's a tough kid, and smart. He'll be fine."

I was about to go into a riff about how ninety-nine percent of those who'd seen combat didn't emerge as "fine." If they weren't wounded physically, they returned with some form of post traumatic stress disorder or were affected by a chronic physical condition, like Vietnam vets with Agent Orange and soldiers who contracted Gulf War syndrome, which resulted in immune disorders, cancer and birth defects. But then CeCe said, "Has anyone talked to or heard from Nick?" and all those scary images flew out of my head, like moths when a drawer opens.

Not that I hadn't been wondering that myself. "How would I know? And why are you asking me?"

"Well, you and Nick have been close for a long time. And he was pretty involved with Paws That Refresh... I thought maybe you called him after things settled down."

I could feel my face getting warm. "Why would I do that? I mean, he just lost his wife." I might as well show up with a casserole at his front door, for fuck's sake.

"That's what friends are for..." Then realization dawned on her furrowless but still careworn face. "Oh, I get it... You have a thing for Nick. And you've grown a pair of chicken wings because now he's available!"

"It's not that simple CeCe," I huffed.

"I can see the two of you together," CeCe mused aloud. "You both love animals and are kind of nerdy, in the best way possible of course. They say opposites attract, but I can say from personal experience it's much easier with someone who has the same worldview... Life is too damn short to fight over whether the roll should be up or down on the toilet paper holder."

And that's how I found myself confiding in CeCe about what happened with Nick so many years ago. His rejection of me was as fresh as if it had been yesterday, and to be honest, his wife dying didn't make much difference. If anything, it probably made me even more threatening since I was single and now, so was he.

"Well, you certainly stood up for him when Elena was murdered," CeCe said, after I finished. "You didn't believe it, not for a second, I could tell. How did you know?"

OK, so it was probably a huge mistake telling her about my meeting with Detective Poller. And mentioning that I might have provided the tip that had helped lead to Nick's release and the apprehension of Elena's real murderer. I of all people knew that while CeCe was never malicious, she dearly loved a good gossip. But damn, what a relief to overshare.

"You really don't know anything about men, do you, Tish? Let me tell you a little secret. *They* don't know what they want. So it's up to us to convince them into thinking it's all their idea even though it's really ours."

Perhaps that was true for CeCe, who never lacked admirers. But not me. Not only had Nick turned me down, but I couldn't even convince my own husband to have sex with me! No, I'd stick to animals, whose reactions were generally predictable. I could love them, and they would never turn away.

*****

The day of the Fur Ball arrived all too soon. My cell and house phone rang constantly with questions and last-minute crises: an advertiser, a major pet store chain, ran out of grooming combs for the goodie bags, so we scrambled to make up the difference with dog-bone-shaped breath mints donated by a local wholesaler. Hopefully the attendees would be too busy having fun to compare swag. Jack Hanna had a family emergency and canceled, and before I could get the word out that we had enough entertainment, my boss Jim Gladstone arranged for a substitute, "Jeremy the Magic Dude," a recent graduate from clown college in Florida (a baccalaureate for Bozos? Who knew?). Since Jim was also on the shelter's Board and had always been so supportive, I could hardly refuse. And it would be a simple matter—and hopefully less disappointing for the attendees—to announce a replacement, rather than a total cancellation, now that the programs were already printed.

But the main ballroom of The Club was hardly conducive to an animal talent/fashion show. The second floor—the space available for members' events and parties—was huge. The ballroom was surrounded by several small rooms—a couple of which had sliding doors—which were where the silent auction and pre-dinner cocktail party would be held. I'd decided to keep the animals in the smaller spaces down the hall from the main area. It was important to contain them, and equally vital to keep the homeless dogs and cats separate from the acts, whose trainers assured me that their animals could handle whatever came their way. But still... What if a performer had an accident and stained the carpet? Or the canines and/or felines got into a rumble, taking the West Side Story theme of the Moscow Cats to a new level? We were on a tight schedule, with very little margin for errors or delays. So I personally had to phone each member of the Club's Board of Directors for permission to lay down inexpensive plywood over where the animals would be walking. Some things you just can't delegate.

However, there were many volunteers to help as we rushed about organizing and setting up. For the first time in my life, I appreciated those women (and some men) who made the overall good of the village a priority. Some may have been busybodies, and others may have been looking to promote their own social standing, but I was pleasantly surprised to find that most were sincere.

CeCe and Evan did their best to calm my nerves. Evan made stupid jokes: "I know ewe think it's a baaad idea that I go to Iraq to work with farm animals, but when I return, I'll go to college and become a Vet vet." Wonder where he got his sense of humor, ha, ha? Not from his dad, who was totally lacking in that department. While on leave, Evan had opted to stay at his friend Clay's house; Clay's parents still lived in New Wellington and had an actual spare room with a real bed instead of an uncomfortable pull-out in the middle of the main living area as was the case with my apartment. After months of living in barracks with no privacy, who could blame him? And CeCe kept trying to distract me by telling me how excited Nick was that the shelter had come to fruition: "He sent in a huge check, and I've arranged for him to sit with us at the head table." Yeah, like *that* would keep me cool and collected.

I went to the designer department at Nordstrom and purchased a strapless green silk gown that highlighted my coloring and few curves (not having to feed a family made it all too easy to stay thin). And I finally broke down and had a session with CeCe's expensive but miracle-working whirlwind of a hairdresser, who bless his heart, gave me a discount because he too was an animal-lover. ("Pugs are where it's at, darling. Everything with them is such a big production! It really helps me put things into perspective!") After all, I told myself, I had to look the part. I would be speaking about the shelter and fundraising in front of a sold-out distinguished audience of 450. Better to incur bills for duds than look like one.

And although I was hesitant to admit it, CeCe had me pumped about Nick. In her eyes, it was inevitable that we would get together; we were perfect for each other, reinforcing what I had always secretly believed. She certainly knew more about men than I, so who was I to argue?

So by the time I put on my clothes and makeup and drove back to The Club for the party, I was feeling beautiful and confident, a rare combination for me. And I remained unruffled, even when Jeremy the

Magic Dude panicked because his rabbit had a fear of felines "Who the hell gets cats to perform?" he demanded. Well, duh, if you train them and dress them up, maybe it might encourage someone to adopt one... So I had to switch him to a room with Tricky Dick's doggies, since we were so tight on space. A table in the auction area collapsed, leaving the items a jumbled-up mess. Fortunately nothing was broken, but sorting it out was a bitch.

Everything else was set. In addition to the animals who were to be present tonight, we'd put together a multimedia slideshow "Happy Tails to You" featuring dogs and cats from other shelters. Proceeds from any adoptions were to be divided between Paws That Refresh and the participating shelter. Once the building was complete, we'd have plenty of strays of our own; but any good adoption was a triumph, as far as I was concerned. The silent auction was to be concluded before dinner; although sit-down service was originally planned, we'd had such a huge response we had to switch to the space-saving buffet, which was actually even more profitable. The MCs, two well-known broadcasters from Channel 6, would host the pet fashion and talent show. And then, there would be dancing afterwards with music provided by the ever-popular Arnett Howard and His Creole Funk Band. Maybe I would take a twirl or two around the floor with Nick; what would it feel like to be in his arms?

Everything was going fabulous. Basically my job was done, so I decided to indulge in another glass of wine—even though all I'd eaten that day was a half a Wendy's salad brought in by a volunteer— and mingle with the guests at the cocktail party. High on the effervescence of alcohol on an empty stomach and watching Paws That Refresh become a reality, I hurried over to greet a tall, salt-and-pepper-haired man. "Nick!" I exclaimed, holding out my arms. "Can you believe we finally pulled this off?"

The man turned around, a total stranger who broke into a grin, revealing an un-Nick-like lack of dental hygiene. "I'm not Nick, but I'll give you a hug anyway."

Before I had a chance to be mortified or even repulsed, Emily, my former coworker and the soon-to-be new office manager for Paws

That Refresh, rushed over. "There you are, Tish! I've been looking for you everywhere. We have a situation." She wiggled her eyebrows Groucho Marx-style, as she always did when an animal started going south or some other major crisis erupted at the clinic. Emily was not one to panic, a major reason why I'd chosen her as my assistant.

Uh-oh. I knew I should have turned down that third (or was it fourth?) glass of wine. But I was the star of the evening and everyone kept buying me drinks and congratulating me. There had been appetizers, of course, but I was too busy schmoozing to take more than an occasional bite.

I excused myself as gracefully as an embarrassed almost-drunk could, and Emily gave me the details as we hurried down the hall to the area where the animals were housed. But I could hear the commotion even before she had a chance to fully explain.

Apparently the Magic Dude's bunny had gotten loose and hopped into the room where the shelter dogs were being prepped for the fashion show. "They went crazy and then Roger rabbited into the cat section and freaked out," she said, referring to the late 1980s movie. Another thing I loved about Emily was her sense of humor, no matter what the situation.

"So why not put on the Tricky Dick dogs first until Jeremy can get his bunny under control?" As the least known act, the latter had been scheduled to open the show.

"But then the other Roger will thinks he's been framed!" she replied, with a sly grin. Although no relation to the late President, this Nixon was political nonetheless and had been very vocal about the fact that he'd been superseded by the "star" of the show, the Moscow Cats. Originally he'd been the main attraction.

I was about to reply that we'd deal with two-legged divas later, when a German Shepherd mix, gussied up as a rap singer, nearly knocked me over. This particular animal was going to be introduced as Snoop Dogg, if I recalled correctly...or not, as his gold chains were scattered about and he'd pretty much torn off his costume, including the "Super Fly" hat with its fake leopard skin rim. At his heels were two cats, who had to be from the performing troupe. Clad in leather vests, one with "Pedigree" across the back in stark white letters and the other with "57," they were followed by their handler, who, when she saw me, stopped and began shouting at me in Russian. Above the din I could also hear rapidly increasing barking, yelling, and meowing. And not only because we were getting closer to the animals. They were headed this way.

My alcohol buzz dissipated as the gravity of the situation began to sink in. There wasn't going to be any entertainment unless I put a stop to this debacle, a veritable flood of animals headed towards the main ballroom. I froze, experiencing a moment of total panic. What were we going to do? The schedule was impossible to begin with and now this havoc... I should never have said yes to that stupid magician...

But here came CeCe hurrying after Snoop. She looked absolutely fabulous in a body-clinging, beaded blue sheath that highlighted her two biggest assets. Her blonde hair was swept up Paris Hilton-style with jewels and the occasional curl around her neck and ears. She grabbed him by his collar. "Ha! You're my bitch now, Dogg." And began picking up Snoop's scattered bling.

And Shelia of all people, pale but healthy looking, rushed over and scooped up the recalcitrant kitties, calming the hissing Russian with apologetic gestures and a few words of the woman's native tongue that she'd apparently picked up from one of her many overseas trips. Most of her hair had grown back—it was less curly and peppered with gray and she seemed stronger than the last time I had seen her, when she told me she was still cancer-free.

Timothy and Evan stood in the hallway, holding back the four legged tidal wave, while various trainers and volunteers sorted out the melee. A mixed-breed terrier with horns and a "Devil dog" cape wriggled away, but I was able to pick him up before he got any further.

"Well, thanks to the Drama Queens, it looks like we've averted a Noah's Ark disaster of Biblical proportions." I flashed a wan, apologetic smile at CeCe and Shelia, as the terrier—one of the fashion show participants—licked my face. "He looks like the dickens but he's an angel in disguise." No one responded; apparently only Emily and I found the situation even slightly amusing. But then, we were the only nonmembers of their precious Club and I was still somewhat tipsy.

But then I realized that they were all staring at something else. The door of the small ballroom, the one space that hadn't been set aside for our event, had opened. I knew that another party had also been planned for the evening but hadn't given it a second thought since it was in a different area, with its own separate entrance. More than once had members gossiped and weighed the politics and advantages over attending two social events the same night in a single venue, although supposedly The Club went to great lengths to avoid such conflicts.

"What is going on here?" Susan emerged, clad in a simple, floor length cream gown. I could hear the babble of guests in the background. I was about to demand the same thing, when the realization sobered me up quicker than if Nick himself had poured a vat of espresso over my head. Brian and Susan were getting married right here, right now at the same time as the fundraiser for Paws That Refresh.

And I could never have seen how we four Drama Queens would ever be together again. Yet, here we were. Karma can be *such* a bitch.

*****

Just like the one who stood here now, looking at me open-mouthed, with that stupid, blank oh-so-helpless-yet-endearing expression that I'd come to know so well. The one that made people stop whatever they were doing and say, "Oh, Susan! That's so terrible! What can I do to help?"

How *dare* they fuck up my moment of triumph? Hadn't they ruined my life, or tried to anyway, with her stupid fear of being alone, and his greed and selfishness? Where was the better halfhole, anyway?

I clenched my right fist and raised it up as if to hit her—although I'd never laid my hands on another adult in my life, even my ex-husband, who, come to think of it, was really the architect of this whole mess, although Susan was equally at fault for going along with it.

"Mom," Evan's voice, cracked with strain, filtered through my red haze of rage. "Mom," he began again. "Dad and Susan didn't know this was the night of the Fur Ball. They planned the rehearsal dinner months ago, long before the new date was set…"

So it was a rehearsal dinner, not the wedding. No wonder Shelia and Todd and a few other of now his but no longer my friends had deigned to attend my event.

Susan now spoke. "I didn't know anything about this," she began. "Brian never told me…"

"Dad tried to switch the date, but it was too late…" Evan said at the same time.

But my hackles were raised, so to speak. I was just about to tell the dumb bitch to shut the fuck up and then follow that up by smacking her. Then I was going to gather all the animals and set them loose in the middle of that room and encourage them to shit and pee and puke and stick their noses up the guest's butts. I didn't care what the circumstances were, and I wasn't interested in any excuses. After I laid Susan out, and then Brian—if the weasel even dared to show his face—my four-legged posse would wreak havoc on their little party—jumping on the tables to get at the food, shredding clothes, barking, meowing, and running wild. Oh, and then I would find Nick and drag him in the middle of the room and somehow talk him into pretending to be my lover… The time for revenge had come, and it was going to be so much sweeter than the catfish banquet I'd originally fantasized about.

But at that precise moment, or close enough to it anyway, Eli and Janice Katz approached our lovely little clusterfuck. "Tish!" Janice gushed, rushing forward to give me a hug. "You have done an unbelievable job of putting this together! What an inspiration and asset you are, to both women and New Wellington, not to mention all those homeless animals!" Eli stood next to her and nodded sagely, one hand folded over the other. He's a lot shorter than I remember, I thought, in spite of my overwhelming fury.

By now, Emily, Timothy and the other volunteers were leading the rest of the escapees back to their respective rooms. The Russian woman had also subsided, cats in arms.

"Isn't she though?" remarked CeCe, adeptly covering for what Janice probably took as stunned gratitude at her recognition of a peon in her husband's fiefdom. "We've known Tish for ten years—actually she was my sister-in-law for a lot longer—and she is a miracle worker! This was her idea, and she persevered until it became a reality."

"Absolutely," Shelia chimed in. "No matter how many setbacks she encountered, she came back stronger than ever. You're a scrapper, Tish, just like me." And the look in her eyes said, don't you dare fuck this moment up. When I rewound the scene in my head later, I realized "survivor" might have been the word I would have chosen.

"This is a wonderful event," Susan chirped. "As I said earlier, I had no idea this was going to coincide with our rehearsal dinner. I'm so very sorry, Tish."

"Of course you had no way of knowing," Janice soothed her quickly. "Although I'm sure your guests may be wondering why all these four-legged invitees are running around!" Everyone laughed, the tension seemingly broken.

So Brian and Susan had seemingly gotten away with it…again. But the moment Janice had said "homeless animals" I knew that my decision to mete out humiliation or revenge or whatever punishment I could incur could never be a reality. Not if I wanted to do anything with my life. I could spend my days plotting revenge, or realize that some things are bigger and more important than personal injustice or even heartbreak. Like making sure 450 distinguished guests are fed and entertained and enough money is raised so that a shelter could be built to help those who can never speak for themselves.

And here came a visibly annoyed Tricky Dick, surrounded by his performing dogs. Apparently Emily had given him the word that he was on first. I turned to my son and the other Drama Queens, although I couldn't bring myself to address Susan directly. "It's no big deal, really. You know what they say—the show must go on!" It was lame, but it was the best I could come up with under the circumstances.

I could sense Janice and Eli's approval as I caught up with Tricky Dick as he headed towards the ballroom. It wasn't as immediately satisfying as letting the dogs out on Brian and Susan, but it was enough.

The rest of the evening was bittersweet. The style show and performances went off without a growl, yack, or even a raised leg. Several animals were adopted from surrounding shelters and enough money was raised to build the shelter and pay my and Emily's salary for a year and a half. Based on the estimates of Emily's accountant fiancé, it would allow us enough time to make sure the shelter was solvent, what with adoptions and other fundraising projects, such as classes and even a little shop to sell necessities like collars, food, litter, and leashes.

Jim Gladstone, my now former boss, assured me that I would always have a job at the Banford clinic. "But I don't see that happening, Tish. In fact, I may come work for you, once I retire!" Which wasn't so far off, although his wife said he'd been talking about it for years.

Nick never showed. His check cleared, but his seat at the head table remained empty. A few weeks after the Fur Ball, I heard that he and his kids moved to California—he'd accepted a teaching position at UC-Davis, where I'd had planned to attend veterinary school so many years ago, when Brian and I first married. Nice ironic touch to his final rejection of me. So much for the whole soul mate thing, fuck you very much. True love, I was beginning to realize was the oeuvre of the young, beautiful, and Botoxed…that, and wealthy older men and ugly rock stars.

But at the end of the day—or in this case what turned out to be a very long and, by everyone else's account, successful evening—I could hardly complain. What good would it do, anyway? I mean, Brian never even told Susan that the Fur Ball fell on the same weekend as their wedding—what kind of relationship was that?

Better to have no relationship at all. And maybe *Brian* was the best revenge—Susan had the whole rest of her life to put up with his bullshit.

And besides, now I was busy running the shelter, and praying that my son would come home safe from Iraq. I didn't agree with what was going on over there, but Evan and his buddies certainly seemed to believe that they were helping. Rather than argue, I downloaded a "Soulja Boy" screensaver that counted the days until his return.

And then Shelia died, and everything changed again.

EPILOGUE AS PROLOGUE

Lassie, Come Home

I had heard that Shelia had been going through treatments again, and made an effort to see her. If organizing and opening a shelter had taught me anything, it was that sometimes "no" is actually "maybe" or even "yes." Although Shelia was a private person and I respected that, she also needed to understand that she had friends who loved and cared for her. So I persisted, and insisted that we go out for lunch once a week, even when she felt too shitty from the chemo to nibble on more than a few crackers. It was much better than sitting in that huge, empty gilded cage of a house. Sometimes CeCe joined us and we'd sit around the New Wellington Grille and swap stories about recalcitrant husbands, exes, and kids. They'd fill me in on gossip from The Club, never mentioning Brian and Susan, except for the juicy bombshell that the happy couple decided to relocate to Boca, supposedly to be near Jack and Brett. "New Wellington is too uncomfortable for them, now that Paws That Refresh is such a success and Tish is a hero," CeCe bragged. Turns out we Drama Queens were better friends than I thought... Well, three of us, anyway.

Toward the end, when Shelia got too sick to go out, I'd stop by and bring her lunch. Although she insisted she didn't want to put me out, I argued that I needed to talk to her; as someone who'd done fundraising for much of her adult life, her expertise and point of view were invaluable. My reasons for coming didn't matter much anyway during the last couple of weeks. She slipped in and out of consciousness; I tried to come by every day and just spend time. I'd really never had the chance to say good-bye to either of my parents—Mable didn't count—so it helped us both a lot.

Several weeks after Shelia's funeral—which in some ways was worse than Gary's because she'd suffered so much for so long, and for seemingly no reason—I received a call from her husband Todd, who wanted to meet at the Weintraub real estate office. "Your lawyer's Timothy Harris, correct?" Todd inquired. "I suggest you bring him along."

"You guys aren't suing me, are you?" Concern, disguised as a joke. Had I somehow offended Shelia's family? I know I'd been insistent on seeing her, but I'd only been trying to be a friend…

In spite of his grief, Todd chuckled. "If anything, it's the opposite."

Hmmm… So Timothy and I showed up at the designated place and time, which was a little weird. We'd dated a few times, but the chemistry simply wasn't there. Which was true of every guy I'd gone out with since my divorce. All two of them. The other was a setup, courtesy of CeCe's cousin. The fifty-year-old bachelor insisted that we meet at a breakfast place where he could use his two-for-one coupon which was limited to certain menu items. He was also allergic to animals. Like that was going to work.

"So what's this all about?" I asked after everyone exchanged pleasantries. Evan was being discharged from the military in a few days and I had lots to do. I'd just purchased a small house and was anxious to get it ready for his homecoming. Thanks to the GI Bill, my son decided to finally go to college and planned to major in veterinary medicine. He'd be living with me for a while, at least during his first couple of quarters at Ohio State.

"Well, I'll make this short and sweet," Todd pulled out a folder with "Weintraub Family Foundation" written across it in gilded script. "Shelia has bequeathed some money to Paws That Refresh."

"What kind of arrangement are we talking about?" Immediately Timothy went on high alert, not unlike his beagle Abbey when she picked up on a scent.

"Well that depends upon how you plan on disbursing the two million," stated Todd's lawyer, whose name I recognized as being the principal of one of the city's most prestigious firms. But my brain stopped after I heard "two million" because there ensued a lively discussion about stocks, bonds, mutual funds, and investments that left me in the dust.

Two million dollars? For Paws That Refresh? We'd never have to worry about raising money, ever again! Not unless the economy did a swirly, flushing the stock market and everyone's money down the toilet, which of course seemed unlikely, given the current booming stock market.

After we left the meeting, Timothy tried to explain to me in layman's language what had transpired. Like a lot of foundations, money was to be held in escrow. He recommended a diverse investment portfolio consisting of IRAs, reliable stocks such as oil, even purchasing land. "You can't go wrong with real estate; people are making big bucks flipping houses and other properties." I, however, was not so anxious to divest myself of the principal. My sister Lisa and her husband Nate had much of their money in Certificates of Deposit; which although were not high-earning, produced a steady yield and were guaranteed by the FDIC. I really needed to talk to Nate before any decisions were made about this windfall. No way was I going to repeat the mistakes I'd made with my inheritance during what seemed like a lifetime ago.

This was unbelievable news, almost as good as my son's safe return from Iraq. I didn't need a relationship to make me feel complete; a steady income and a job that I loved, family and good friends were enough.

*****

Several months later, I was asked to speak at the OSU Veterinary School. Through internships and clinics with students at Paws That Refresh, I'd gotten to know Dean McAllister rather well and was finally able to take him up on his offer to talk to a third-year class about the realities of working in and managing an animal shelter. Now that Paws That Refresh was solvent, and I didn't have to put in such long hours, it was great to have more time for outreach, to help educate people on caring for homeless animals, and vets and other professionals on dealing with situations involving abuse. Although I still spent a lot of time at the shelter, making sure animals were properly taken care of and that the place remained clean and well-run, I knew I could delegate certain tasks to Emily and a couple of trusted volunteers. Jim Gladstone, my former boss, made good on his threat to retire and was also working part-time as a vet, although he was stretched thin serving as an advisor to the OSU interns.

Evan had finally found an apartment in a reasonably safe neighborhood nearby and I planned to meet him for lunch on campus after my talk. But then he cancelled at the last minute, allegedly to finish a paper. I suspected a girl was involved, since he'd stopped coming around for meals, and weekends were now off-limits, except for an occasional Sunday afternoon movie. But that was fine; Evan was a 23-year-old man, a vet-almost-vet and entitled to his own life. I'd gotten used to being on my own, anyway and after five years of being divorced, couldn't imagine living with another person, much less sharing a bed and most of my free time with him. I don't know how I'd managed with Brian, and certainly couldn't think of anyone I wanted to replace him with. Most men and a lot of women, I'd learned, couldn't stand being alone. I'd come to realize that I was the exception.

And that was how I ended up standing in the hallway of the OSU Veterinary School, engaged in a long discussion with Vern McAllister about finding an advisor for our growing cadre of interns. Although there were ten slots for internships, almost three times that number had applied. And even though we certainly needed the help, a veterinarian advisor was also necessary to oversee their work. "I have just the person," he said. "He started teaching this semester. In fact, he just moved back here. Here he comes now." And his face lit up with a smile.

I knew it was Nick before I even turned around. A subtle change in the atmosphere, a lightening of the soul, or maybe just romantic bullshit.

"Hey, Vern, Tish," he said. Same deep set-eyes, same smooth caramel voice. Difference: Inner peace, and a man comfortable with himself. Me, too, except that I lacked a penis.

"Hey, Nick." I couldn't help myself; my whole inner being lit up. Damn it, he was still gorgeous.

"You two know each other?" The Dean had receded into the

background, speaking from the same tunnel as the students hurrying around us on their way to their next class.

Well, duh, yeah, I thought, isn't it obvious? But I said, "Nick was instrumental during the early planning stages of Paws That Refresh until his wife was mur...I mean until he moved to California to teach." What was it about this man that always made me blurt the wrong or at least stupid things? It never changed—from the moment I met him as a harried mother and country club wife in a tennis outfit until now, my dream achieved, director of a successful animal shelter and an independent, self-supporting woman.

"You can say it, Tish, it's OK." Nick appeared unruffled. He either had gotten some seriously good therapy or major psychotropic drugs. Or maybe he was just used to my tactless comments by now. "My wife was killed a few years ago and Tish helped exonerate me," he told the Dean. "So of course I would love to be involved again with Paws That Refresh." His radiant smile resembled that African-American senator from Illinois with the weird name, the one who Hillary Clinton was beating in most of the primaries. His chances of becoming the next President were about as likely as my ending up with Nick.

"I came back for a lot of reasons, not the least of which was reconnecting with my friends and colleagues," Nick continued. "I realized that my leaving so abruptly after Elena's murder was just running away. It wasn't fair to myself, my children or our families. Columbus is home for all of us. And of course, I wanted to see you, Tish, and thank you for all you've done."

"Well," said Vern. "I have a meeting, so I'll leave you two kids to figure out the details. I'll need your schedule Nick, so we can adjust your office hours." He hurried away.

To say that I was overwhelmed would be an understatement. First of all, how did Nick know I provided information leading to his acquittal? And second, he was implying that his reason for coming back here—or at least part of it—was because of me.

"I didn't know how to approach you, Tish, because I actually wanted to call you," Nick said now, almost but not quite reading my thoughts. "I mean, we've both been through so much…" He left the sentence unfinished.

It was hard to meet his gaze and see what was in his eyes, because it was looked an awful lot like what I wanted for so many years and thought I'd never have. What if I was lying to myself and deceiving myself…again? I didn't exactly have the world's greatest track record when it came to reading men.

But at least I could start by being honest. And I had a question or two of my own. "How did you know that I went to the police? I swore that detective to secrecy. And CeCe too—she was the only other person I told." And then I realized—of course. Along with her breasts and a few other artificial parts, the thing that remained indomitable about CeCe was her inability to keep a secret. Especially when she thought was she helping along a romance.

"I see from your expression that you already know the answer. Not that you have to be a brain or even a veterinary surgeon to figure that out. You know, Tish, we really need to sit down and talk. And not just about Paws That Refresh. I think we have a lot to catch up on."

"Well." I recovered my remaining shreds of composure and pulled them up around me. "Of course we would benefit from a meeting. You've always had such great ideas, Nick, and we worked well together in the past. But before we take this any further, I have one other question."

"And what would that be?" I'd forgotten about the adorable way he tilted his head when he was curious. Sort of like a big, shaggy retriever that you would always love, even if he chewed up your shoes or peed on your carpet, neither of which Nick would do, unless he was 105 years old and had dementia.

I took a deep breath. Well, I thought, here goes… "Do you prefer your toilet paper roll up or down?"

The smile that pulled at the corner of his mouth started in his eyes and actually looked more like hysterical laughter. As in, yes, this woman is as loony as I remember, and life is never dull around her. "Well, actually I don't give a shit, if you pardon the expression. It's got to be two-ply though, but if you prefer the more expensive brand, I'd pay the difference. Aren't we getting a little ahead of ourselves here?"

"Not if you believe CeCe. She's the one who says you have to be on the same page and that life is too short to fight over little things."

"She's got a point." He looked at his watch. "Oh hell, I've got a class in 5 minutes. Do you mind if we start walking?"

"Sure. Let's exchange numbers and figure out when to meet." Then I worried, was I being too forward? Was he just trying to hook up with the animal shelter again and not me? After all, I was his get out of jail free card. Sort of.

"Actually, I was thinking more about dinner Saturday night. I just moved to a loft Downtown—my kids transferred to Columbus Academy so school districts don't matter. It was hard to move back to Powell, and so we decided to make new memories while keeping some of the familiar ones..."

His voice changed to the seductive tone I remembered so well. "I can walk to wherever you want to eat and meet you there; there are a lot of great restaurants nearby." Later I would find out his "loft" was a 4000-square-foot condo at Miranova, Columbus's most exclusive and expensive high-rise. It was custom-built not only to accommodate his teenagers but his two dogs and a cat which he'd managed to transport safely across the country—twice. As with my pets, Nick's animals were part of the family, and whither he goest, they went.

"So let me ask you this," Nick said now. "What *is* the difference between the toilet paper roll being up or down?"

"You know, I could never figure that out. My ex-husband Brian always yelled at me about it, though. That and moving the shower head so that water sprayed on the floor whenever he opened the sliding glass door. Like I deliberately skulked around the bathroom, waiting for it to go everywhere and getting my jollies," I chuckled. Many of the issues that seemed so important during my marriage were now inconsequential, although when I looked back on them, they were a reflection of much larger problems. A good thing, being able to laugh about this. The best revenge.

Author Information

Sandra Gurvis is the author of fifteen books, including *America's Strangest Museums* and *Careers for Nonconformists*, which was a selection of the Quality Paperback Book Club. Her books have been featured in newspapers, television, and radio stations across the country. Sandra has been selected for residencies and fellowships and is a member of the American Society of Journalists and Authors (ASJA). She has one home—in Columbus, Westerville, and New Albany, Ohio. For more information about Sandra, check out her websites:

www.sgurvis.com,
www.booksaboutthe60s.com

Publisher Information

VISIT THE LOCONEAL BLOG AT

www.loconeal.com

Breaking News

Forthcoming Releases

Links to Author Sites

Loconeal Events

Made in the USA
Monee, IL
27 August 2019